Scandal in the Pews III

The Aftermath

National Best Selling Author

Tracey T. Cooper

Published by Crowned Heir Publications INC.

DEDICATIONS

This won't be your ordinary dedication, simply because as I put my pen to paper; I prayed and asked God to give me a story that was nothing short of extraordinary. As a sign that he honored my prayer, he gave me "The Aftermath" and a message which has ultimately turned into my dedications.

This Book is dedicated to every young woman who has looked back on her choices and shook her head thinking, "*what the hell did I just do?*" Whether you struggled in secret to clean up your mess, or hid your face in shame praying no one knew.

To those that chose the wrong "HIM" a few dozen times, praying he would love you organically until you someday learned to love you.

To the vulnerable queen who sacrificed her self-worth without the realization that dropping your price tag still wouldn't deem him worthy of you. Sis, this one is for you!

To those who grew up in prim and proper homes yet made some poor decisions along the way, which were judged harshly by those around you. They bore the face of disappointment and chagrin while looking down on you, Doll face this one is for you.

Lastly, to all the sisters out there drowning in a sea of debt because you've chosen an addiction to high end labels as your drug of choice to mask an inner void... Choosing your outward appearance over sensitive matters of the heart. Daily presenting yourself as a struggle who is well draped in designer, while going spiritually and mentally bankrupt hoping to find a fresh start, this one too is for you.

I can admit I have been right where you are and back again a time or two, but this unorthodox dedication comes to bear good news. All your bad choices will only permanently define you if you allow them to. For it is the essence in which you handle the "Aftermath" that will speak volumes in truth. I'll have you know the calamity created amidst your decisions will work together for your good if you own them.

Here, is one more exciting thing for you to look forward to… Your faith is about to have a head on collision with your destiny if you keep moving forward and shedding all of the bad habits of yesterday and your comfort zone of used to. Head Up, Shoulders back, be brave, be poised, be resilient! Wear your crown well and B.I.G (Believe in God) you can't fail when he's within you. Oh, and here is your bonus, I believe in you too......Which is why I have dedicated this novel to the queen in you.

Keep Queening, Love Always,

~ Tee

CHAPTER ONE

Do I Ever Cross Your Mind

"I can't remember why we fell apart, From something that was meant to be, yeah……Forever was the promise in our hearts, Now more and more I wonder where you are……do I ever cross your mind anytime, Do you ever wake up reaching out for me? Do I ever cross your mind anytime….I miss you?"

Sheila Denise

"I need a towel, Reds." Gregory called out as he stood in the doorway of the bathroom.

As the water glistened from his body, I struggled to drop my gaze. I pulled myself from the bed and pulled the sash on the short silk robe just a little tighter as I moved closer to him. A grin appeared on his face as I walked over to the linen closet, retrieving a towel for him.

The moment I placed the towel in his hands, the sides of his lips curled sexily. And, with a swift movement of muscle; his face changed from the grin to a full-on smile as he pulled me close to him. His lips met mine, kissing me passionately. Our tongues clashed with one another, the taste of mouthwash still lingering in his mouth. I felt his hands slip from my lower back to the round of my hip effortlessly.

I silently prayed my kitty wasn't purring loud enough for him to know I wanted him just as much as he wanted me. The simple pleasure of being in his arms was the most inviting and intoxicating thing I had experienced in a while. I felt slightly high from his touch alone as I put my lips to the very spot on his chest where a tattoo of my name used to be.

"What are you thinking Reds?" Gregory asked as he planted kisses from my forehead to my chin.

"I don't want you to leave." I whispered vulnerably.

"You don't ever have to worry about that. I know where I belong, baby." Gregory spun me around until I faced the floor length mirror in front of me.

What I felt in my heart, felt right. But what I saw in the reflection, were two very different things. The better of the two visions, was me being held again by the man that I loved most... well close second to my father. And the latter vision, was me back in the arms of the same snake that had once bitten me.

His lips kissed the back of my neck, sending my spine into a tingling fit. One hand slipped into my robe while the other worked on pulling the knot from the sash. The moment my sash fell loose and my robe opened, exposing my naked body; Gregory grinned from ear to ear with much satisfaction. He palmed my breast with his hands, as he whispered in my ear how he loved me and only me.

"*Shit.*" The alarm buzzed loudly as I rolled over.

Groggily, I sat up in bed; utterly confused. I truly couldn't distinguish if that was a damn dream or a nightmare I'd just had. Slick and I, together again? I couldn't picture that, not even if it were taken with a *Kodak*. Now, I would never say never because you never know what God has planned but I'm sure he hears my thoughts and my prayers! And, believe me at this point; they were for a younger, wealthier man.

CHAPTER TWO

Creep

"If he knew the things I did he couldn't handle me, and I choose to keep him protected.... So I creep, yeah, just creepin on....... But I'll know 'crept nobody is supposed to know, so I'll creep, yeah, because he doesn't know what I do.... And no attention goes to show."

Nadira Sy'Mone

"*It's funny how the tables turn. You just never know in life when the next plot change will be starring you.*" I brushed away my thoughts along with a single strand of hair that dangled in between my eyes.

Refocused, I reached out to receive the keys to the hotel room from the front desk agent who was tending to me.

"Thank You." I smiled, slipping the key into my *Chanel* bag.

"No problem. Have a great stay, Mrs. Fortune." The agent replied, as I inched closer to the elevator.

I quickly looked around for any listening ears who may have

heard her. I stepped into the elevator and hit the button marked eighteen. I was ever so grateful we were in the penthouse suite and I didn't have worry about running into anyone in the hallways.

I couldn't help the smile that crept on my face as I walked into the room and took in the amazing scenery. There were long stem roses, and my absolute favorite chocolate covered strawberries from Godiva. I began to undress in the living room area, stripping down to my *La' Pearla* high waist lace panties, bra and pearl necklace.

I decided to keep on my heels, although they were killing me. I was a tad bit self-conscious about sporting a thicker version of me due to my pregnancy.

"Hey! Took you long enough, Sexy. I was starting to think you weren't coming." He said as he stood up from the edge of the bed and walked toward me.

His physique towered over my tiny frame as he bent down and kissed me. I surprised him by kissing him back. Usually, kissing on the mouth was something neither of us did. Immediately, his hands found their way into my panties, and I became putty in his hands. My hormones were raging from my pregnancy.

His fingers began exploring my throbbing clit while his mouth met with my hardened nipples. The satisfaction was so surreal I could cry.

"You ready for Daddy, huh?" he asked as he pulled his fingers from my panties and tasted me.

I grinned as I took him by the hand, leading him over to the bed. He sat down in front of me while I stepped out of my panties. The towel he wore around his waist, was no more. His joystick stood thick, milk chocolate and on full display for me. I tried to keep my cool even though my juice box was dripping. This moment had been a long time coming. He grabbed me by the hand and laid me back on the bed gently before climbing on top of me, spreading my legs gently with his knee.

"Not so fast." I cooed, as he grabbed at his erection.

"What? What's up baby?" He asked, his face full of confusion.

"Where are your manners, young man? I'm sure your mother taught you to speak first when you enter someone's home. Well, the same rules apply to my kitty. She likes to be spoken to…"

"In tongues, please." I added, licking my lips seductively.

He didn't put up a fight at all. He crawled into the place between my knees and began a conversation with my pearl tongue.

"You taste better than I imagined." He smiled, licking every bit of me from his lips.

I eagerly opened my legs to receive him. I bit down on my bottom lip to keep from crying as he entered me; he was working with a monster to say the least. He held the sides of my face, gently placing kisses on my lips as he worked himself into my prized jewel. The more he grinded, the more my legs shook in response to his girth. The moment my body adjusted to him completely, it was on.

He lifted my leg over his shoulders, diving deep within my love tunnel. My nails dug in his back, as he continued stroking ever so passionately. I couldn't suppress the orgasm that was building so I did my best to make sure he came right along with me. I threw back the kitty the same way he was hitting me. Before long, I was releasing my love as he released; shooting his babies on my stomach.

“Damn, that pussy is amazing!” He screamed as he rolled over beside me.

I smirked to myself. Hell, it wasn't like it was something I hadn't heard before.

I looked down at the *Rolex Date* on my wrist and sat up quickly. I had one hour to make it to my meeting. I hurried to the bathroom and grabbed a washcloth to clean up quickly. I shook my head at the thought of taking what Isha’s grandmother used to refer to as a ‘hoe bath’ but my choices were slim. A few short minutes later, I emerged from the bathroom struggling to zip my dress and slip into my shoes simultaneously.

“Damn bae, where are you going?” He asked as he rolled over in the bed to look at me.

“A meeting,” I answered as I pulled on my blazer and grabbed my keys.

“So that's how you’re going to do me?”

“I’m sorry, Keon. Thanks for lunch.” I winked as I made my way to the door.

“Damn, you cold. Just love me and leave me?” Keon held his chest as if I’d hurt him deeply.

“That’s the nature of the game we are playing. Later baby,” I called out as the elevator doors closed.

CHAPTER THREE

"Bless your soul you got your head in the clouds, You made a fool out of you and Boy she's bringing you down."

Sheila Denise McClure

There is something so intricate about a woman's stride.

Her walk is a strong indication of who she is as a woman. Her current mood, her all around character, and her level of self-confidence. In her stride, she has the power to turn heads. Capture glares of envy and/or admiration, and put a slight crook in even the stiffest of necks. Today, my walk was as loud as a lion's roar and as graceful as a trained ballet dancer yet as confident as a colorful peacock. The Brian Atwood shoes that adorned my size eight and a half feet hit the tiled floor beneath me, creating a melodic rhythm that could only be interpreted as woman on a mission.

As I reached the large oak double doors, I was ushered into a conference room with large leather seats; most of which were already occupied. My eyes scanned the room, taking in the face of each of the board members present. The room was filled with the governing body of BOLD Brand.

In my divorce three years ago, I graciously surrendered several things; from properties to my precious last name. However, you could bet your last dollar that Sheila Denise was no fool. I would by no means give up my share of BOLD Brand, after all it's a cash cow. I took my seat at the head of the table offering a polite smile and head nod to those at the table.

I was seated at the head of the table with Nadira sitting directly across from me. My ex-husband Gregory sat in the head seat to my left, shoulders squared and looking debonair as always.

"Let's begin, shall we?" Nadira stood adjusting her blazer to cover the pregnant belly she was sporting.

"Many of you are aware of the purpose of today's meeting. And, for those of you who are still in the dark please allow me to enlighten you briefly. BOLD Brand has been presented with an incredibly lucrative opportunity that I'm sure many of you will be most excited about. Over the past thirteen years, BOLD Brand has set a precedence in innovation, profitability, ingenuity and growth. It is now time to raise the bar and take this brand to a new level as we explore unchartered territories. Excuse me," Nadira paused to take a drank of water.

"As I was saying, with the consent of the founding members of the Board; we will officially launch our IPO or Initial Public Offering. For those of you who have not done your homework before this meeting, launching an IPO would mean BOLD Brand would become an internationally traded public company. This would raise our capital and expand the business on a level that is unheard of for a faith based organization. Outlined before you on the projectors are the benefits of this launch. It is imperative that we concentrate on making a sound decision that will greatly benefit the future of each of our families as well as BOLD Brand as a whole." Nadira concluded as she took her seat.

Ronald Mayer secretary of BOLD Brand quickly stood as the room began to whisper quietly about the presentation.

"Ladies and Gentlemen, I ask that you take a minute to gather your votes so that we might proceed expeditiously. For all of those in favor, would you please raise your hand and say I." Ronald instructed. Everyone in the room raised their hands, well except me of course.

My vote carried weight and I knew it! I was about to make them pay like they weighed today if they hoped to get it.

'Sheila?" Ronald spoke my name seeing that I was the only one in the room who hadn't raised my hand.

Raising my hand would be out of the question. However, I was about to raise eyebrows, questions and most of all the moral conscience of everyone in the room. I was no longer the mousy wife that would go along to get along. I had a voice and I was going to use it.

"Do we have your vote as well?" Ronald asked humbly.

"That's going to be hell no for me. And, might I add…Contrary to popular belief, there are disadvantages to going public as well." I stated as I stood, straightening my Navy-Blue Pinstripe *Balenciaga* suit.

“I'd like to call your attention back to the projector before you.” I pulled on my eyeglasses and stepped to the front of the room.

“On the slide before you are some very important elements of going public that Mrs. Fortune forgot to mention. I ask that the members of this board would be so kind as to read over them carefully and understand that all money is not good money.” I could feel Nadira’s eyes burning a hole through my soul.

Still, I was unmoved as the chatter in the room began. After fifteen long minutes of discussion, the room was divided… Just as I had planned. My mission was simple. I was about to teach little Mrs. Fortune a lesson today she wouldn't soon forget.

“May I have your attention please?” Gregory said, finally breaking his silence.

“I propose that each of us take all that what we have learned today, home and chew on it. It may be best if we reconvene here later, in effort to come to a mutual consensus. Same time next week, I suppose?” Gregory said stroking his beard.

The members of the board agreed with his proposal as many of them stood to leave; still chattering amongst themselves. I sat back in my chair, poised with a sophisticated smirk gracing my lips.

Nadira

"Was that necessary?" I barked behind Sheila as she made her way to her car.

"Simmer Down. All that unnecessary aggression still won't get you my vote. I see you still playing checkers, silly of me for believing that you were smart enough to know that we big girls play chess. Now enjoy the rest of the day. And, uh before you go back in that building… I suggest you check that stain on your dress. The Monica Lewinsky look went out in the nineties." Sheila winked.

I wanted to fire back but I didn't have the words. I watched her back as she sashayed to her car, leaving me standing in the middle of the parking lot looking like a fool for the second time today.

I didn't bother to walk back inside the church, instead I walked over to my car and climbed inside. I wanted to vanish before I had to face my husband one on one. As I started up the engine, I looked up to see him standing outside of my car door.

"Hey, you okay?" Gregory asked as he leaned into the driver's side window, his hand tapping the roof of the car.

"Yes, I'm just a little tired. I'll call you a little later." I replied, barely looking up at him.

"Okay. Be careful." He tapped the hood and watched as I pulled out of the parking lot.

My conscience was kicking my ass, but I refused to let it win. Instead, I turned the radio up to drown it away.

Gregory

Smooth, wasn't she today?

Daily, I was watching her slip away. It was like she was here, but a million miles away. Sometimes, I wondered would things ever be the same between her and I. We needed someone to talk to and seemingly God had been my only confidant over the last few months.

I reached into my sport coat and grabbed my phone.

I dialed the one person I knew without a shadow of doubt could be trusted regardless of what terms we were on.

"Good Afternoon Bishop, to what do I owe the pleasure?" Sheila answered sarcastically.

"Just wanted to say that was a hell of a show you put on today. I didn't know you were so well versed in stocks. That was impressive, Reds." I commented, thinking back to the presentation Sheila made.

"A woman can't let what a man brings to the table be all she eats, Bishop. I've dabbled in the market for quite some time, you might have known that if your head weren't in the clouds." Sheila spoke.

"Head in the clouds?" I asked, confused as to why she felt that way.

"Correct. It's been that way for a long time too, Slick. You can't see her wrong because you're too busy trying to convince yourself that she's Mrs. Right. You better remember Samson and Delilah and wake up a bit Gregory." Sheila warned.

In thirty plus years of knowing her, I knew one very important thing and that was not to question her when she was spitting game.

"I hear you, Reds. On a lighter note, what have you got planned for the weekend?"

"Now, now… I don't think I owe you an answer to that question. Besides, I wouldn't want to offend the good Bishop. So, what I will say is have a good evening. I'm headed out, but please do me a favor and don't make light of what I said." Sheila stated sternly before ending the call.

I laughed a little to myself. Sheila's mouth was still as slick as the day we met. Some things would never change. I was just grateful we were in a good place. I took in the events of the day as I headed out of the car to pick up Heaven. She was my piece of sunshine through my current storm.

CHAPTER FOUR

Your Body's Callin'

"These hands have been longing to touch you baby. And now you've come around seeing it my way. You won't forget baby and you surely won't regret it baby."

Indiya

In this current moment, I knew exactly what R. Kelly was trying to convey when he said, "*My minds telling me no, but my body is telling me yes!*"

I have never been so ready to jump on somebody in my life. It had been four months since the fiasco with Mekhi, and I had been chilling hard…Well, until about six weeks ago when I met Cameron. He wasn't a guy I could take home to my parents, however; he was a bad guy who looked so damn good and he treated me well. His lifestyle was one I wasn't used to at all. Of course, Mekhi used to nickel and dime in the selling game, but he wasn't nearly on the same level as Cam.

I yawned loudly hoping to get Cam's attention as he sat on the floor playing a game of *Madden 2K16* on the *Xbox* while I laid at the top of the bed, stretched out and fully dressed.

"If you want my attention baby girl, you're going to have to come and get it." Cam said smoothly.

Right then, I knew I was going to have to step it up and make a big girl move. I moved to the edge of the bed as I proceeded to take off the *H&M* basic dress I wore and my sandals.

Sexily, I walked over to Cam wearing just my panties and bra. I secretly hoped I didn't look like a fool trying to imitate the walk I'd seen my step mother do for my father on numerous occasions.

"Now that's how you get a nigga attention, Ma." Cam said pulling me down in front of him.

His hands roamed all over me before he unhooked my bra, allowing it to fall to the floor. He took each of my breast into his mouth, one at a time as his other hand massaged my juice box through my panties. I was super wet and ready for the next move. I guess Cam could sense my eagerness as he made his way out of the T-shirt and ball shorts he wore. His joystick was rock hard and standing at full attention as he pulled my panties to the side and slid me on top of it.

"*Ahh.*" I bit down on my lip.

My hands cupped the side of his face, as I kissed him on the lips and rocked back and forth on top of him. Cam ran his fingers down my back as his sucked on my neck. My juice box was doing things it never did before, making noises that almost made me embarrassed. But, the pleasure I was feeling, topped all of that.

"Turn around and arch your back." Cam whispered with much authority.

I complied with joy, making sure to fully arch my back as I turned around in front of him. He wasted no time plunging inside of me.

"Damn…Baby!" I moaned as Cam began stroking rough and steady from behind.

"You like that don't you?" Cam asked, as he held onto my waist tightly.

"*Mmm hmm*," I moaned.

I tried my best to throw it back on him. I was no Porto when it came to sex but I had been watching enough videos to know just what to do. As Cam sped up his pace, I slipped my hand between my legs and did exactly what I did on many lonely nights. I began stroking my clit until I felt what could only be described as electricity; shot down my spine. Cam pulled out quickly, releasing his load on my lower back.

I laid back, panting heavily.

CHAPTER FIVE

War

"He's attacking everyday but I'm watching while I pray……No matter the attack I won't turn back……This means War."

Myka

Eighty-One…

It had been eighty-one long days since Isha's death and it still felt like it happened yesterday.

There was still such an eerie nature whenever Nadira and I spoke about her that I tried my best not to bring her up in conversation. The aftermath of her death hit everyone hard. But, one person was struggling with her death more than anyone I knew, and that was Nadira. I guess knowing she was gone… And, watching her blow her brains out was different. Today, like most days after work I had taken the drive to Nadira's to keep her company and visit with Heaven. When I arrived, I was surprised to find that Dira was still out at her meeting while Heaven played with the Nanny.

I had just gotten down on the floor to join Heaven at play when Dira walked in the room.

"Hey Lady, how was your meeting?" I asked, looking up at her.

The scowl on her face told me that things didn't go as planned. She shook her head from side to side and then nodded toward her bedroom.

"I'll be in, in a second." I said as I hugged on Heaven who was bubbling over with joy.

I made my way to Dira's bedroom as my cellphone began to vibrate. I knew it would be only Sean. He had been feeling very neglected over the last few months. I spent a lot more time at Nadira's than I did at home and that was causing a lot of strife in our relationship.

"So, what's up? How'd the meeting go?" I asked again as I appeared in the doorway.

"Nothing like I planned." Nadira revealed, taking a seat on the bed.

"You want to talk about it?" I asked as I inched closer into the room.

My phone began to vibrate for a second time. I pulled it from my pocket to see the flashing caller ID display read Sean.

"Not really and stop ignoring that man, Myka. We are fine here. Go spend some time with him." Nadira fussed.

"Okay, Okay… I will. Are you sure you don't want to talk about the meeting before I go?" I asked once again.

“There’s nothing to talk about except the fact that Sheila is an old bitch. She completely ruined the meeting by telling the board members that an IPO wouldn’t be a good move for BOLD Brand.”

“Wait, I thought you two were on good terms? Like damn near best friends just a few months ago?”

“Lesson learned. Being cordial with a person doesn’t make them your best friend, any more than standing in a garage makes you a car. Now get going, Myka.” Nadira said, shoeing me out the door.

I didn’t resist. I walked into Heaven’s room and kissed her little face before jogging down the stairs and out the door.

CHAPTER SIX

Forever Don't Last

"I had high hopes for us baby, Like I was on dope for us baby……Chasing after a high that I'd never get back again."

Nadira

One Month Later…

The sun beamed down on my face as I walked out of the front door and into an awaiting car.

Today, was the first time I had left the house since the meeting with the board of directors. If it were physically possible, I would've continued to avoid the world from the confines of my bedroom; where I had been for weeks. I really had no contact with anyone outside of Keon, who I only hit up when I was in the mood, and my Mother. I hopped into the back seat for the lengthy ride ahead.

I purchased a newly built home in New Jersey just weeks after Isha's death, I couldn't bear the thought of returning to my home in Royersford after the incident. The mere thought of what happened in my driveway sent my heart into a frenzy. Daily, I did my best to show no signs of trauma, although on the inside I was an emotional wreck. I was suffering from PTSD (also known as Post Traumatic Stress Disorder) which had almost crippled my daily living. Much of what made me independent, had been stripped from me due to it.

I inhaled deeply as my ride came to an end and Emilio, my driver pulled in front of the Medical building which housed Dr. Winans's office.

“I'll be ready to go in about an hour.” I said, as Emilio opened the door for me to exit the truck.

I pressed against the wall as the elevator climbed to the eighth floor. Dr. Winans's office was typically closed on Friday's, however she agreed to see me when I stressed to her that it was an emergency. I walked through the double doors into the empty waiting room. Dr. Winans rose from her seat behind the receptionist desk the moment she saw me.

“Nadira, you're pregnant?” She asked, though it was more of a rhetorical question.

The white linen pants and white tank I wore did very little to hide the fact that I was expecting.

“Follow me dear.” She led the way to an exam room.

I sat my *Gucci* handbag in a chair and took a seat on the exam table. I wasn't in the mood to answer a bunch of questions. I knew exactly why I had come here today.

“I'll give you a minute to change into the gown on the table, I'll be back in just a minute.” Dr. Winans wore a puzzled look on her face as she stepped out of the room and I couldn't blame her. She'd been my doctor since I was a teen and I hadn't informed her of my pregnancy at all.

I changed quickly before being greeted by the medical assistant who had come to draw blood for labs.

Moments later, Dr. Winans returned with a tech and a portable Ultrasound machine.

"We are going to have a look," she smiled slightly while applying the cold jelly to my stomach.

I neared tears as I turned my face away from the screen. The baby's heartbeat was strong and almost soothing to me. But still, I had no peace.

"Congratulations," Dr. Winans said as she cleaned me off.

"Are you excited, Mrs. Fortune?" she sat down on her stool and scooted close to the exam table.

"How far along am I?" I questioned, not really sharing in her excitement.

"Well, from the looks of things you're about sixteen weeks." Dr. Winans announced.

"I know it's late but what are my options at this juncture?" I said reluctantly.

The air in the room immediately became thick. I watched as Dr. Winans eyebrows rose.

"Nadira, when you say options what exactly are you asking me?" She questioned with concern in her eyes.

"You're not thinking about terminating, are you?"

"I am. I'm just not in a great place and I think this baby has suffered enough." I answered reluctantly.

The truth of the matter was every time I was with Keon, I felt guilty carrying this baby.

"Nadira, you are bigger than every obstacle that you are facing right now. I can't imagine the hurt you must feel after Isha's death but what I can say is that it gets easier. You and Gregory will work through your issues and you will get back to living before you know it. Don't make a permanent decision, in a temporary circumstance. Besides, a late term abortion could ruin any chances of conceiving in the future. So, let's skip that thought all together. Please," Dr. Winans reached out and touched my hand gently.

"I will get your prescriptions and some paperwork and be right back." I watched as she walked out of the room.

I pulled on my clothes in a hurry and grabbed my bag from the chair. I was slightly embarrassed that I had even asked for options. That wasn't what I really wanted. However, I did want the hurt to stop.

CHAPTER SEVEN

Never Loved A Man The Way I Love You

"You're a no good heart breaker, You're a liar and you're a cheat... And I don't know why, I let you do these things to me... My friends keep telling that you ain't no good, But oh they don't know I'd leave you if I could."

Sheila

"Sheila Denise. It's been a while since I last saw you." Anita rose to her feet to greet me.

She was right. It had been a long a time since I saw her last, partially because I felt like I could finally fly without seeing her. I felt like I had put all my issues on the table and I was good. Well, until I had that dream of Gregory a few nights ago. Now, don't get me wrong I didn't want him back and I didn't really miss him; at least not in my conscious mind.

"It has been a minute but I had some things on my mind that I needed some help sorting out." I admitted.

"Well, that's what I'm here for. Let's talk. What's been up?" Anita said, welcoming me to open up my heart to her.

"I've been dreaming of my ex-husband a lot lately." I began to speak, a bit embarrassed.

"You seem reluctant to be dreaming about him, Sheila. Exactly what kind of dreams are you having?" Anita moved to the edge of her seat.

"The kind where he and I are happy together. And, sometimes rather nasty ones. You know… in a sexual way." I divulged.

"Well, sometimes our dreams are our subconscious mind preparing us for things to come in our waking life. And, other times dreams are our repressed memories finding a way to escape our hearts. So, tell me… Is there any part of you that misses, Gregory?" Anita asked.

I paused to think for a moment, and earnestly had to fight with an onset of tears. I wasn't even sure where they were coming from.

"The truth is, sometimes I miss Gregory. He was my high school sweetheart, my first lover, my daughters father and all else. But, what I don't miss is the other side of Gregory… The lying, cheating dog." I grimaced.

CHAPTER EIGHT

Do Right Man

"Take me to heart and I'll always love you, and nobody can make me do wrong. Take me for granted, leaving love unsure. Makes willpower weak and temptation strong. A woman's only human this you should understand. She's not just a plaything, she's flesh and blood just like her man. So if you want a so right all day's woman. You got to be a do right all nights man."

Sheila Denise

1996…

It was no ordinary Sunday morning in the Fortune household. Our usual Sunday morning Gospel had been replaced by the sounds of Aretha Franklin. There was no breakfast being prepared and no shirts being ironed. I looked at the clock on the nightstand which read 9:20 a.m.

My husband had lost his way home, again. It was becoming a regular occurrence in our household.

My hand grazed the back of my one-year old daughter who lie asleep on my lap. The door handle turned and the door crept open slowly. Gregory stood in the doorway with his tie hanging loosely around his neck, grinning from ear to ear; as if all were right with the world.

"Good Morning, Beautiful." Gregory crooned.

"Why aren't you up, getting ready for church?" He questioned.

"The children and I aren't going." I replied softly.

I recalled one of my grandmother's favorite scriptures which read "Soft words turn away wrath."

"Why not? A First Lady should always be on her post." Gregory stated, as he rummaged through the closet for a suit to wear.

"That's a loaded statement for a pastor who so often neglects his post." I rolled my eyes disgusted by Gregory's utter disdain for our household.

"The devil sure is woke and busy this morning." Gregory chuckled.

"Seems to me he pulled an all-nighter, seeing as one of us got lost on the way home. But, I'm sure you found refuge from the cold under some willing skirt." I retorted.

"Keep your voice down, Reds." Gregory said above a whisper, looking at me sternly.

"Keep your dick in your pants, Gregory." I spat bitterly in return.

"Why do you always want to fight?" Gregory asked.

"Well, that depends... Do you always want to lie and cheat? Or does the urge just overtake you suddenly?" I was growing tired of our conversation by the minute.

"Sheila, do you think that this is easy for me? You think this is the way I want things to be? When was the last time you showed me some affection? Or made me feel good as a man? "Gregory replied, trying his hand at reverse psychology.

"She, whomever this one was... must've screwed your brains out last night if you think for one minute that I'm about to sit here and pacify that load of crap you just used to justify cheating. It's bad enough that you do what you will behind my back, but what you won't do is stand here and play in my damn face. Now, since you asked... Let me remind you of the last time that I showed your ass some affection and made you feel good as man; I ended up with Chlamydia while carrying our precious little daughter. Which simply means you were doing you, even when you were doing me. It's obvious that one home isn't enough for you. You're selfish and you're greedy and since your needs aren't being met here... Do me a favor baby? When you walk out that door today and leave me lonely, do it permanently. Because having you here robs me of the joy and happiness that having a husband who is a true Man of God should bring." I scolded.

"I don't want to lose you, Sheila." Gregory pled.

"You sure don't want to keep me either. Have you any idea what it's like to be in church praying and counseling the same women that are really laughing at me? I've been your fool for much too long baby. So, the greatest gift you can give me in the moment is to walk your ass out that door and restore my peace, please." I finished throwing my hand in the way to block any response Gregory may have wanted to offer. Relief fell over me

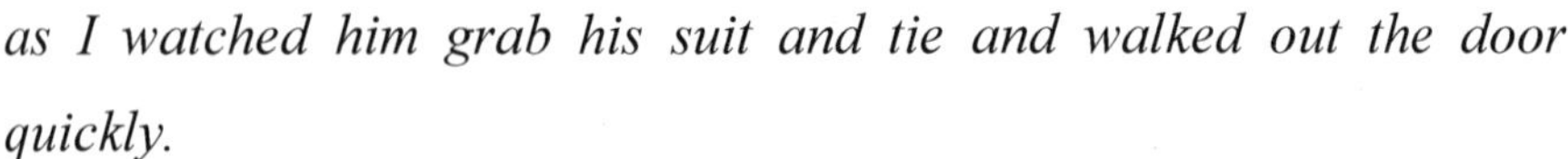

as I watched him grab his suit and tie and walked out the door quickly.

CHAPTER NINE

Party

"I may be young but I'm ready to give you all my love, I told my girls you can get it. Don't slow it down. Just let it go."

Indiya

"Hey! Where are you going, sexy?" Dij doubled back into my bedroom door.

I stood in the middle of the floor putting the finishing touches on my face. I wasn't big on makeup but tonight I needed my face to be beat down like a boxer, if I wanted to party amongst the city's elite.

"Get dressed." I said, barely looking back at her.

"Yes Honey, you don't have to tell me twice." Dij disappeared from the doorway quickly, as I took a step back from the mirror and gave my complete look the once over.

I had stopped by my stepmother's house earlier to see her but since she wasn't home I borrowed her ID as well as a couple of hot pieces from her closet. My own closet was nowhere near her level. Everything that she owned had a label… She gave true meaning to drape in all designer. My body was filling out the black silk *Balmain* jumpsuit I wore. And, my new haircut added a couple years to my baby face. My feet were laced with Nadira's signature *Giuseppe Zanotti* heels, that I knew I had to return tomorrow morning. I smoothed on a little Matte red lipstick before spritzing all over with *Gucci "Guilty"* before grabbing my clutch and my keys and walked down the hall. I stopped at Khadija's bedroom door and was pleasantly surprised when I looked inside. Dij was dressed in a white tank body con dress that fit like a second skin. I could tell the way the dressed hugged every curve that Dij had little to nothing on underneath. Her short haircut reminded me of rapper, Dej Loaf.

My mouth hung slightly agape as I watched Dij slipped her feet into a brand-new pair of Steve Madden heels. This was something new. Dij was a tomboy of sorts, she had her own unique sense of style that typically consisted of jeans and the latest sneakers.

"Don't say nothing," Dij laughed as we walked out the front door.

"Okay, but you cute though." I said looking her over again.

"Might even catch you something tonight, boo." Dij and I laughed hard as we slid into my car.

"So, are you going to say where it is we are headed or is it a surprise?" Dij said impatiently.

I pulled the tickets to the celebrity black out party from the visor and put them in her lap.

"Oh, bae! you know some folks that know some folks huh?" Dij eyes were wide and I could tell she was just as excited to be in the mix as me. Cam had gifted the tickets to me earlier this week and I surely didn't want to go alone so who better to share the night with than my best friend.

CHAPTER TEN Jealous

"I wish that you were me, so you could feel this feeling. I never broke one promise, I know when you're not honest"

Nadira

My doctor's appointment today, left my head even foggier than before I went. I swear I was emotionally and mentally bankrupt. Crying out, for some type of stimulus to relieve me of my burdens. In my thoughts today, I realized my husband wasn't unfaithful; he just wasn't forthcoming and that hurt. I believed every word that Gregory had ever allowed to roll off his lips and I guess that was my mistake.

My phone vibrated on the side of the tub. I peeked over at the caller ID and decided to answer since it was my Mom. I just prayed she didn't have a speech for me today.

"Hello," I answered

"Hey, baby girl. How are you doing?" she inquired.

"I'm okay, Mom. What's up?" I began pulling myself from the bathtub.

"Sounds like you're over there crying again. Do you need me?" My mom was a rider.

She'd been right by my side the last few weeks, tending to my needs, helping me through the grief process and most of all rooting for her son in law.

"I'm good Ma, I promise." I wrapped in a towel and walked into my bedroom.

"Yeah, okay. Tell me anything. You know, I was sitting out on the porch doing some thinking the other night. And, I was trying to figure out why all of this seemed like Deja Vu and then it hit me. You're punishing Gregory for more than just his past. You're punishing him for Cokes' short comings too. I remember it like yesterday when he hurt you," My mother paused.

Nadira

2003...

"Aye babe! How long is it going to take you to get ready?" Coke called out as he sat on the bed in my condo while I took my time getting dressed in the mirror.

Tonight, he and I were going to celebrate my progression from intern to employee. I was just weeks away from graduation and already making boss moves.

"I'm hungry as hell girl! Can you please come on." Coke appeared, blocking the bathroom doorway with his massive presence.

He stood 6'4, two hundred and fifty pounds. He flashed his beautiful smile, the same smile that always caused me to melt like putty in his hands.

"You look good enough to eat," Coke said as he wrapped his big arms around me.

I felt safe in his presence. Many feared Coke, because he was notorious in the streets for being merciless. He was a kingpin, a boss in his own right with connections whose names held major clout. However, Coke did his best to keep that part of his world away from me. When we were together, he was Darren... A thug and a gentleman. Coke and I walked hand in hand, to his awaiting Mercedes Benz.

"Where do you want to eat baby? Coke questioned as he massaged the back of my neck.

"Maggianos," I smiled excitedly. It was my favorite spot to eat.

"You love that nasty ass Italian food, and that crazy ass downtown traffic." Coke laughed.

"Anything for my baby though." Coke put his hand under my chin and lifted my face to look at him. I smiled back at him as we arrived in Center City. Coke parked in the garage, close to the Gallery.

"Can we go inside baby? " I looked over at Coke, already knowing he would never say no. He shook his head yes and pulled his gun from the trunk to his waist.

"Here and make it quick too. I told you a nigga hungry." Coke pulled a wad of hundred-dollar bills apart from the knot in he'd taken out of his pocket and handed it over to me.

I walked inside of New York and Co. and went to town on the racks. When I could no longer carry the pieces that were draped across my arm I made my way to the register to pay for my clothes. After my damage was tallied up and paid for, I happily walked to the door of the store. I was about to exit, but become frozen in place as I watched Coke exchange heated word with a unknown woman. Beside the woman, was a crying child who looked to be about two years old. I adjusted the bags in my hand and walked closer to where they stood. I really prayed I didn't have to beat this bitch ass today.

"I take care of my son, and that's all you should be worried about!" Coke screamed as I stood beside him.

"You're a damn lie, Darren! You're too busy running behind this little ass girl to even know where the hell your son is half the

time." The woman screamed in Cokes' face, mushing him in the head with her finger.

I looked back and forth between the both of them. I had heard so much, yet I still felt like I hadn't heard enough. Coke didn't have children? We had this conversation about having kids on numerous occasions and he had never even mentioned a son. He begged me to wait, claimed he wanted to marry me before we had children. This bastard hadn't even touched me in all these years and now he has a son.

"Get the hell out of here, Keisha! I take care of my son. You're mad that I don't want to be with your ass no more, that's all." Coke picked up the crying little boy from beside him and hugged him tight. He instantly laid his head on his shoulder and stopped crying.

"You know what Darren, you right. Let this little ass girl stash your drugs. Let her deal with all your trifling ways and most of all let her wear your damn ring. I'm done! You can keep your son, too." she said before taking off in the other direction.

Coke stood there with his son on his shoulder, saying nothing. I looked at him for an answer yet he said nothing. We spent five years together, how could I not know he conceived a baby and that he was living another life while I was believing his shit didn't stink.

*****

I couldn't have been happier when my mother finished her spill. After saying our goodbyes, I hurried to my bedroom and dried off quickly. I rummaged through my drawers, pulling out a pair of *Victoria's Secret 'Pink'* leggings and a T-shirt. I swiftly got dressed and then slipped into my *Chanel* track sneakers before running down the steps. I grabbed my car keys from the desk in the den and walked toward the front door.

Within minutes, I reached my destination; *The Ritz Carlton Residences* in Philly. I drove into the parking lot. My conscience had now stepped into high gear as it did every time I arrived here. This place had become my refuge on the nights when my mind wouldn't stop racing.

I fought to silence my thoughts as I got out of the car and stepped onto the private elevator. When I reached the top floor, I slid the key card I had been given across the reader and stepped inside. I could hear the shower running as I walked further into the apartment. I was tense and my body was sore. I needed some relief.

"Hey! You cool?" Keon asked as he walked into the living room and stood behind the chair where I sat.

I nodded my head yes.

"I'll be right back," Keon backed out of the room wearing only his towel.

I knew I was playing with fire each time I came here. Still, I ignored my better judgement and came looking for comfort anyway. In the back off my mind, I was already aware that Keon was only comforting me; in hopes of having a chance with me. Still, I kept coming.

"Come here." Keon reached out his hand to me as he stepped back into the living room wearing only his *Calvin Klein* boxer briefs.

I had to admit he was fine… But, he wasn't my husband. At least that's what I kept telling myself. I rose from the sofa and slowly walked toward him; finally connecting my hand with his.

"Relax man, you know I don't bite. Unless you want me to… I think you know that by now." he said with a smile as he led the way to his bedroom.

He helped me out of my clothes and shoes, then into the bed. He covered me with the throw blanket that sat at the bottom of the bed. "Close your eyes, your safe with me." He kissed the back of my neck, sending chills down my spine.

I maintained my composure as I lay in his arms. I didn't want sex tonight, I just wanted his comfort; someone to spoon with me and make me feel safe and secure.

"You seem tense, turn over for me." He instructed.

I did as he asked, watching him grab a bottle of baby oil from the night stand drawer.

His hands began kneading out all the knots of discomfort I was feeling; soothing both my aches and my roaming mind. Hot tears rolled down my face that was buried in the pillow and soft moans escaped my lips. The war was on! Internally, my mind wanted him to stop but my body was begging for him to keep going.

CHAPTER ELEVEN Disrespectful

"If my girl found out you was on her side of the bed she'll kill you."

Keon

Nadira was fast asleep in my arms after I put these hands all over her body. I was restless, though. I couldn't get any sleep as I kept thinking about how I'd stupidly gave her a key to my place. Yes, I enjoyed her company… And, I loved having her in my arms whenever she chose to come by. But, there was someone who would go crazy if they even thought I was allowing another woman to get this close to me.

I pulled Nadira closer to me as I watched her stiffen in her sleep. Her breathing pattern changed and she clutched my arm tightly, I knew she was fighting through another one of her night terrors. I couldn't lie, I enjoyed being her knight in shining armor though Nadira on the surface would swear to you that she was no damsel in distress.

I rubbed her small belly and kissed her in her sleep, careful not to wake her… You never really knew what you were going to get with Nadira. Sometimes, she comes off like all she wants is company and maybe some conversation. And then, other times she'd show up in some sexy shit ready to fuck me and leave. I respected her though. We are both adults with complicated situations but I was along for the ride. Wherever she wanted to go from here, I was going to follow her sexy ass.

I muted my phone which had begun to vibrate on the nightstand, yet again. My girlfriend Dani was calling me back to back. I couldn’t explain this thing I was caught up in with Nadira to her if I tried. Rather than give it anymore thought, I silenced the calls the best way possible by turning the phone off.

CHAPTER TWELVE

Somebody's Sleeping In My Bed

"I've got this feeling and I just can't turn it loose, that somebodies been getting next to you."

Gregory

I had a nagging feeling this morning as I got Heaven and myself dressed for the day. Something just wasn't right. I had been trying to reach my wife for hours but was met with the voicemail each time I called.

"Come on daddy's girl. Let's go check on, Mommy." I said as I carried Heaven to the car.

I pulled out my phone and dialed Nadira one last time before backing out of my parking space in the garage. I was grateful Heaven wasn't old enough to understand what Nadira and I were going through.

As we pulled up to the home my wife newly purchased, I looked back at my daughter who was fast asleep in her car seat. I walked to the backseat and picked her up as we headed up the stairs to the front door. I rang the doorbell and was greeted by Marta, Heaven's Nanny or Au pair as Nadira liked to call her.

"Good Morning, Mr. Fortune. Do you want me to take the baby? Mrs. Fortune isn't in this morning." She offered as she reached out her hands to take Heaven.

I was a bit alarmed by my wife's absence, wondering where she could have been at this time of morning.

"Did Mrs. Fortune leave for work already? I asked, prying a bit.

"That I'm not sure of, Sir. She wasn't in this morning when I arrived." Marta said as she rocked Heaven in her arms.

"Okay, Thank you. I will check on Heaven later today." I said as I walked to the front of the house.

I opened the front door just in time to see Nadira walking up the stairs to come inside. She looked startled by my presence as I stared at her.

"Good Morning." I greeted, stepping into her path.

"Good Morning." Nadira said as she tried to avoid my gaze.

"Are you okay?" I asked looking down at her attire.

It wasn't her norm, but I knew I couldn't go right at her and ask her where she had been although I wanted to.

"I just dropped Heaven off, I can come by and get her later when I'm finished at my office if you need me." I assured her.

"I'll call you later if it's necessary." She spoke quickly, never making eye contact with me.

"Alright. Try to enjoy your day." I encouraged as I walked down the steps to my car.

C H A P T E R T H I R T E E N

Angel

"My heart is without a home, I don't want to be alone.... I gotta find me an angel in my life."

Sheila

"Humph....I call bullshit." I said aloud reading through an article in Glamour magazine about dating over fifty.

I discarded the magazine on the table that sat on the balcony beside me. I heard my friends that are close to my age say how happy they are to be single and just living life to the fullest. I had to say my views were torn on the subject. Being single was still new to me. Being married for more than half of my life meant relearning and reworking the way I did everything from cooking dinner to laundry, even the things I watched on television.

Somedays, I felt like I didn't do single well. I longed for a hyphen to my last name and a man that I could come home to every night. Until, I remember the peace of mind and the joy I feel while lying in the bed at night knowing there isn't a damn soul out there cheating on me because I don't belong to anyone. There was freedom and liberation in being single that was for damn sure. My needs came first for the first time in a very long time, and I was slowly regaining the pieces of me that I once lost.

My phone vibrated on the table beside me, annoying me slightly.

"Damn… Can't a girl think in peace?" I blurted out before answering.

It would've been too much like right to look at the caller ID display before answering because now I was stuck on the phone with a caller I had been avoiding well for months.

"Hey there, Stranger! I finally got through to you." Vic chimed cheerfully.

I rolled my eyes and shook my head.

"*Be nice, Sheila.*" I convinced myself.

"Hey Vic. How are you?" I greeted in return.

"I'm well. I miss you. It's good to hear your voice again." He replied, laying it on thick.

I wish I could return all those sentiments but I was detoxing from him. I couldn't afford to mess up my karma again.

"What can I do for you, Victor?" I asked sweetly.

"Meet me for lunch." He answered quickly.

"I don't know if that's a good idea." I sneered.

"Why not? What harm could lunch do?" Vic challenged.

"Well that depends, are you still married Victor?" I asked sarcastically.

“I am and my wife is gravely ill, Sheila. But you know that.” Vic replied.

“You're exactly right. I do know that Vic and you know what, that's reason enough for you to be by her side versus scheduling lunch dates.” I sighed.

“Well, if you change your mind my number is still the same.” Vic said before ending the call.

I wish I could deny that I was thinking long and hard about saying yes while I had him on the phone, but it was inevitable. I missed him too. Only time would tell where Victor and I stood.

*****

Indiya

It was just a little after two in the afternoon when I arrived at my apartment on campus; last night was a wild one. Dij and I attended a Black Out party in Philly that was bananas. I don't remember much but I woke up next to Cam which made my morning a great one. I put my key in the door and turned the knob. As I stepped inside, I found Dij laying on the couch watching "Power."

"Hey," I said walking over and sitting on the couch beside her.

I had to look over to make sure she wasn't sleep since she didn't respond when I spoke the first time. Instead, she jumped up off the couch and walked back to her bedroom with an attitude.

"*Here we go with the dumb shit.*" I thought to myself as I headed to my room to take a shower.

I slipped in the shower after peeling off the clothes I wore, to wash away the residue of a long night.

After a quick shower and change, I walked down the hall and stood in Khadijah's bed room door to find out what her deal was this afternoon.

"So, what's up with you?" I asked, still annoyed that she ignored me earlier.

Dij sat scrolling on her iPhone, still saying nothing.

"Uh, hello? Do you not see me standing here?" I snapped.

"Get the hell away from my door, Indiya." Dij rolled her eyes.

"What did I do to you now, Khadijah? I'm tired of catering to your funky attitude constantly." I folded my arms across my chest, as I waited for an answer.

"That's funny because I'm tired of you constantly being a flake, who worries about nothing or no one except her damn self." Dij sat up and looked at me with anger written all over her face.

"What are you talking about?" I was now confused because I hadn't done anything, at least not to my knowledge.

"Stop playing dumb, Indiya! You invited me out last night and then disappeared as usual, leaving me stranded miles away from home. You didn't even have the courtesy to let me know that you were leaving with some random ass dude. Or, how about last week when you begged me to go to a party all the way out in New York City and conveniently forgot about me being there with you the whole night." Dij spat.

"Okay, so first off I never forced you to go anywhere. Secondly, this is college. People come to have fun. Lighten up, Dij. It's not that deep, really. If you can't go with the flow, I won't ask you to go out with me anymore." I was getting more pissed off by the minute.

"You're a real bitch, you know that Indiya? I'm not sure what world you live in, Indiya however you're selfish and inconsiderate. If we go somewhere together, there is a simple courtesy of letting me know that you have alternate plans afterwards so I can plan accordingly. That would be the adult thing to do. Now, get the hell out of my room." Dij snapped.

I slammed Khadija's door and walked down the hall. My night was too good to be arguing with her about some dumb shit. As she said, we were both adults and I didn't owe her a damn thing. I walked back into my bedroom and packed a small overnight bag before heading back out the door. I would get some rest when I got to my next destination. I was way too mad to sleep at this point.

CHAPTER FOURTEEN

Got Me Waiting

"You got me waiting, you got me waiting.... When I tell you everything you need to hear like baby come now, You got me waiting but I can't keep waiting on you acting like whatever I'm gone always be around."

Myka

"Hey, are you about to go out?" Sean asked from behind me as I stood in the mirror putting on my earrings.

His question was one I'm sure he already knew the answer to. It was Sunday morning and of course I was headed to church just as I had every Sunday since he and I met.

"I'm going to church. Would you like to join me?" I offered.

I already knew what his answer would be, however I thought that the offer to join me would combat any argument of me attending.

"You haven't spent any time with me all week long. Church isn't really the place I want to spend time with you, Myka." Sean groaned.

"We can spend the entire afternoon together after service." I offered.

"Why am I prone to getting your leftovers, Myka?" Sean shook his head in frustration.

"My leftovers?" I asked, confused.

"Yes, your leftovers. The little bit of fuel or time that you have left when you come in from spending the entire day up under Nadira. Or, the time you have left after ministry. Or, whatever else it is that you are devoted to now!" Sean spat.

"I'm sorry, I didn't know that you felt that way. I know I have been spending an awful lot of time with Nadira these last few weeks. It's just that we are both grieving because of Isha and it just makes it easier to grieve together. But, I hear you completely." I paused and thought for a moment as the realization of my neglecting of Sean settled in.

"I'll tell you what, let's go to church and have a date night this evening. I promise I will be more mindful of you when I'm scheduling out my days and nights." I tried my best to smooth the situation over. I wasn't up for arguing, besides the taste of metal in my mouth was getting the best of me.

"Okay, church it is." Sean conceded before kissing me on the forehead.

I was happy to know he could compromise too. I took note to consider him a bit more than I recently have, as well.

CHAPTER FIFTEEN

Grown Woman

"I'm so sexy remain a mystery, Cause everybody want what they can't see. And what they can't have, and what they can't grab and what they can't see and baby that's me."

Sheila

"Good Morning. Time to get your ass up and out of my bed," I sang standing over the fine chocolate Adonis that was laid up in my bed like he was king of the castle.

"*Sheila, you have to stop with the cougar nonsense.*" I shook my head, laughing at my own thoughts as he rolled over disoriented.

Q was young and fine, he had a strong back and muscular arms. Looking at him, he could be one of my sons.

"*Damn shame, Sheil.*" I thought to myself.

"What's up with breakfast?" he asked, wiping sleep from his eyes as he rolled to the side of the bed.

"Boy, please. What you need some money? Here, you go. McDonalds serves breakfast all day long." I said reaching into my *Isabel Murant Linen* pants and pulling out a fifty-dollar bill.

"Your mouth is so slick, it's cool. I'll just eat you." Q picked me up by my waist and threw me onto the bed before I had a chance to react.

He snatched off my pants and my panties in one flick of the wrist.

"*Ah Shit!"* my conscious was kicking my ass, but every endorphin in my body was fighting back for this pleasure like hell.

Q was known on the basketball court as "The Bully" and that I could agree with. He was definitely a bedroom bully. He held my waist firmly in place and explored me, using only his tongue. Chills ran down my spine as he focused in on my throbbing clit. He slurped hard before tongue kissing it gently. Then, he inserted two fingers inside of me while making love to my clit. His finger explored my G-spot.

"Damn it, Q! Stop it, you know I have to go out." I pleaded, as I pretended to put up a fight but I really wanted some of that bomb loving I knew I was about to get.

I pushed Q's face away only to have him pin my arms above my head.

"Hold still, and shut up." he commanded, discarding his Armani Boxer briefs.

He lifted both of my legs over his shoulders and snaked between my thighs; making sure to enter me fully.

"You get on my damn nerves." I said aloud.

I was soaking wet and dripping with pleasure as he stroked away. I had plans on carrying my tired ass to church this morning to surprise Kat but from the looks of things, that wasn't happening. Q slapped me on the ass, signaling for me to turn over. I crawled on my knees, seductively throwing my ass in the air. He wrapped one of his tatted arms around my neck, choking me lightly; I slapped his arm away.

The dick was good but this fool was not about to try that new age kinky stuff on me. His grip returned to my waist where he slammed into me repeatedly. He alternated his pace from fast and hard to grinding slowly, which drove me crazy. I had to show him that an old girl could flex. While tightening my muscles around his shaft, I reached back and gripped his balls; massaging them gently.

"I love when you do that shit," Q moaned.

It was in that moment, that I knew I had captured his damn soul. Q pulled out quickly as I rolled over on my back, releasing his fluid on top of me. I sighed with both pleasure and relief. My ass was getting too old for this acrobatic sex.

"How about breakfast now?" Q rolled over on his back panting hard.

I took a minute to recover before crawling off the bed.

"How about a washcloth so you can carry your ass home?" I snickered as I walked into the bathroom to clean up.

"Damn! No hope for breakfast, I see." Q said, as he sat on the edge of the bed.

"Not at all. And, um Quentin… Your ass is fine and all… However, the next time you decide to choke me… I'll be reaching for a lot more than your balls." I winked as I closed the bathroom door.

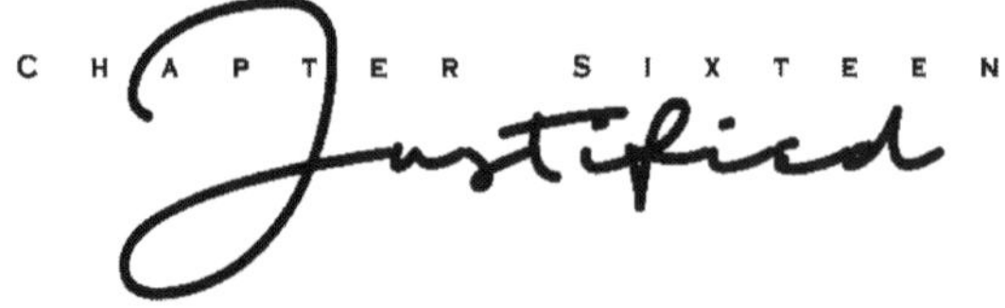

CHAPTER SIXTEEN

"Justified me, Glorified me. Paid my ransom, I've been redeemed by his blood."

Gregory

"*Paid a price, for my life. And all that was wrong his love made it right. Now what greater sign can any man show. That know with his blood, He made me whole.*" The words of the song penetrated my heart as EFM spirit of praise sang during the altar call.

I was overwhelmed. Almost near tears as I held tightly to my wife's hand while she sat poised beside me. EFM spirit of praise ministering in song brought conviction and confirmation for me.

Nadira squeezed my hand slightly, reassuring me that she had not completely checked out on me. I turned my head to look at my wife who sat with glassy tear-filled eyes, while trying to remain strong. Part of me wanted the tears to fall so that I could comfort her for the first time in months, but there was this other part of me feared that behind that ball of emotions would be hurtful words exchanged like divorce. She and I stood together as the associate pastor called the congregation to stand for the benediction.

“Hug someone and tell them you're glad to see them here.” Pastor Garrett instructed.

I reached over and hugged my wife tightly. It was the first embrace she and I’d shared in a while. She was accepting of my hug, not pushing me away as I thought she would. Though the smirk on her face read, her favorite tagline of “You tried it.” I missed her touch, her scent and her laugh more than I could express. Everything about her was intoxicating to me and I needed her. The little tug on my pants caused me to snap out of my thoughts. I looked down into the face of my little girl.

“Daddy's, little girl. I've missed you.” I lifted Heaven from the floor and kissed her face, as Dira excused herself congregating with a few members before disappearing into her office.

Nadira

"Good Afternoon, Lady Fortune." Myka smiled as she walked into my office.

I looked up at Myka who's face which rendered a sea of emotions. I saw Myka almost daily when she visited, but today I saw her with fresh eyes. I could finally see that she too had some needs and some issues plaguing her.

"Hey Sis, what's good? Come in and have a seat." I sat back in my chair as Myka stepped into my office further and took a seat at my desk.

"I just wanted to say hello and check on you before I left. You look good today, Dira. I'm glad you came to church." Myka smiled.

"It felt good to be here." I admitted with a slight grin as well.

"Bishop, couldn't be happier to have you here. I saw all the sneak glances he was giving you. That man misses you sorely. Can you please just stop being evil, and give him some."

"All that word going forth and that's what you got out of the sermon?" I laughed as Myka fished through the candy bowl on the desk filled with Lindor truffles.

"You like it. I'm sure in that big head of yours, you were sitting up there thinking *you want me don't you daddy?"* Myka popped a truffle in her mouth before looking for another to devour.

"Maybe, maybe not. Only time will tell." I replied, sitting back folding my hands in my lap.

"When did you start liking chocolate though, Myka?" I raised my eyebrow at her.

“Since, I missed my period a month ago.” Myka rolled her eyes in her head.

“So, what are you saying here my love?” I squinted, at Myka trying to read in between the invisible lines.

“Time will tell.” Myka mocked me.

“Time and a EPT test, heifer.” I remarked.

“Don't look so frightened, Myka. Babies are a blessing and this is something you looked forward to right?” I said, digging a little deeper.

“Once upon a time, I surely did. I just don't know where my current situation with Sean is going. We had a little rift this morning, but I’m hoping for the best.” Myka smiled.

“All couples do. It shall be well.” As I finished my last words, Gees, Sean and Heaven appeared in the doorway.

“There's Mommy.” Gees exclaimed, as he placed Heaven in my arms.

“Well family, we are going to be getting out of your way. Enjoy the rest of your Sunday.” Myka said before kissing Heaven on the cheek and walking out the door with Sean in tow.

“Heaven and I are about to get out of here, too.” I picked up my handbag from my desk, just as Gees walked over and stood in front of me.

He smiled before kissing me forcefully. I allowed him to get a second one in before pulling away. Gregory was wearing me down.

“Are you going to join us for dinner?” I invited innocently.

I couldn’t lie after that kiss, I wanted his company.

"Sure thing." Gees said making sure to brush up against me as I walked out of the door.

I just shook my head and put on a happy face as we walked to the car, stopping momentarily to shake hands and hug many of our members; like a happy first family should.

CHAPTER SEVENTEEN

Until You Come Back To Me

"Why did you have to decide, you had to set me free…I'm gonna swallow my pride, I'm gonna beg you (please baby please) see me. I'm gonna walk by myself…. Just to prove that my love is true…. Oh, for you baby, til you come back to me…That's what I'm gonna do."

Sheila Denise

The day had gotten away from me.

I lay in the bed sore from the countless rounds of rough nasty sex I had in the last twenty-four hours with, Quentin. I was too sore to even walk, I counted today a day well spent in bed. From the *Bose`* sound system played *Sade* which took me into a realm of thinking that was much too heavy for a Sunday afternoon.

I sat up in the bed as my Mother Kat appeared in the doorway. She stopped by for a visit as she typically did on Sunday. As always, she was filling my house with wisdom, cheer and the smell of delicious Sunday dinner that she prepared for me weekly.

"What has you so deep in thought baby girl?" She asked as she approached the bed and took a seat.

Kat didn't miss a beat. She could read me backward and forward and there was nothing I could hide from her. She ran her hand through my hair which had grown into a shoulder length bob.

"Just thinking. That's all, mom." I lied, trying to conceal the nature of my true thoughts.

"You do know I'm not new to this, right?" Kat said, cocking her head to one side.

She was as sassy as a seventy-three-year-old came, and still sharp as a tack.

"I'm just wondering if I'll ever really love again, that's all." I finally mustered up the courage to say.

"Do you want to hear the truth?" Kat asked, staring me in the eye.

"Yes, the whole truth and nothing but the truth." I laughed.

"Sheila Denise, I have watched for the past three years while you reinvented yourself. You began seeing someone new, and you started doing all the things that you said you would do when you were younger. You even started seeing that fancy head doctor, but the truth is… You never stopped loving, Gregory. The largest part of your heart still beats for him. You love his rights and his wrongs. Girl, you love that man's dirty drawers." Kat laughed hard.

"You know what else Sheila Denise? You even befriended his wife, while putting on your super hero cape and played strong.

Never stopping to realize just why it was that you were trying to save her, did you?" she stopped to ask with her hand on top of mine.

"No, ma'am." I answered afraid of what was coming next.

"You were trying to shield another young woman from ending up like you. You gave a selfish man one-hundred percent while he barely gave you two. But you know what? Your father taught me a lesson many years ago that I will never forget. Sometimes, the other woman comes along to teach him how to be a better man to you. Don't be discouraged Sheila, you too have a ship coming soon. And, there won't be any sharing treasures this time. Now come on downstairs and let's eat." Kat slapped me on the knee walking out of the door just as quickly as she came.

I shook my head in admiration. I loved having her around. She was like my own personal superhero. Yet, she wore no cape and she didn't fly. But, she always seemed to show up just in the nick of time to fix whatever was broken or rescue me in my times of need.

Gregory

I was soaking up time like a sponge with my family, today. Heaven had finally gone to sleep and Indiya was back in her room studying as I made my way down the stairs; hoping for a few minutes alone with my wife.

"Do you want some coffee?" Nadira asked softly.

"Yes, please." I took a seat at the island while she prepared the Keurig.

"I have a doctor's appointment for a test this week." She announced as she sat the mug in front of me.

"I'll be there." I said without hesitation.

I looked at my wife. She began to grab at her chest, her breathing was sporadic and her chest heaved in and out heavily. .

"Are you okay?"

"I just need a minute." She said, quickly.

She hurried out of the kitchen and I followed closely behind. She went into the bathroom and closed the door behind her.

"*What just happened?*" My brow furrowed.

I slowly opened the door and entered the bathroom. I found Nadira gasping for air with tears running heavily down her face as she leaned against the sink. I wrapped my arms around her instinctively. She and I had talked on many nights about the sudden panic attacks but because of my absence, this was the first one I'd witnessed.

"I got you, baby." I lead her upstairs to the bedroom.

Her panicked breathing pattern slowed as I lie down beside her. I stroked her hair and held her against my chest. Her nails dug into my arm as she gripped me tightly.

“Do you want me to get your medicine?” I asked.

“No, just stay with me.” she said through her tears.

*****

Nadira

I awoke at 3:40 a.m., securely nestled in Gees arms.

I quietly moved out of his arms, careful not to wake him and went into the bathroom. I stripped out of my clothes. The smell of his cologne all over me, made me realize just how much I'd missed his scent, his touch and even his presence around the house. After my shower, I grabbed my robe and took a seat at my vanity for a second to check my phone. No missed calls or text worthy to be answered at this hour.

When I returned to the bedroom, I found Gees seated at the edge of the bed. I sat beside him, rotating my neck hoping to alleviate some of the stiffness.

"Are you alright, Smooth?" Gregory asked, as he caressed the back of my neck.

"Yes. Thanks for staying with me." I spoke softly.

"What are we going to do, Smooth?" Gregory asked sincerely.

"We can talk about it. But, not tonight. I'm sore and tired." I answered, wanting to avoid the conversation all together.

Suddenly, he kissed me. His tongue was tangoed with mine as his hands found their way inside my robe. I didn't push him away. Instead, I lie back against the pillows and awaited his next move; there'd be no fight from me tonight. He began kissing me from head to toe, and the feeling was intoxicating.

My head began fighting with my flesh, and currently my flesh was winning. He went from licking to sucking, while I fought to maintain a straight face. His lips trailed down to my stomach as he planted gentle kisses, before parting the lips of my kitty. I had gotten a fresh wax just a day ago and was in desperate need of his attention.

He French kissed my throbbing clit while rubbing my breast with both of his hands. I arched my back and sat up on my elbows, pushing my juice box further into his face. It didn't take long for me to reach the point of no return as I climaxed. Sex with Keon couldn't equate to the intimacy I shared with my husband.

"Better now?" Gees asked, moving my hair away from my face.

I nodded my head yes and drifted off to dream land.

CHAPTER EIGHTEEN

Trap Queen

"Married to the money, Introduced her to my stove.... Showed her how to whip it now she remixing for low."

Indiya

I wondered if anyone else could see my heart beating through my chest.

It felt like I had a set of African drums in my shirt. The train conductor's announcement that we would soon be arriving at my destination in five minutes was like music to my ears. I stood up from my seat trying not to seem noticeably anxious as I grabbed the *Louis Vuitton* duffle bag that sat in the overhead rack just an hour prior when leaving Baltimore. I used my front facing camera to check my appearance. I wanted to be sure not to look too disheveled by my nervousness.

The *Carrera* shades and Ombre Blonde bob cut wig I wore gave me a brand-new identity. I was certain no one I knew would recognize me even if I were staring them in the face. The moment the train screeched into the station, my feet hit the platform. I blended in with the crowd as Cam had advised, breezing through the station. I moved steadily toward the exit watching my surroundings as I made my way to his awaiting car.

"What up's Bae?" I smiled finally able to relax.

My nerves had been on edge since he asked me to make the run for him a few days ago. Truth be told. I was just as excited as I was nervous.

"*He trusts me.*" I thought as I put the duffle bag full of cash and product in the backseat.

"Proud of you." He smiled as he whipped onto the street.

Cam drove a few blocks away onto Powellton street where I had parked my car earlier. He grabbed the duffle bag from the back and pulled out three stacks of bills all wrapped in $2,000 bands before kissing me on the cheek.

"Buy some sexy shit." He smirked dropping the money into my *Louis Vuitton* purse.

"Thanks, Bae. Am I going to see you later?" I asked with my hand on the door handle.

"For Sure." He nodded before kissing me on the cheek.

I walked to my car smiling like a Cheshire Cat. I knew what I had just done was dangerous but it gave me such a rush. In my head, I knew that without hesitation that when he asked me to; I would do it all over again.

CHAPTER NINETEEN

All Men Lie

"Baby it's the truth I know the grass ain't greener on the other side."

Nadira

Monica's 'Code Red' Album was banging through the speakers of my *Maybach.*

I had finally gotten some act right and felt strong enough to return to business as usual. During my hiatus, my duties at work had fell in Janelle's lap and I was most impressed at the way she carried on without me. I checked my hair in the mirror as I pulled into my space in the parking garage, making a mental note to make an appointment with my stylist a little later today.

Today's attire screamed, "She's Back!" as my perfectly tailored *Pyscadelic Emilio Pucci* two-piece suit and *Versace Medusa* heels gave the perfect mix of summer time fun and professional slay. I arrived at the twenty-second floor and the elevator doors opened wide. I stood quietly in front of Janelle's' desk while she sat engrossed in a finance book.

"Honey, they did say when the cat is a way the mouse will play." I took a seat in one of the chairs occupying the reception area.

"Oh my God, what are you doing here?" Janelle jumped up and ran around the desk to hug me.

"Welcome back, Boss lady. You have been sorely missed around this place." she picked up my briefcase from the floor in front of me.

"Humph... I can't tell. The way you were reading that book leads me to believe that you have it all under control." I teased as we walked back to my office.

"That's because you taught me so well." Janelle complimented.

"Seriously, I didn't think that you were coming back so soon." Janelle gathered the briefs that sat on my desk and placing them in order of importance for me.

"It was time for me to get my head back in the game. The Skype meeting and conference calls were cool but I wanted to join the rest of the functioning world again." I logged into my email and began responding to them quickly as well as putting my partners on notice that I was back in the office.

"I never had an opportunity to really tell you how sorry I am about, Isha. I admire your strength. Just being here, in your right mind after the fact… That takes a lot. Anything you need, just let me know. I'm here." Janelle said sincerely.

"Thank you, Janelle. Do me one favor today make sure that no one else comes in here talking to me about Isha's death. I'm craving some normalcy. The only thing I want to talk about today is money. Now, can you please order me some breakfast and also… Take this number and make this call for me as soon as possible." I said as I scribbled a name and number on a post it, along with instructions.

"Sure thing. I'll be back in a few." Janelle exited my office to fulfill her task.

If there was one thing I appreciated about Janelle, it was her commitment to me. In due time, I knew I would have to reward her diligence with a position that matched her level of dedication.

******

Sheila Denise

I stepped off the elevator already irritated.

I bypassed the Administrative Assistant who was typing away and made found my way toward the door labeled *Office of Vice President*. There sat Nadira, phone glued to her ear and a scowl painted on her face.

"Hang up the damn phone." I spoke softly and slowly.

Nadira ended her call after a few more words before looking up at me. She folded her hands in her lap.

"Have a seat, Sheila." She said calmly, as she sat straight up in her chair.

I took a seat in the chair before her desk and crossed my legs, taking a minute to admire my *Carlos Santana* shoes.

"What's good? You summoned me, right? Get to talking." I said with an attitude.

I was pissed at the fact that she didn't have the decency to call me herself.

"My, my… Aren't we testy, today?" Nadira joked.

"However, you don't seem inclined to be in my company long… So, I'll get right to it. I called you here today for two reasons. The first is business. Since, you aren't on board with BOLD Brand going public, I am prepared to buy you out. There is no need in stagnating the movement, for the sake of one person." She pushed an envelope in my direction.

I ripped open the seal with my nails and looked down at the offer inside. I began to laugh so hard that I choked.

"You just offered peanuts to an elephant. BOLD Brand is a multi-billion-dollar company. If you want to buy me out, you're going to have to pay like you weigh 'Boss Lady'." I huffed as Nadira grimaced.

She knew there wasn't a chance in hell I was about to make this easy.

"Sheila, nothing stays the same for forever. If we want to grow as a company, we must take risk. You're the one being selfish, blocking what could be a dynamic move for BOLD brand. Why not just sell your share?" Nadira retorted.

"When you make an offer that isn't insulting to me then maybe I'll consider it. But, until then darling… I suggest you carry on to your next order of business." I smirked.

"Whatever you wish. The second is personal. The other day when I saw you at the meeting, it jogged a memory that I have been trying to subtract from the depths of my mind. But, I couldn't let it go because it finally added up and it equaled you. At the meeting, the other day when you brushed past me, you left behind remnants of a very distinct fragrance… "*Flash*" by *Jimmy Choo*. It happens to be the same scent my husband smelled of after spending all day with you. The directions to your home that he map quested, should have been my first clue but the bigger issue at hand is why none of this was ever mentioned by you?" Nadira spat.

"Girl, bye! Miss me with this shit here. I have been the wife, which means I will never be the other woman. You know why?" I sounded.

"No, why?" Nadira asked, baffled.

"Because, that would make me just like you! You're sorry, you know that. I get it now. You spent ten years as that man's mistress and you contracted OWS, short for other woman syndrome. That's why you can't enjoy your damn marriage or see that he's doing his best to be a decent man to you. Once upon a time, I thought of you as wise. Now, I see you're nothing more than a well-dressed fool." I snapped.

"Gregory and I had lunch, that part is true but that nigga couldn't do me with a ten-foot pole after all the shit he's put me through. Now, if you're looking for an exit baby girl… Be smart enough to just use the door. Because the window you just tried to leap out of on me, is going to land your ass flat on your face. I'm through entertaining you for the afternoon, I must go now. Enjoy the rest of your day." I stood up from the seat I was occupying and threw Nadira a kiss over my shoulder, as she sat stuck trying to pick up her face.

CHAPTER TWENTY

Cake

"Baby this might sound rude, I'm taken but I want you……And I don't want to play by the book no rules.... You say you can't have cake and eat it too, But ain't that what you supposed to do?"

Nadira

"Hey, are you busy?" I asked the minute he answered the phone.

"Never too busy for you." He answered.

His answer calmed my nerves almost instantly as I sat in the parking lot, speaking to him through the Bluetooth stereo system.

"Why are you so quiet?" Keon asked, snapping me out of my own thoughts.

"No reason," I lied.

"So, what's up? You didn't call to hear me breath I'm sure. I know you don't like me that much." He joked.

"I just had a long first day back in the office. And, I needed someone to talk to… That's all. How is L.A.?" I asked, switching subjects quickly.

"L.A. is cool. But about this long day… Are you alright? Do you need anything?" Keon asked sweetly.

"No, I'm okay. Just wanted to hear your voice and see how everything was going."

"I know what you need." He suggested.

"Oh, do you?" I asked, curiously

"I do. Where are you right now? He inquired.

"In my car, in the parking lot." I responded.

"Put your seat back." He instructed slowly.

I pushed back the seat without any knowledge of where this was going.

"Okay." I whispered.

"Now, take a breath first. Breath in and out, and imagine me there rubbing your shoulders, helping to take your stress away." I did just as he said, inhaling and exhaling all the events of today.

"Open your legs up wide for me." Keon urged.

My eyes shot open wondering what was next, still I did as he asked.

"*Mmm hmm.*" I cooed into the phone.

My head pressed against the headrest as I unbuttoned my pants and licked my MAC covered lips awaiting further instructions.

"I want you to slip your hand down in them pretty panties I know your wearing and in between those thick lips. Now, tell me is it warm and wet?"

“Yes.” I answered as my fingers ran across my clit and explored my kitty. I was dripping wet and ready for whatever now.

“Pull your hand back out and taste it. Let me hear you moan while you take your other hand and rub on your nipples. Imagine my mouth on them, licking and sucking them while I play with your pussy.” Keon added.

My fingers kept roaming until they found their way inside. I wished like hell it was Keon between my legs but for now my fingers would do. I moaned softly letting Keon know I was still there.

“Stroke that pussy good for me and say my name when you do it.” He interjected.

I was in a state of total ecstasy. I found myself moaning his name as I felt an orgasm building in the pit of my stomach.

“Yea, don't stop baby. Cum for me,” Keon said, as a gush of wetness hit my hand.

I was left speechless from my own pleasure. Nonetheless, I was now satisfied and could get through the rest of the day.

CHAPTER TWENTY-ONE

Womanifesto

"I'm not gon lie and pacify, I am arms to hold. I am lips to speak

I am a Motherfu&%$#@ G."

Sheila Denise

"Still shaking the damn table, I see." I shook my head at Gladys who sat on the porch dressed in a Moo-Moo and slippers while puffing on a Newport.

Age and a rough life were both catching up to her. She didn't bare the sight of that hideous red wig she usually wore. Instead, today her hair was neatly braided in gray cornrows.

"Quit staring at me like that, Reds. We can't all age like fine wine." She smirked.

"What are you doing in my territory anyway?" She crushed the lit cigarette beneath her foot and stared up at me.

I took a seat on the top step with my back facing Gladys. I didn't care to look at her more than I had to.

"You know I really used to hate your ass. You were always so nasty and hateful to me. It seemed like from a child to an adult, your goal was to make me as miserable as you were. As a little girl, you tried your best to break me. And, as an adult woman when you revealed to me that you were expecting a baby by my then husband you almost did. It wasn't until I came into this space I occupy currently as a woman, that I fully understood just what you were doing. You're one of those hurt people that like to hurt other people. It's about time you stopped tracking your dirt into other people's homes. The reality is, you have more days behind you than you have in front of you. I would hate to have to come back through this block. The next time, it will be Reds that visits you and that's a promise." I rose from the steps and started towards my car.

My visit to my sister, to the naked eye would seem as if it were for Nadira and Gregory's sake but truly it was personal. Everything I said today, was something I long wanted her to know. Before pulling off, I took one final glance at the porch where Gladys sat with her head hung low. She knew exactly what I was referring to without me ever making mention of it. My feelings for Gladys were bittersweet, I loved her as a sister but I hated the monster that lived within her. Maybe it was selfish of me to feel that way when she was forced to do many things before she ever had a choice. But, I could no longer allow that to be her excuse now especially as a woman in her late fifties. It was time to exercise better choices.

CHAPTER TWENTY-TWO

Brand New

"Then I buy a cheap dress every Friday, cause I go to every show on the weekend."

Indiya

"Yes, honey! Push through!" I said aloud to myself as I checked out my outfit in the mirror.

The money Cam through me went to good use on my trip to the mall earlier; I felt like I had been upgraded while I looked at the cut off *Joe* jeans and *Stella McCartney* denim shirt I wore. I had even splurged on a pair of "*L.A.M.B.*" shoes by *Gwen Steffani*. I was meeting Cam in an hour for a concert and I had to say that I was stoked. I loved spending time with him one on one.

I awkwardly walked down the hall hoping to avoid Dij. We'd been beefing non-stop since the Black Out Party. Everything I did got on her damn nerves. I was certain my grandmother would be a better roommate for her boring, safe ass than me at this point.

"*Shit.*" I thought as I walked smack dead into her as I reached the living room.

"Hey," I said, trying to sound as friendly as possible.

"Sup." She returned.

Her attitude was one of the main reasons I couldn't get down with her like I used too.

"Cooling." I replied, as I checked my bag once more to make sure I had everything I needed.

"Another day, another party huh?" Dij remarked sarcastically.

"You know what Khadijah; your life would be a lot more interesting if you focused more on you and less on me. Enjoy your night." I said, flipping her the bird before walking out the door.

She wasn't about to piss in my Cheerios. I had fly shoes on my feet, money in my pocket and a man waiting on me… Life was good. My mom always told me, people come into your life for a reason and/or a season. Maybe, me and Khadijah's season was just over.

CHAPTER TWENTY-THREE

Not A Lie Bit

"How'd I believe that this time would be different......How'd I believe that you changed."

Sheila

Vic had finally worn me down and convinced me to meet him for dinner.

He was *Keith Sweat* style begging me daily until I finally said yes. I now regretted going against my better judgement. He had stepped off numerous times to take the multiple calls he was receiving. His face showed signs of worry still I didn't ask him any questions. I figured he would tell me what he wanted me to know.

"Sheila, I'm sorry. That was my wife's nurse. She's declining fast. I'm going to have to be go. I'll make this date up, I promise." He said pleading with his eyes.

I could have kicked myself for getting all dressed up and putting myself through this foolishness again. I couldn't lie, I was feeling some kind of way but I wasn't heartless.

“Go.” My lips were tight as I spoke.

Vic stood from the table and made his way to the exit. His head hung low as he disappeared out of the door. I wasn’t about to waste a perfectly good outfit pouting. I signaled the waiter to bring me another glass of wine, while I pulled out my phone to surf the web. If I couldn’t be in the company of the one I loved, I’d damn sure take advantage of the opportunity to enjoy the one that loved me most; my damn self.

CHAPTER TWENTY-FOUR

"Peace and Blessings manifest with every lesson learned. If your knowledge was your worth then it would be well earned..."

Nadira

The moment my eyes shot open, a pain went through my heart.

Today is Isha's birthday and she isn't here to celebrate it. The end of our friendship was extremely bitter for the both of us, still that didn't stop me from missing her. I wanted to call and wish her a Happy Birthday, possibly call her ass old as I would normally do but today that was humanly impossible. I pulled myself from beneath the *Silk Duvet* and into the bathroom to begin preparing for the day.

As I stepped into the bathroom and my feet touched the cold marble clad floor, I instantly thought of someone else I was missing as well; my husband. This was one of those kinds of mornings I would love to crawl back into the bed and cuddle with him but I was still acting like a damn fool.

"*Pull it together, girl.*" I spoke to myself as I turned on the shower jets and stepped inside.

The water rolled away a few of my cares just before I turned off the water and stepped out to begin getting dressed. A few minutes later, I emerged from my bedroom ready to take on the day.

"Heaven, it's time to go baby." I called out as I reached the landing.

"Coming, mommy." Heaven called back excitedly, as she made her way down the stairs on Indiya's hip.

"Indiya, Heaven and I are headed to the city. I will see you later baby doll." I kissed her forehead as I walked toward the door. Emilio stood outside the car awaiting Heaven and me.

"Afternoon, Mrs. Fortune and Baby Fortune." Emilio said as he helped us into the car.

The moment I settled into the seat, a million thoughts began to swirl through my mind. I needed to hear my husband's voice. I took a deep breath and closed the partition as I pulled out my phone.

"Smooth." Gregory answered quickly.

"Hey." I said trying to keep myself from crying.

"I miss you." he said, genuinely.

"Yeah. I miss you too, Poppa." I admitted.

"You do?" Gregory answered surprised.

"I do. I'm ready to be whole again. There's a void in my heart without you. I don't want to be married and living like a single parent and estranged wife anymore." I sighed.

"You're right, Smooth. You don't deserve to feel that way. I would do anything to turn back the hands of time but that part is out of my control. The only thing I have the power to do, is rebuild where we are broken. I'm not the man that I used to be, you helped me to be a better me and I need you to trust that I will never return to who I once was. Forgive me for not allowing you completely into my world. I never want you or anyone else I love to hurt because of my actions. I'm ready to come home, Smooth. Let's work it out, please?" Gregory pleaded.

"Ok." I said through the knot in my throat.

"I'll see you later. I love you," I said, as we pulled in front of the restaurant.

"I love you too. Kiss my little lady for me." Gees said, before hanging up.

I patted away the tears from my cheek as Emilio opened the door for me.

"Hi, pretty girl." Myka exclaimed, completely ignoring me while reaching for Heaven.

She and I shared a one arm embrace as I got out of the car.

"She's just adorable, I can't wait to see what little one in the oven looks like." Myka commented, as we were seated at our table.

"Hopefully, it's a boy." I said shortly.

"So, how about you? Have you taken that test yet?"

"I have and I'm actually hoping for the same. But, I won't put much emphasis on sex as long as the baby's healthy."

"Congratulations, officially. How are you feeling?" I asked, noticing she wasn't smiling at all.

"I've accepted it. Like you said last week children are a blessing. Sean and I are trying, we have our spats here and there but I'm certain he will be happy too." Myka admitted reluctantly.

"Hey, you don't have to explain lovers' quarrels to me especially not when there are hormones involved." I shrugged a little, thinking on my marriage.

"You've got a good man, Dira. Who loves you unconditionally, you're just stubborn." Myka said, matter of factly.

"Would you like to be the pot or the kettle today, Myka?" I teased.

I knew she meant well.

"Whichever one is right." Myka laughed.

"Okay, kettle. You're right. Gregory's coming home today, I couldn't make it through another day without him no matter how stubborn I try to be. I miss him. I don't like who I am without him." I paused thinking on the little tryst I'd been carrying on with Keon.

"It's just time." I continued.

"Honey, that just made my day. I have been rooting for you two since the day you told me you walked away. I guess that means I will be babysitting tonight." Myka smiled hard.

"Please and Thank You." I agreed.

"Okay, on a lighter note… Let's order some dessert for our girl, since it is her birthday and all." I said with a slight smile.

"Aww, yes! Let's…I woke up missing her so much this morning." Myka admitted.

"Girl, tell me about it. I cried like a baby when I realized what day it was." I confided.

"It gets easier, at least that's what I keep telling myself. Everything else we have endured has gotten easier, why wouldn't this?" Myka reasoned.

"I'm just going to trust that you're right." I said, as the waiter returned to the table with the cake we ordered and a candle lit.

As the rest of the staff moved to our table singing "Happy Birthday", I fought back tears. If Isha were here, she would be soaking up all this attention up and grinning from ear to ear.

"You want to make the wish?" Myka asked wiping tears from her eyes.

"Let's do it together." I suggested as we blew out the candle.

Myka and I held hands and blew out the candle. I wasn't sure what her wish was but I prayed God would honor them both in time.

CHAPTER TWENTY-FIVE

I Can Love You

"You work more body than Jane Fonda.... Physical Fitness, Mary Blige be my witness.... Under Pressure I lie for ya, die for ya.... Reuger by the side right hand high for you."

Indiya

My stomach was doing back flips as I rode the NJ Turnpike on the way to my father and step mother's house.

I had just made another run for Cam, this time to Brooklyn. My heart was in my shoes every time I rode past a state trooper. I had a trunk full of work and was carrying a gun for the first time in my life. Cam insisted that I needed to have protection on me always when I was out handling business for him in the streets.

Cam loved that I was down to do whatever for him. He bragged that it let him know that I was in it for more than just the money and that I was unlike any other girls he had dealt with in the past. Knowing all of that, made it hard for me to say no to him no matter how afraid I was. Today, I wasn't dressed in a disguise of any kind. I was driving my own car, looking the part of a college student. My hair was pulled up in a messy bun and I had on a West Chester University T-shirt and leggings; hoping in the instance I was pulled over I would be viewed as a student on their way home for the weekend.

I entered the gated community relieved that I had made it. I wondered if anyone was home as I climbed the outside stairs.

"*Thank You God.*" I thought as I walked inside with the duffle bag on my arm.

I peeked in every room, no one was home. That gave me time to slow down my heart rate and stash this work until I met up with Cam in a few days.

CHAPTER TWENTY-SIX

"Oh baby, I'm not asking for the world , maybe….You can give me what I want, Baby come hold me tight and when I'm drowning save me……Give it to me on a daily."

Nadira

My next stop was one I was looking forward to; quick stop at *Saks*. I wanted something new to wear for Gees this evening.

When I arrived at Saks, I walked straight to the lingerie section. Nothing but *La Pearla* or *L'Agent Provacteur* would do.

"May I help you with something?" The young saleswoman asked.

"I'm looking for something special for the evening." I said, still skimming the section.

"Oh, right this way." she said.

"I love this one, it just came in. It's called *Layla* and it goes perfect with the *Denver* robe." she said pointing out the display behind us.

"I'll take it in a medium." I said, stepping to the side while she went to grab the robe, armed with my *Saks 5th Avenue* charge card. When she returned, she quickly wrapped up my purchase for me.

"Here you are, Mrs. Fortune. I'm Julianna, if you ever need help in this section again look for me. Have a good night," she said politely.

"Thanks, Julianna. Enjoy the rest of your day." My mission was to get home and prepare for the evening before Gregory arrived.

I walked out the door to find Emilio stationed in the SUV reading his newspaper.

"Is this there something in that bag for me?" Keon said, as he casually strolled up next to me.

"Uh no." I said, startled as I turned to see Keon.

He looked good. His skin was smooth, his teeth were perfect and the *Armani* suit he sported was laying perfectly. But, what else was new. I was a wee bit nervous to be in his presence since I had been avoiding contact with him.

"Looks like someone has big things planned for tonight," he joked pointing at the *L'Agent Provacteur* bags.

"Didn't think I would see you here." I retorted, slightly embarrassed.

Here I was, standing beside the man I'd been seeing regularly over the past three months with boxes of lingerie that I planned to wear for my husband. My heart knew it was time to put this affair to rest if I wanted things to work between Gregory and me.

"You've been avoiding me hard enough. I guess the universe set this up." Keon laughed.

"Hmm…if you say so." I stepped closer to the SUV and opened the door ready to get inside.

"Non-believer in the universe, are you? That's cool just make sure you send me some pictures in that fancy lingerie you just bought."

"Omg. You're nuts! That is not going to be happening again." I laughed as Emilio helped me into the SUV.

"And, you're caramel." he licked his lips.

And, your point is?" I asked as I stepped into the car.

"We make a good sundae." he said as I rolled down the window.

"I'm sorry babe, I'll always be his favorite topping." I winked as Emilio pulled out the space.

Before we could hit the highway, my phone was ringing in my purse. I asked Emilio to pull up the partition as I took the call.

"Hello." I answered casually.

"So, I'm guessing that you and him, are back together?" Keon started in right away.

"He's my husband." I answered, feeling a slight conviction for the first time.

"You're right about that but you do remember that you were just saying my name last week, don't you?" Keon asked smoothly.

"Look, I'm sorry if I've been leading you on. I love him. He and I have a family and there is nothing easy about walking away from that. So, I'm choosing to run towards it instead." I said taking a breath.

"Good luck, and enjoy your night." Keon returned.

Before I could speak a word back he had ended the call in my ear. I tucked my phone safely back in my handbag and closed my eyes for the rest of the ride.

Indiya

"I said you looking like the bomb." I imitated *Martin* as Dira walked through the door.

"You like it?" Dira asked swinging her hair from side to side.

"Yessss, Honey! You slay." I said, walking closer to get a good look.

"Thanks cupcake. So, what do you have planned for tonight?" Dira asked kicking off her shoes.

"Girl, I'm about to get a three piece and biscuit, and binge watch *Orange is the new Black.*" I lied, I was about to hit the streets hard.

"Well, let's make a deal. Here's a five piece." she said handing me five one hundred-dollar bills.

"Go, have a good time. Besides, we pay for a very expensive apartment, you should be spending more time in it." Dira said on her way up the stairs.

"Dang! You don't want my company?" I threw on a fake pout.

I had already done what I came here to do, I was just killing time at this point.

"No, I don't want your company. Daddy's coming home tonight." she said as she walked into her bedroom with me on her heels.

"That's fine. I ain't want to hear you screaming 'Oouuu Poppa' all night long anyway." I laughed so hard my stomach hurt.

"Get the hell out." Dira said trying not to laugh.

"Okay, have a goodnight girl." I waved as I took to the stairs to make my exit.

CHAPTER TWENTY-SEVEN

Need You Bad

"I was so foolish to ever leave your side, searching for what was right before my eyes."

Nadira

At exactly 7:30 p.m., I dressed in my fly lingerie and *Giuseppe Coline* shoes.

I dusted my face with just a little bronzer and smoothed on some *MAC* myth lipstick. Gregory had sent a text a few minutes prior letting me know that he'd be arriving shortly. My excitement was evident as I ran down the steps toward the door. I was about to make up for the time we spent apart, in every position possible. When I swung open the door, Gees stood looking like a Greek God. Dressed in all black from his *Armani* shirt and slacks to his *Ferragamo* belt and loafers.

"Wow." Gees shook his head in awe as he spun me around.

"You look amazing, baby. I've missed you so much." Gees said, inhaling my scent.

"I missed you too baby." Gregory picked me up and placed me on top of the counter as we entered the kitchen.

I palmed the sides of his face with my hands and kissed the top of his head. His mouth met mine as he kissed me so passionately that I lost my breath. He kissed a trail from my neck and stopped when he was face to face with my love box. He kissed my kitty through the lace before sliding my bodysuit to one side.

I was shaking with both anticipation and nervousness as if it were the first time. He threw my legs over his shoulders and dove in face first, licking and slurping my juices. He was sexing me with his tongue while he rubbed my clit with the pad of his thumb.

"I missed you so, so much." I moaned.

"Oh yeah?" Gees asked as he continued sucking.

"Tell me how much?"

Ahh...this much" I screamed as I finally reached the point of no return.

"That ain't enough." Gees said, still teasing my clit.

"Damn daddy..." I screamed.

I began rotating my hips, and grinding on his face. I needed to cum again.

"Play with it." He demanded.

He stood up in front of me and slipped my erect nipple into his mouth.

I gladly obliged as my hand traveled down to my slippery center. I bit my lip seductively as I began massaging my kitty.

“Why you so wet?” G's whispered in my ear.

“Because I want you.” I whispered back.

“Show me.” His shirt hit the floor.

I licked my lips before climbing off the counter top. I dropped to my knees in front of him and pulled his joystick from his *Armani* boxers. I ran it across my lips, allowing his pre-cum to glaze them. I planted a kiss on the head, took him all the way in my mouth and then spit him back out while looking up at him. I licked his shaft and massaged his balls gently. He was about to get all of this million-dollar mouth.

'That's it, Smooth.” Gees said, grabbing my hair in his hands.

“Shut up.” I said as I continued.

I knew he was close to climaxing and I wanted the gold. I shoved his dick back in my mouth and began deep throating him. I felt his leg stiffen as he gripped my hair tighter. Gees shot a load of cum down my throat so big I fought to keep from choking as he pulled me up from the floor.

“Put it in the air.” he said bending me over the table.

He wasted no time ramming into me from behind.

“Ahh.” I cooed.

Gees stroked hard from behind. He gripped me by my waist and plunged all the way inside, I couldn't even catch my damn breath. Gees was punishing me for all the months I punished him.

“Babe, slow down.” I said trying to keep my legs from shaking.

“No.” He returned sternly before pulling all the way out and going right back in deeper.

I couldn't even throw it back, he had my waist held so tight.

"Do you love daddy?" Gees asked biting my neck.

"Yes, I love you daddy." I cried out, feeling the mix of pain and pleasure.

"Cum for daddy." He commanded.

"Mmm hmmm." I moaned.

Gees slipped his free hand down to my clit and began rubbing it like he was waiting for a genie to pop out. Instead, I coated his hand and joystick with liquid candy. Gees pulled me by my hair down to the floor and shot his cream on my lips. I licked every drop before standing up to kiss him.

"I love you." Gees said holding my waist.

"I love you more." I said holding his hand as we made our way upstairs.

CHAPTER TWENTY-EIGHT

Do You Mind If I Stroke You Up

"Dim the lights unplug the phone and turn the radio on, I've got what you need.... So put your trust in me, And I won't let you down So give me your love right now."

Sheila Denise

"Can I get you something to drink?" I asked Q as I sauntered into the space between his legs.

"Nah, you got everything I need right here." His hands ran over the round of my hips as he lay back at the foot of the bed.

I took that as my cue to have my way. I seductively kneeled in front of him, and tugged on his *Hermes* belt. He laid back with his hands folded behind his head as I reached into his boxers and pulled out his dick which stood at full attention. I licked my lips before pulling it towards them.

Pre-cum glazed my already glossed lips while I moaned like I it was the best meal I had eaten in weeks. Skillfully, I guided him into my mouth.

Tonight, I was full of tricks. Hell, if I had to suck a dick I might as well make it interesting.

"Close your eyes baby." I purred.

I smiled devilishly as I reached between my breast and retrieved the grapefruit with a hole cut in the center that I had placed there. YouTube was one hell of a teacher and a forty-nine-year-old woman could certainly stand to learn some new tricks. I massaged the grapefruit up and down his shaft, giving him the effect of my walls. The way this nigga was moaning let me know that *Aunt Angela's* technique was a winner. I circled the head of his dick with my tongue while moving the grapefruit up and down with ease.

"What are you doing to me?" He cried out between breaths.

I withdrew my mouth and kept stroking slowly as Que shot cum straight in the air.

"That was the reaction I was going for." I said sticking out my tongue at him as I stood from the floor.

"I'm tearing that ass up as soon as I catch my breath." Que panted. Quite frankly, I was depleted of energy so if he rolled over and went to sleep it would be all good with me as long as he woke me up for some fun later.

C H A P T E R T W E N T Y - N I N E

What Kind Of Man Would I Be

"The feeling is strong and we know it, But we got to see past the moment."

Gregory

I sat up on the side of the bed while my wife slept beside me. I was happy we'd finally made up, yet there was discontentment in my heart. There were some things I still needed to get off my chest. I was tired of wearing my track shoes and running from issues I should've had the courage to face some time ago. Every moment, I spent out of this house was one I used to resolve within myself that I would never be away from my family again.

Being a man of God or a pastor is noble, but the temptation that comes with it is frightening. Everything that tempts every other man daily seems to tempt preacher's times ten. Money, sex, drugs and the biggest temptress of all… women. They almost seem to magnify the more you rejected them.

I've always thought of myself much too strong to give into any of those things. I guess that's the thing about temptation, you never visualize yourself falling into it until after you've already become a victim.

******

Gregory

1986…

"Alright man, this is my last round." I said as Bernie waved down the waiter.

"You ready to go so soon, Slick?" Bernie asked as if he was disappointed.

"Yea, I got an early day tomorrow." I lied, I just didn't feel like the hell I know my wife would raise if I came in the house staggering again tonight.

We had been going through it the last few months for reasons I couldn't even explain. It was almost as if couldn't do anything to satisfy, Sheila. The things that used to make her happy, were now the same things that enraged her. And, forget getting next to her. The couch and I now had an indescribable bond because I had been banned from the bed with her for about a month.

"I'm no fool man, I know you're in a rush to get home to the wife. I'll tell you what if my lady looked anything like Reds I would be in a rush to get home to her too." Bernie joked.

I don't know what it was about his comment that sort of rubbed me the wrong way but I did my best to dismiss it.

"I know you said this was the last one man, but one more round and then I'll roll with you."

I nodded my head as the barmaid poured our last drinks. I wasn't a big drinker and I had long ago reached my limit, but never one to be outdone; I took a chance and swallowed back the last round.

"Take a walk with me right fast, Slick." Bernie said as he threw money down on the bar.

I tried my best to hold it together as I walked down Baltimore avenue with Bernie. If my mind served me right I knew just where Bernie was headed. My mind was telling me to run the other way but my drunken feet just kept going.

The moment we approached the house, I shook my head. I was right, and if I knew nothing else I knew my wife would kill me if she knew I was at the whore house as she so often called it. It was her childhood home, and the dealings that were done there when she was a child hadn't stopped. Whoring was passed down to another generation instead. Bernie knocked on the door while I stood on the porch.

"Come on man." Bernie said, looking back at me.

"Nah man, go ahead and make it quick. I'll be out here." I said looking around.

"Man, come on." Bernie insisted.

I shook my head as I walked inside. This man always had me into some shit I had no business in. I watched as Bernie whispered something in the ear of the woman that opened the door and she offered me a wide grin.

"Relax. We got something special for you, Slick." I followed the two of them up a set of stairs.

The woman pointed into a doorway on the right and nodded her head for me to go inside.

I opened the door and stepped inside the dark room that was lit by a candle only. I was nervous as hell, sweating bullets as I took a seat on the twin bed.

"What the hell did I let Bernie get my ass into now?" I thought as I brushed my hand over my head.

It wasn't too late to leave but my feet felt like lead and then the door opened.

"Well, ain't this some shit? They said we had a VIP. You ready for me, Slick?" Sheila's sister Gladys said as she walked inside the room closing the door behind her.

She wasn't a looker by far, dressed scantily in black thigh high stockings and a robe that did little to hide that she was wearing nothing underneath.

"Take off your damn pants, Slick. I ain't got all night." Gladys said as she walked over to the bed, stopping to get on her knees in front of me.

She grabbed hold of my belt and began to perform the same task that she commanded me to do. She was forceful, and I couldn't get my mind to communicate resistance to my body. So instead, I lay back with my hands folded behind my head while she climbed on top of me.

It only took five short minutes for the ordeal to end. Still, I sat speechless as Gladys cleaned herself off in front of me.

"Don't worry, I won't tell your little wife either." she said as she exited the room.

I made my exit right behind her, holding onto the wall as I made me way down the stairs and out the door. I felt like I was going to be sick, the moment I hit the porch. I threw up the entire content of my stomach the moment my feet touched the pavement and I looked back at the house. My wife had been distant, mean and a bit unbearable at times but she didn't deserve this.

CHAPTER THIRTY

"I'm doin me, this time around......I'm doin me, I've finally found.... I'd rather be by myself...I'm doin me."

Sheila

The chiming of the doorbell, woke me out of my sleep just before five in the morning.

Once again, Q had worn my ass out before slipping off into the night. I crawled out of bed and grabbed the black silk robe that was thrown across a chair in the corner of the room. My wild night was evident by the look of my hair which was tossed all over my head. I carefully walked down the stairs in the darkness. I resolved within myself that I was going to kick Indiya's ass if she'd left her keys again as I hit the bottom step.

I peeped through the curtain on the side window and instantly became flustered. It was, Vic. I thought about the last time I was awaken out my bed at this time of morning. It was by his wife, while he lay asleep in my bed. Humph... his ass would be just standing there. After all, he knew how I hated visitors just dropping by unannounced.

"*Shit.*" I said to myself as I tip toed closer to the stairs.

Just as my foot touched the bottom staircase, Vic rang the bell again, knocking this time as well. I placed my hand on the door knob in front of me and pulled it open. There stood Vic with a face full of tears. His shoulders shuddered as he tried to form a sentence.

"She's…She's gone." He finally said falling into my arms.

My heart hurt almost instantaneously. Vic stood upright again, trying to dry the tears that were continuously streaming down his face. What was I supposed to do now? Vic stepped further into the doorway.

"I need you." He cried.

I didn't blink, I simply closed the door before leading him into the family room.

"*Thank the heaven's, Q left when he did. Things would've have been very awkward here, tonight.*" I thought, as I offered Vic some tissues to dry his face.

C H A P T E R   T H I R T Y - O N E

"One of these mornings the chains is gonna break... But up until the day, I'm gonna take all I can take."

Nadira

The cool summer breeze blew through our bedroom window as I lay in the bed behind Gregory, who was sitting up with his back to me. I peeked over at my phone on the nightstand and tapped the home key. I had a slew of missed calls and text from Keon. I turned my phone face down immediately. I couldn't allow Gregory to remotely get the sense that there was anyone else in my world.

"Good Morning," I said softly as I pressed my head up against his rib cage.

Gregory reached back and pulled me close to his chest.

He kissed the top of my head before greeting me "Good Morning." in return.

"How did you sleep?" He asked as his fingers walked up my spine.

"I slept wonderful next to you. It's good to have you home." I commented.

"It's good to be home baby, good to be home." Gregory retorted.

In my head, I wanted to discuss all the details of why he and I were separated in the first place but my own indiscretions kept me from saying a word. I couldn't allow my own guilt to steal the moment so I swallowed my words instead.

"Smooth, we been apart for much too long and I never want us to go down that path again. I need you to make me one promise, that no matter what it is that we go through it won't be my past that you hold me hostage to. If we are fighting, let it be about something worth it. Something that's brand new. The truth is my past ain't pretty. But, it is my past nonetheless and I would hope that you don't hold me to mine, the same way I would never hold you to yours. Let's get back to loving one another." Gregory stated pulling me onto his lap.

I agreed, fully kissing him on the lips as my phone vibrated again in the background. I cupped his face in my hands and laid him back ready to make love to him all over again.

CHAPTER THIRTY-TWO

Love Don't Love Nobody

"Sometimes a girl will come and go....You reach for love, but life won't let ya know .... That in the end you'll still be lovin her but then she's gone and You're all alone."

Sheila

Three Weeks Later…

"Good Morning, sister dear." I greeted Sha who sat at the island in my kitchen drinking coffee.

Uninvited guest had been coming in a multitude, over the last few days. But Sha, I didn't mind. We didn't spend much time together outside of our weekly phone calls.

"Good Morning, Sunshine. Finally pulled yourself together, I see." Sha said giving me the eye.

When she arrived this morning, I was a wreck. I was juggling nights with Quentin and days helping Vic with his grief.

"It's been a long few days." I sighed joining Sha at the island with my protein shake.

"Yuck! What the hell is that?" Sha said, with a disgusted look on her face regarding my shake.

"This is here, is the magic potion. It's much of the reason I looked older at the age of twenty-nine than I do right now at forty-nine. Oh, this and the fact that I traded my husband in for this stress-free life over here in the sun." I snickered.

"So, are you saying you never want to be married again?" Sha asked seriously.

"I'm saying, I thoroughly enjoy doing me. The peace of mind over on this side of town is plentiful. And, I never want to be without it. Never, ever again." I emphasized.

"Is that right? So, what's up with that ring on your finger?" Sha asked referring to the ring on my right hand.

Vic had given me a ring a few days ago. Truth was, I was in no way impressed by the proposal. However, the diamond and the clarity were second to none.

"It's beautiful, isn't it?" I asked condescendingly.

I really wasn't in the mood for a heavy conversation today.

"Where did it come from, Reds?' Sha persisted.

"Victor." I answered shortly.

"Damn! Now, y'all know y'all wrong. You could have at least let the damn lady get settled in her grave before you began wearing a ring from that man." Sha fussed.

“Tuh! Honey, what the hell does the dead have to do with the living? I can't enjoy this beautiful ring because she went on to Glory. Selfish.” I huffed jokingly.

“And, it's on my right-hand Sha’. I’m not hurting no damn body. You don't see me planning a wedding or trying on a last name. I’m just living that's all. Join me, boo.”

Sha rolled her eyes before she fell out laughing. “Damn! divorce created a monster, didn't it?”

“Call it what you will, just know that the evolution of a woman is real. Things I would have never thought I'd do once upon a time, I regret saying never to now. The best thing I could have ever found in life Sha, is me. Once a woman finds herself, she can conquer anything.” I insisted.

Sha shook her head. Though we shared the same face and many of the same physical features, we differed in opinion and experience.

“It's been years since, Bell died and I don’t think I've found me yet.” Sha admitted painfully.

“Well, it's all a matter of choice. Some women don't want to make the discovery. Simply because finding yourself, doesn't just mean you strap an S on your chest and suddenly your super woman. It means that you uncover all the things about yourself that kept you in the dark and more importantly exercise accountability for your actions past, present and future.

“That's powerful, Sis.” Sha agreed

“Women are powerful creatures; don't you ever forget that. And, this mighty warrior right here has some errands to run and some business to tend to so you can stay as long as you want just make sure you lock up." I said as I grabbed my keys and handbag from the island.

Gregory

I stood face to face with the headstone of my best friend of over forty years.

My thoughts early this morning lead me to this place. There was so much unresolved in my heart and mind. And, though I had shut down that conversation with my wife; I needed resolution within myself.

"I never thought that this would be the place I would have to meet you to tell you my thoughts. I guess that's the funny thing about God's will, we never know where we will end up in time. I made the mistake of allowing you too much access to my life in the time that I spent with you. I mistook you for a sheep, when you were really a wolf. You were the man that presided over my second marriage, but you also had a hand in destroying my first. I guess the old saying is right. You can never be friends with someone who wants your life. The God in me wishes you were sleeping in peace, but the human side of me prays you're experiencing the same kind of hell you unleashed in my life." I kicked dirt from under my feet over the headstone in front of me.

I took a chance and came to visit the cemetery today. Some years ago, Bernie convinced Sheila and I to buy plots in the very same cemetery where he and his wife had. The untimely death of Isaac resulted in the plot being used as his final resting place instead of myself or Sheila. I walked a few steps away and kneeled at the freshly placed headstone rubbing my hand over it. My heart ached for the first time in years. I was open to sharing a moment with the son that I raised, yet he was no longer here.

“I may not have been your father by nature, but you were always my son in my heart. Sleep on son.” I brushed away a single tear quickly as I stood to my feet.

“That was some conversation you were having over there, Slick.” I turned to see Sheila making her way up the small hill behind me.

“I wasn't expecting to see you here, today.” I said as she made her way to Isaac's headstone.

I stepped back as she kneeled and placed flowers in front of it and spoke softly. I didn't want to interrupt her private moment.

“Whenever I feel too far away from him, this is where I come to reconnect and reflect on the memories that we shared.” Sheila said wiping tears from under her sunglasses.

“On somedays, it's therapeutic. On other days, it's torture.”

“That I can understand.” I nodded my head in agreement as we made our way back down the hill. “

“Aye slick, you know what therapy has taught me?” Sheila looked back at me and asked.

“What's that, Reds?” I asked as we finally made it to her car.

“It's much easier to get closure from the things that we own.” Sheila said staring up into the sky.

While I stood beside her with my back resting against her car, I took in every word she said. Somehow or another, she knew just what I needed to here; not just right now but always.

“You’re exactly right, Reds. A short while ago I wanted to quit ministry because I didn't know how I could keep preaching and laying hands while doing the same things that sinners do. Or, how I could overcome all the calamity I created in my past. But, there was something that kept me going. In the back of my mind, I always felt like someone was praying for me. Now, I know that someone was you.” I admitted.

“Always have and always will, Slick. The calamity of your choices will only derail your destiny if you allow them to. You have a lot of living and soul saving ahead of you. Stay in the race and in own your lane, you’ll be just fine.” Sheila encouraged as she slipped inside of her car.

I tapped the hood and watched her drive off just as quickly as she came while I was left to chew on the words she left behind.

CHAPTER THIRTY-THREE

Slippin

"Now don't you know that they want to catch you slipping with no protection……lead you in the wrong direction every nigga around you is a reflection…. Of you when you were at your lowest point in your life."

Indiya

"*One more run*" is what I kept telling myself, as I got off the bus at Grand Central Station.

I was scared shitless today. Usually, I never unzipped the bag. Today, curiosity go the best of me. Here I was, carrying a *Louis Vuitton* duffle that held eight birds or eight kilos of high grade cocaine. I wanted to leave this bag in the nearest restroom and run for the damn hills. I had a bad feeling down in the pit of my stomach. I had called Cam a hundred times, and all my calls seemed to go to voicemail.

I walked up to the baggage counter as I had done several times over the last few weeks and handed over the bag that I carried on my shoulder. The clerk took the bag placing a tag on the handle. She handed the claim tag over to me and awaited the five dollars in which I quickly retrieved from my bag.

"Have a good day." She smiled as she placed the bag on a cart behind her.

If she knew what was in that bag she wouldn't be smiling. I hurriedly walked toward the pay phones in the center of the station as I was instructed on the many occasions I made this same drop. I picked up the receiver putting it to my ear, I dialed the number written in the palm of my hand. The phone rang twice before I replaced the receiver in the cradle. I slid the baggage claim check on top of the phone booth before walking away casually.

My pace sped up a little as I made my way onto the Manhattan street. The moment my feet touched the concrete, I spewed the content of my guts.

"*Damnit! My nerves had gotten the best of me.*" I thought as I strolled down Forty-Second Street.

"Dear God, thanks for keeping me." I said aloud as I walked into busy Time Square.

To most, those words would seem hypocritical. However, I knew who was really looking out for me.

C H A P T E R T H I R T Y - F O U R

I Apologize

"Operator it was like a bad dream, Lord you should have heard the way he shouted and the way I screamed……I regret it cause I was unfair I took it all out on him."

Sheila Denise

The most dangerous place in the world for a woman to be, is in her feelings.

I had messed up royally, took a wrong turn and somehow ended up there. There was an emotional tug of war waging on the inside of me. The battle for my heart was on, and while the heart had a tendency to want things that weren't always good for it; the mind usually knew better. I took a deep breath before walking to the front door. I didn't have to look through the window or the peephole, my guest today was an invited one.

"Hey." I said as I swung open the door slowly to see Vic standing behind it.

In his hand was a bouquet of sunflowers, that were beautiful to say the least.

"How are you?" He asked as I stepped to the side for him to enter the foyer.

"I'm well." I answered pleasantly.

I wanted today to be a lighthearted one for us no matter how hard the news I needed to break to him was.

"Do you want something to drink?" I offered as I sat on the couch beside him.

"The flowers are beautiful, Victor. I'll put them in water in just a second." I said holding them on my lap.

"So, what's up baby? You look like you have something on your mind?" Vic observed.

"I most certainly do, and before I say this I want you to know that there is really no easy way to put things. I have to give you this back." I said handing him the ring box that sat behind a pillow on the sofa.

"But, Sheila why? I thought this is was why you stuck by me through everything with my wife." Vic wore a confused look on his face.

"I wanted you, Vic. Marriage is a far cry. I honestly just feel like it's too soon for a ring of any kind."

"Sheila, are you saying you don't want to marry me?" Vic bellowed.

I could see this conversation was going to go in the same direction as the last one. So, I stood to retrieve the ring I had placed back in the box just a few hours earlier.

"Vic, what I am saying is I'm not ready to marry you. And, in all fairness to yourself you aren't ready to marry me either. You haven't allowed yourself anytime to breath and or grieve your wife." I spoke humbly.

"I wouldn't have given you a ring if I wasn't ready to marry you, Sheila." Vic retorted quickly.

"I don't want to marry you or anyone else right now, Victor." As much as I hated to admit it, Sha's comments the other day really put things in perspective for me.

"So, what is it that you want, Sheila?" Vic asked exasperated.

"To continue enjoying life, Vic. Is that too much to ask?" I asked coyly.

"I don't get it, what do you mean by that?" Vic's brow furrowed.

"Take off your clothes, Vic." I stood up from the seat I occupied.

I threw the oversized shirt I wore to the side as I walked closer to him. His eyes met with mine as he wrapped his arms around my waist. If I knew nothing else about disagreements, I had learned and mastered the fact that it was hard to fight naked.

CHAPTER THIRTY-FIVE

"Baby, I know you got moves to make. But I ain't leaving til I get another taste...I ain't ashamed to say you got a nigga open babe... I'ma need some more before you get away."

Gregory

"Daddy, that's enough." Smooth squealed beneath me.

I was in overdrive since our reconciliation. Being apart for weeks only made my love for her stronger. My lips brushed against her bare skin as I inhaled her scent. I ran my hands across her stomach and kissed it gently.

"You want to get up?" I asked in between kisses.

"Yes." Smooth answered dryly, surprising me.

I could tell that she wasn't into it. As of lately, I wasn't sure of what or who I would get when we were together. She was hot one minute and cold the next.

"You don't want to spend the morning with me?" I asked as I slipped between her legs.

"Baby, I would love too. But I have to go to work, Gregory." Smooth said kissing me on the nose..

"Smooth, you have plenty of time. You used to love cuddling and playing with me in the morning." I said kissing her hardened nipples hoping to get her in the mood.

Nadira looked over at the clock to confirm my words and pushed my head toward her love box, signaling me to do my thing. I crawled between her legs with pleasure. I was glad she was willing to be my breakfast.

CHAPTER THIRTY-SIX

Desperado

"If you wasn't we could be runaways...Running from and it's out of luck. Yeah...Yeah, there ain't nothing...There ain't nothing here for me.... There ain't nothing here for me anymore.... But I don't want to be alone."

Nadira

I finally managed to crawl out of bed and away from my husband. His clinginess was killing me. Since coming back home he wanted to spend every waking moment under me. I dressed as fast as possible in my *Stella McCartney* mid-length wrap dress and *Miu Miu* heels before skipping down the stairs quickly. I didn't bother kissing Gregory, he'd had enough of that this morning. Since Gregory's return home, I quit Keon cold-turkey, and believe me it was no easy plight.

My body was yearning to see him. I sometimes spent hours at my desk hoping he would call or text so I'd have a reason to talk to him.

"*Head in the game.*" I scolded myself as I pulled into my parking space at the office.

Today, I had meetings of important nature and I needed to be present in more than just the physical sense.

"Good Morning, Madam. Don't you look lovely." Janelle smiled as I stepped off the elevator.

"Good Morning, cupcake." I said quickly as I slipped through the double doors and down the hallway to my office.

I went straight to work the moment I sat down in my chair, reading over the memos that sat on my desk first.

"Uh, Mrs. Fortune. There is someone here to see you." Janelle chimed over the intercom.

"*Damn, I just got here.*" I thought to myself as I began looking over the briefs that sat in front of me.

I sighed at the thought of who was here to see me, though I never thought to ask Janelle for details.

"Uh, Mrs. Fortune?" Janelle chimed again impatiently after my delayed answer.

"Send them in, Janelle." I murmured sitting upright in my chair.

A few seconds later, I was joined in my office by a woman in her late thirties who was tall. She stood in the doorway dressed in jeans, a simple grey V-neck shirt and sneakers; nothing fancy.

"Come in and have a seat." I invited while my eyes stayed fixed on the paperwork in front of me.

Out the corner of my eye, I watched as the woman walked over to my desk and took a seat in front of me with her hands tucked inside her pockets.

"How can I help you?" I asked, finally looking up .

"Mrs. Fortune, I presume?" The woman sitting in front of me asked.

"Correct." I responded

"Dani." She said extending her hand to me.

"What can I do for you, Dani." I retorted, ignoring her extended hand

"Mrs. Fortune, I know you're a busy woman. But, I just need you to answer a couple of questions for me." She cleared her throat, earning my complete attention.

"Like?" I asked cocking my head to one side.

I was growing increasingly agitated. I should have screened this visit before allowing this woman into my office.

"Like, how do you know my man?" She barked ferociously.

"Your man?" I asked with my eyebrows raised.

"Keon Walsh." She sneered.

"Your man is my client, he and I have a business relationship. Anything else?" I snapped.

"A client? Do you call every man that you sleep with a client or is Keon just lucky?" She chuckled.

"As a business woman, I would think that you'd be a lot more savvy in this technological era in which we live. I've seen your cute little text you've sent him, about all of your little meet ups, and low-key dates." Dani muttered.

"Dani, is it? Maybe you didn't understand me the first time I said it, but I'm going to repeat myself and make it very clear for your gravely insecure ass. Keon is a client. We have a working relationship. Now, let me take this a bit further. Because he is a client, there are times that I need to see him, advise and/or consult with him on business matters. If you find my cute little text offensive, please excuse the boss in me." I spat.

"You're not fooling anyone but yourself. Hiding behind this desk and allowing your position to be your cloak in order to bait wealthy men into your clutches. Well, I'm here to let you know that the man your trying to sink your claws into belongs to me. Now, you may be the boss around here but when it comes to my man, I run shit." Dani informed.

I laughed hysterically, this chick was crazy. But, Nadira Sy'Mone didn't scare easily. I wanted to be evil and tell her I could have her man for good if I just said the word but I was too amused to even be a bitch at this point.

"Do we understand each other?" Dani roared , rolling her eyes.

I looked down at my phone that just dinged signifying I had a text. My finger swiped the home key unlocking the phone in front of me. On the screen, a text from Keon which read: *Long time no see, I'm at the Four-Season Penthouse Suite come see me.*

"Got you, Dani. We certainly have an understanding." I winked as I stood from behind my desk, grabbing my Chanel bag and phone on the way out the door.

CHAPTER THIRTY-SEVEN

Between The Sheets

"Oh, Girl let me hold you tight.... Oh, and I'll make you feel alright, Oh baby just cling to me and let your mind be free....... While making love between the sheets."

Keon

"You know your little girlfriend came to visit me at my office, today?" Nadira spat as soon as she walked in the door.

I pulled her in close by the sash that hung from the side of her dress. She stood between my legs with her eyes piercing through me and her hands placed on her hips.

"She's wild. Don't pay her no mind." I wasn't interested in talking about Dani and/or Gregory when it was she and I alone. We were the only two people in the world that mattered to me when it was just us.

"Pay her no mind? She walked into my place of business issuing threats about her man, and you want me to pay her no mind?" Nadira's voice elevated.

I could tell Dani had gotten under her skin.

“I’m right here with you. So, yes. Pay her no mind.” I tried my best to sound secure with my words.

“I’m done with this, Keon. Handle your big foot bitch, please. I’m pregnant but my aim is good.” Nadira warned.

“You know what else has good aim?” I asked, rubbing my hand over her thigh.

“This dick.” I grinned before pulling it out.

Nadira didn’t find my antics amusing at all. Instead, she stood up and disappeared out the door just as fast as she came.

CHAPTER THIRTY-EIGHT

Hope She Cheats On You

"Don't know the difference between a touchdown and a lay-up.... Got you on Viagra in order for you to stay up, I may sound bitter I'm a little bitter......Just a little bitter because you were with her.... I'm Salt Lake City now I'm up on out the picture remember how it was when I was with ya."

Sheila Denise

"*Rock Steady, baby. That's what I feel now. Just call this song exactly what it is. Just move your hips with a feeling from side to side. Sit yourself down in your car and take a ride. While your moving rock steady, Rock Steady baby."* I felt like a million dollars plus tax as I rode down the city streets listening to Aretha Franklin.

I felt so good that I'd forgot about all the other drivers and pedestrians who could see me grooving to the beat. I was swinging my hair from side to side, snapping and rocking to the beat. I cut out of my office early and couldn't wait to have a steak dinner and a glass of wine. Most of all, I couldn't wait to see, Quentin. He'd just returned to the city from an away game.

I felt like a whole woman for the first time in eons. I was rolling with life and all of its punches good, bad or indifferent and I was loving it. I looked down at my watch as I sat at the traffic light just a few blocks away from the hotel. Quentin, though young had a thing for time. He believed it was a sign of respect and I couldn't disagree with that, although I had a horrible tendency of running late.

I reached the hotel with just five minutes to spare. I impatiently tapped my finger against the steering wheel as I waited for the long line of cars that were being valeted before me to move. Cars began honking the horn behind me as I sat frozen in my car, unable to move. My eyes locked on a couple standing in front of the hotel engaged in what looked like a heated conversation. My heart jumped as I recognized the face of the woman. I watched as he kissed her on the cheek, seemingly ending the argument that they were having.

"Nadira" I said through the window, gaining her attention.

I could tell she was immediately startled by my presence. She stared in my direction momentarily but didn't bother to part her lips to speak. I suddenly recognized the gentleman she was speaking with as well. It was the football player from lunch some time ago.

"*Everything ain't what it seems, Reds.*" I reminded myself trying to settle my own swirling thoughts.

CHAPTER THIRTY-NINE

Me, Hennessy and You

"You, me and Hennessy, look what you did to me.... I say my head keep on spinning.... Me, Hennessy and You.... Aye this what happens when we ."

Indiya

The music in the room seemed to vibrate through my body as I sat in a booth in VIP next to Cam. The private section in which we occupied was filled with his team. We were all out celebrating the successful week we'd just had. I had to include myself since I had taken on the task of making runs to New York for him. My eyes were super low as I was high as a giraffe's ass from smoking weed for the first time in life, tonight. I'd also been sipping Hennessy right along with Cam, pretending I wasn't a light weight.

"You ready to go babe?" Cam asked, rubbing his hand over my thigh. His touch made the hairs on the back of my neck, and my nipples stand at full attention.

“Yes.” I softly kissed Cam’s tattooed neck.

“Let's roll.” He said, standing up.

I stood beside him with my hand tucked in his as we proceeded to the door of the club. Cam and I arrived at our car and he made sure to open the door for me. I loved that, it reminded me of my daddy every time he did it. He wasn't a perfect guy but at least he was a gentleman.

“Did you have a good time tonight?” Cam asked intertwining his finger with mine as we rode down the street.

“I did.” I smiled.

Suddenly, I saw red and blue lights in the rearview mirror. I prayed they would just go around us. Cam pulled over to the side of the road.

“Be cool, we should be moving again in a minute.” Cam reassured as the police officer walked up on the side of the car.

Cam presented him with his license and registration information. I was sweating, trying to conceal the fact that I was panicking inside. Meanwhile, Cam sat beside me cool as a can be.

“Listen, if they search the car… There's work in the trunk, play dumb. Got me,” Cam informed.

My heart almost leaped out of my chest.

“*God, please let this be over soon.*” I prayed silently as the officers appeared on again.

“Sir, Ma'am... Step out of the car, please.” The officer demanded.

I felt like I would pee myself as another patrol car appeared behind the one that already pulled us over. The female officer searched me quickly before cuffing me, and sitting me on the curb. The male officer proceeded to do the same thing with Cam.

"Bingo." The male officer yelled as he rummaged through the trunk. Moments later, Cam and I were word read our rights and placed in separate patrol cars. I sat in the back of a police car for the first time in my life, with hot steamy tears running down my face. This wasn't how things were supposed to turn out. I just wanted to have a good time, I never thought Cam would be foolish enough to carry weight out while we were supposed to be having a good time.

I thought back to all the weeks of me carrying weight back and forth in my car and on the bus, making moves I should've went down for... But instead, here I was about to go down for some shit I had no control over.

Sheila Denise

Khadijah squirmed uncomfortably in the passenger seat. She called me two hours ago, waking me out of my sleep with the news that Indiya had been arrested. Internally, I felt like a fire breathing dragon. While externally, I remained as calm as I could. I could assure you of one thing, the moment Indiya was within my reach I was going to slap fire out of her. I was disappointed to say the least, Indiya promised me after her last hiccup that she was going to focus on her education.

"What can you really expect Sheila? she's still young." I tried to convince myself but I was still bothered.

I didn't call Gregory, I could handle this one on my own. I would inform him later. We arrived at the roundhouse where Indiya was being held things went from tense to awkward when I got out of my Range Rover to see Nadira standing in front of her car.

"You called this funky bitch?" I asked Khadijah as we moved closer to her.

"I'm sorry. I didn't know who to call so I called both of you." Dij explained nervously.

"Okay. Remind me to beat your ass, too." I said to Khadijah, never taking my eyes off Nadira.

"She'll be out in a minute; my lawyer took care of everything." Nadira said looking up from her phone finally.

I really wanted to get in her ass. But, I would play her game until I saw my daughter walk from beyond those doors.

"What's the damage?" I asked pulling out my checkbook.

"It's taken care of." Nadira remarked.

Her attitude was haughty and I was more than ready to humble this bitch. At that moment, I was having a very hard time deciding whose ass I wanted to beat more.

"Thanks. Um does Gregory know that you're here picking up Indiya or do you always keep late hours." I smirked.

"That's not necessary." Nadira replied, slightly embarrassed.

"Perhaps you're right. Just thought I'd ask. Khadijah do me a favor and walk away." I instructed, ready to pull the trigger on this conversation.

"It's not what you think." Nadira spat quickly, trying to shut down any notion I may have had about seeing her.

I nodded my head letting her know that I heard her as Indiya walked out toward us, accompanied by Nadira's lawyer.

"Mom." Indiya called out as she walked toward me. Her face was full of tears but I was unmoved and my natural reflexes caused me to slap her ass so hard that she stumbled.

"Get in the damn car now." I commanded.

"Sheila, please. I know you are angry right now. Just please let me take her home with me tonight." Nadira intervened, stepping between Indiya and I.

"You got it." I said biting my tongue for now.

CHAPTER FORTY

Waterfalls

"Don't go chasing waterfalls, please stick to the rivers and the lakes that you're used to.... I know that you're gonna have it your way or nothing at all but I think you're moving too fast."

Nadira

I looked over at Indiya who was in the passenger side, balling her eyes out. Although I agreed with Sheila's anger, I was stuck between a rock and a hard place. I too knew what it was like to be young and dumb. My anxiety levels were on high from the instance with Dani this morning, to seeing Keon this afternoon, right down to Indiya's arrest late this evening.

I took a deep breath thinking back to a simpler time when I was Indiya. I was a lot more street smart but guilty of the same mistakes nonetheless.

"You know Indiya, I cried those same tears you're shedding when I was arrested many years ago. But there was subtle difference between you and me. I didn't have the audacity to call my mom, a girlfriend or anyone else for that matter. I remember sitting in the cell, shivering while waiting for them to call my name; praying someone posted bail for me. That call didn't come for me, until two days later. You see, I understood the consequences of dating a street nigga. It's all a part of the lifestyle. If you get caught holding the bag, you keep your mouth shut and hold him down… The same way he's been doing you. And, most importantly… You never, ever call mommy. These were your choices, and as a big girl they should be your consequences too. You like that fly shit he been lacing you with? You like the fancy cars he lets you drive? Or that bomb ass dope nigga dick he putting on you? If so, you better know that all of that comes with a price and the very next time… You may pay with your life. Wise up, little girl. And pray that the charges get wiped away from your record quickly." I admonished, as we finally pulled through the gate of our home.

CHAPTER FORTY-ONE

Adorn

"Let my love adorn you, Don't you ever, don't let nobody tell you different baby……I'll always adore you."

Gregory

"*Mmm…* What a way to wake up." I moaned.

Smooth was on top of me, rocking back and forth. Her hips were winding to a beat of their own, while her wetness made sounds like the ocean with every rock.

"Morning daddy." Smooth whispered in my ear.

She didn't miss a beat as she spun around with me still inside her. She began riding reverse cowgirl, giving me a look at her baby soft skin and perfectly shape behind that peeked from under my T-Shirt that she wore. Her finger gripped the sheets beneath her as she seemingly pulled me further into her, using only her muscles.

My mind wandered to the days when Sheila would scold me saying, "Nadira had Voodoo pussy." The way she was putting it on me right now, I would be the first to testify that it was the truth. My hands gripped Smooth's waist from behind, guiding her to speed up the pace a bit.

"Ah, Poppi." Smoothed moaned as I turned her over kissing her on the lips while I entered her.

We were chest to breast as I moved in and out of her. Her legs were wrapped tightly around my waist as she placed her hands gently on the sides of my face and pulled me into to kiss her again. This was a refreshing change, because Smooth had been a bit distant lately.

"Cum for me, daddy." Smooth whispered in my ear just before I gave up and gave her just what she was asking for.

I kissed her lips as I rolled over beside her. She lay beside me, rubbing my chest and kissing my neck gently.

"You better stop playing before you get what you're asking for." I joked.

"You know you want another round." Smooth said, sticking out her tongue at me. She wasn't lying.

I pulled her back in the bed as she sat up on the side and did the only thing I knew to do… Start on round two.

CHAPTER FORTY-TWO

I Don't Love You Anymore

"I'll take care of my responsibilities.... I'll send you your money, every month you can depend on that.... You better believe that you can."

Myka

I must have rehearsed my spill a thousand times in the mirror. Sean and I hadn't seen one another in weeks. His warnings to spend more time with him and check back into this relationship had fallen on deaf ears as I became consumed with fear over my newly found pregnancy. I was apprehensive about everything, even telling him. My mind couldn't escape Trent and how he treated me when I became pregnant.

The doorbell chimed, I shook my thoughts and took one last look in the mirror as I headed down the stairs.

"Hey." He finally spoke once he was inside and sitting on the couch.

"Hey." I retorted.

"So, what's up?" He seemed a bit hasty.

"I called you over because I think it's time for us to finally talk." I swallowed.

A look of confusion, spread across his face.

"Sean, first and foremost I want you to know that I'm really sorry that I've been so distant from you late—"

"Save the speech, Myka." Sean voice boomed, cutting me off mid-sentence

"I know you brought me here to break up with me. But, I got some news for you… I don't want you. And, you won't want me until you watch me doing all the things that I was trying to do with you, with someone new."

"Sean, I'm pregnant." I finally blurted.

My words seemed to sober Sean up instantly as he sat up in his seat and placed his head in his hands.

"When did you find out? He asked.

His voice much calmer than it was just minutes ago.

"A few weeks ago." I admitted.

"Myka, I'll be here for whatever you need me for. But, I don't think things are going to work between you and me. You have work to do… You still haven't gotten rid of him in your heart." Sean nodded his head toward a wedding picture of me and Trent on the table.

"Call me when it's time for your appointments, I'll be there. And, if there is anything you need… I'll be there too. As for the work, you must do on you… Myka, that's personal." Sean stood to his feet and kissed me on the cheek.

He didn't say another word, he simply walked out the door; leaving me to be one with my thoughts.

CHAPTER FORTY-THREE

Sitting On The Dock Of The Bay

"Sittin' in the mornin' sun, I'll be sittin' when the evenin' comes....Watchin' the ships roll in, Then I watch' em roll away again, yeah…....I'm sittin on there dock of the bay....Watchin the tide roll away. Ooo...I'm sittin on the dock of the bay, Wastin time."

Sheila Denise

I sat on the waterfront, occupying a space between my mother and my twin sister Sha'. It was a rare moment to have the three of us in one place at the same time. Our family dynamic wasn't a perfect one, yet it was a real one.

"So, what's new girls?" Sha asked looking over at Kat and I.

"Nothing new this way," Kat remarked.

"I almost killed Indiya, the other day." I admitted for the first time.

I had been tight lipped on sharing the news of her arrest with anyone up until this point.

"What?" Kat and Sha exclaimed in unison.

"She got arrested a few nights ago, along with her new drug dealing boyfriend. Apparently, he had several kilos of cocaine in the car. And, dig this… She didn't even call me, she called Khadijah." I reflected, shaking my head.

"Not the little princess." Sha' said sarcastically.

Both Sha and my mother had a soft spot for Indiya. In their eyes, she did no wrong. No matter how bad she messed up.

"Poor, little girl. Maybe she didn't know he had that junk in the car. Sheila, she's a smart girl. But, the three of us know that when it comes to men; every woman has been guilty of making a few dumb decisions." Kat stated.

"I know I have." Sha agreed.

"Hell, me too." I agreed reluctantly.

"I remember when I was Indiya's age, I prided myself on living with no regrets. I didn't care what my actions cost me. And, some of those decisions had a hell of a price to pay." Kat sighed.

"Do you regret any of your choices?" I asked with my hand on top of hers.

"Honey, in my seventy plus years of life I have reflected, deflected and reflected some more… And, believe me… I used to regret things like not going to college, getting married late in life, choosing the street life over family life and a real career. But, let me let you tow in on something. One day in my prayers, God revealed this to me. Every one of those choices served a purpose. I didn't go to college but baby I learned lessons that a professor could never teach, at the school of hard knocks. I got married late in life but had I done so early I would have mishandled the man of God that was sent to me. Choosing the street life, birthed an entrepreneurial spirit in me. I know how to get and a keep a dollar in ways the average millionaire has yet to uncover." Kat explained.

"What about your girls? Do you have any regrets?" Kat asked looking over at Sha' and I.

I looked over at Sha, who sat to my left deadly silent. I could tell she was deep in thought.

"I do." I admitted painfully.

"And, what's that Sheila Denise?"

"I regret putting up a fight for the wrong things in my life while letting the right things go much too easily." I reflected.

"Mmm, I hear that. I have been guilty of the same. It's funny, at times we fight for those things that we are bound by instead of releasing them."

"I concur. I once fought tooth and nail to hold on to the notion that I was a victim of rape and had every right to be angry, bitter, hateful, mean, and even resentful. I never took the time to understand that the same cause I was fighting for was one that helped knock my marriage right out the ring. It's funny, three years later and I can finally admit that I wish that I had put up a better fight before just allowing Gregory to walk out my life."

"Sheila, you don't feel like you put up a good fight?"

"Hell no! I should have put up a Jennifer Holiday good ole, *Darling there's no way I'm living without you. No, No, No, no way I'm living without you* fight." I sang.

Kat and Sha' both laughed so hard they were holding at their sides.

"Tuh... You two are laughing and I am as serious as a heart attack. The Sheila I was before my divorce was a weakling, But, this evolved Sheila would be looking for Gregory's ass with a flashlight in a daytime, and snatching wigs if a heifer looked at him sideways. He's looking pretty good for an old man right now." I joked, making Sha and Kat laugh even harder.

"Sheila Denise, snatching wigs isn't allowed at this age. You're too graceful for that." Kat said, still tickled.

"Maybe not snatching wigs, but a few of them disrespectful wenches sure should have been checked without hesitation. I guess that's all water under the bridge now though. What about you Sha, do you have any regrets?" I asked snapping her out of her thoughts.

Sha took a deep breath and exhaled while chewing on her lip a little. I could tell whatever was on her mind was heavy.

"I have one regret." She sighed.

"I'm not ready to share it, although it plagues me daily. I just hope and pray that God lets me live long enough to fix it." Sha explained.

The mood around our cheerful girl time became a somber one. I looked to my right where Kat sat with her head hung low. I knew for certain whatever Sha was dealing with, Kat was already in the know. I wouldn't pry in the moment. I had a strong belief that time reveals every player's hands so I would just allow this one to play out on its own.

Indiya

"Aye, girl! Hold your head up and stop worrying. Didn't I tell you that I got you?" Cam asked with his hand under my chin.

His advice to stop worrying was of no use since every time I thought about the pending court date; my mind went into a frenzy. I could really lose everything behind this stupid mistake.

My eyes began to water, the more I sat and thought about everything and my heart ached at the thought of the look on my father's face when I told him I was arrested. Disappointment wasn't enough to describe his reaction. I had eluded my mother thus far. I hadn't spoken to her since the day of my arrest. I worked so hard to show her how well I was doing only to disappoint her again. The only person that seemed to understand was Nadira and I loved her for that. She gave me tough love but schooled me to the game at the same time.

"Indiya, I'm going to take the charges. You know, that right?" Cam questioned.

"I told you from the beginning, you can put it all on me. We gon' be good baby girl. As long as while I'm down you ain't out here giving my pussy away." Cam licked his lips before slipping his hand in my shirt.

I wasn't really in the mood to have sex but then again maybe it would lighten my mood. I laid back against the pillows and allowed Cam to climb on top of me. He skillfully pulled off the leggings I was wearing and pulled my shirt over my head. His hand roamed down between my legs as I closed my eyes ready to receive the pleasure he was about to bring.

"I love you." Cam whispered in my ear.

I swear the words made my juice box overflow. It was the very first time Cam had ever said it and it felt amazing.

"I love you too." I said with tears in my eyes.

"Say it like you mean it." Cam said, stroking me deeper.

"I love you baby." I cried as Cam filled me with his fluid.

"You my rider baby. Don't forget it." Cam kissed my forehead and rolled over on his back panting heavily.

I sat up on the side of the bed and checked a text from Khadijah.

Sheila

I poked around in Indiya's apartment as I waited for her to arrive. At the advice of my mother and sister, I gave it sometime before showing up. I planned to be sensible yet stern when Indiya walked through the door. This matter was more than serious, she could be disqualified from her program at school. Not to mention, the hassle of trying to get a job with a felony record.

I crossed my legs and began scrolling through the emails on my phone, trying to exercise some patience. Khadijah told me almost two hours ago that Indiya's last class had ended before noon. Just as my finger began tapping, Indiya walked through the door. Her eyes widened on sight. I could tell she was afraid of what was about to happen. But, I didn't want her to fear me. I wanted her to respect me.

"Come, have a seat Toots." I said patting the cushion beside me.

Indiya walked over slowly and took a seat on the other side of the sofa.

"Baby girl, you're going to need to bring yourself a little bit closer… Just in case I need to reach out and touch you during this conversation." I warned.

Indiya inched closer, staring me in the eye with much guilt. I could tell she was fighting back tears. But, I was more interested in the passion mark that adorned her damn neck.

"Indiya, I don't need to go through a whole speech about how disappointed I am in you. I'm certain you know that. I have come to the painful realization that you are an adult and punishment is out of the question. So, dear daughter… I didn't come with some outlandish punishment today but some very, very tough love that hurts even mommy.

"You want to behave like an adult, I'm going to treat you as such. Now, run me the keys to that car, and the Amex and Visa all of which I pay the bills for monthly." I said holding out my hand.

"But mom." Indiya exclaimed.

"But nothing, run it." I rolled my eyes.

Indiya stood up to retrieve the items I asked for from her purse. She quickly placed them in my hands and resumed her seat beside me.

"You're about to quickly find out that this big world out here ain't no place for a little girl to play in. Those big boys you out here playing with, will use you until you last drop. You better wake up quick little sister and pull your shit together. The very next time you lay down with a snake and get bit, there may not be anyone around to suck out the poison." I warned as I stood to walk to the door.

"Do you think this is easy for me? Did you ever stop to think… how has Indiya dealt with all the things that our family has gone through? Did you forget about the days when I wanted your attention but you were too busy crying about my father? You think it's weak of me getting bit by men? How did you think I felt watching you, for all those years while he did slimy shit to you? Did you ever stop living your new life long enough to think about your daughter who watched someone blow their brains out just a few months ago? Or, that I had an abortion just a few hours prior to that because I was too afraid to tell my holier than thou parents, who can't seem to get right their damn selves. No one checks for Indiya, yet everybody wants to check, Indiya. Well, you know what… It's fine. Check for me no longer, I'm a big girl. I'll be good." Indiya revealed with tears in her eyes.

I felt like I had the devil on one shoulder and an angel on the other, keeping me from wrapping my hands around her neck.

"Indiya, you can say what you want and you are most certainly entitled to your opinion but disrespect is what I won't have. Everything that I have ever done since the day you were born, I did for you. Not walking away from your father while you were young was a sacrifice that I made because I wanted my children to have both of their parents in their household. Little girl, it was my sacrifice that afforded you this plush little world you live in. And, if we must speak of parenting… I do believe that I, Sheila Denise did one hell of a job with the little in life I was given. The only mistake I ever made, is giving your spoiled ass too damn much. But, you will soon learn it's a cold world. And, the streets ain't for everybody baby, be mindful. That's why they made sidewalks. Now, enjoy the allowance I left for you." I slammed the door behind me.

Right now, the rebellious side of my daughter wanted to fight against the lesson I was trying to teach her but in due time she would understand.

CHAPTER FORTY-FOUR

Neither One Of Us

"When it comes to saying goodbye.... That's a simple word I just cannot say, there can be no way, there can be no way.... This can have a happy ending (Happy ending) ...So we just go on (we go on) hurting and pretending and convincing ourselves to give it just one more try Because Neither one of us wants to be the first to say Goodbye."

Sheila Denise

2000...

I looked around the neatly cleaned room at Queen's house that I lived in as a child. My mind was running a million miles an hour on the childhood memories alone. This house held a special place in my heart, as I recalled Sunday dinners, sleepovers with my siblings, and even the first time Gregory and I had sex while I played hooky from school. Currently, this house was my place of refuge. One week ago, I packed everything I needed for Indiya and I to survive along with my bleeding heart and came here. I always said I would leave him but I would come up with thousands of reasons why I had to stay.

My top three reasons were the ones that held me captive to a marriage I almost felt like was destroying me. I was afraid to be alone, I was afraid of what people would say and the most hurtful of all, I no longer felt like a whole woman after having a full hysterectomy at just thirty-three after contracting HPV (Human Papilloma Virus). Yet, another sexually transmitted disease my husband had brought home to me. In the back of my mind, I couldn't fathom who would want me.

"Sheila Denise." Queen called from the bottom of the stairs.

"Yes." I answered leaning over the bannister. I rarely came out of the room other than at meal time. I wasn't up for much of anything these days.

"Come down here for a minute, baby." She said kindly.

"Coming." I called in response.

I walked slowly down the staircase and was met by the same face that I had walked away from just eight days prior. He smiled slightly as my feet hit the landing.

"I'll leave you two alone for a minute." Queen said excusing herself from the room.

I wanted to run after her and beg her to stay. I was weak for Gregory when no one was looking.

"You've got a minute to talk to me, Reds?" Gregory asked, in his usual smooth tone.

I nodded my head and led him onto the enclosed porch. I didn't want Indiya to see her dad here. That would only make me feel worst about leaving him, she was a true daddy's girl.

"How you been?" Gregory asked, pulling loose hairs away from my face.

"I'm okay." I lied.

I was hurting like hell but I would never admit that to him.

"I miss you." He whispered, taking a hold of my hand.

"Damn it Sheila, don't melt." I warned myself.

"Reds, I don't know what I can say to win you back. I never meant for us to get to this point. I know that as a man, I've messed up time and time again and I really don't deserve you. But, you must understand that you're all I want in this world. It's been painful not having you and my little girl to come home to every night and I can only blame myself for that. I need you, Reds. I need us. I can't sleep without you, I haven't been right since you left." Gregory confessed.

I took a breath. I had to be strong. I couldn't let this time be like times before.

"How can you want me and all you do is cheat and lie Gregory? And, you say you can't sleep without me... Well, I find that hard to believe because you don't sleep with me. You seem to find another bed to sleep in almost every night." My voice cracked as I spoke.

"I know I hurt you, baby. I don't know why I do the things that I do. But, what I do know is that I want to be a better man to you. I want to make up for all the hurt that I put you through. Will you give me that chance?" Gregory begged.

"I can't." I said through my tears.

"So, you're just going to walk away from me Reds?"

"Walk away from you? Gregory, you walk over me like I am a door mat daily. You take no consideration to my feelings and you're so bold with your blatant disrespect that you even have the nerve to track your muddy feet over me. Gregory, I am tired. I have learned to remove myself from any table where love is no longer being served." I said, batting away my tears as Indiya appeared in the doorway of the porch.

"Daddy!" She exclaimed running into his arms.

Gregory picked her up, immediately kissing and hugging her.

"I miss you so much daddy." She giggled.

"I miss you too, Sweet Pea. How much do you miss your dad?" Gregory asked looking over at me.

"Sooooo Much. I want to come home with you, daddy." Indiya said with her arms around Gregory's neck.

"Tell your Mommy that you want to come home to your Daddy." Gregory said looking over at me with pleading eyes.

"I want to go to our house with Daddy." Indiya cheered.

"I got ya toots. Go play for a little bit, while Mommy and Daddy finish talking." I said shoeing Indiya away.

I waited until she scurried back into the house before turning to look at Gregory.

"I promise it will all be different this time." Gregory pleaded, placing his hand atop of mine."

"Give me one reason why it will all be different?" I asked, trying to look through to Gregory's soul.

"Because, I'm different baby." Gregory said before kissing me. My heart melted and it was all I needed to seal the deal.

CHAPTER FORTY-FIVE

I Know You're Going To Make It

"You gotta square your shoulders and dry your tears, No room for doubt……Say goodbye to your fears…..You're more than a conqueror, you were born to win…..Things are going to get better, I believe they will."

Myka

"Glory." I lifted my hands in praise as the choir sang, Norman Hutchins 'I know you're going to make it.'

The words were ministering to my very soul. Though everything wasn't alright, I was confident in God enough to know that everything would soon be made alright. My mind wondered back three and a half years ago, when I started going through my own trials and tribulations. I didn't know how I was going to get through, but looking back I know it was nothing but the grace of God and the love of family and friends that has carried me this far.

That and the fact, that I took Nadira's words she spoke to me in her home one day during a tea session to heart. I can remember like it was yesterday…

"*Myka, when a person doesn't love you anymore they just don't. You either let them go or be dragged trying to hold on.*" Well, I had some letting go to do.

"Look at your neighbor and tell them I know you're going to make it." Bishop Fortune exhorted as he stood behind the podium.

The congregation erupted with high praise. I couldn't help but to throw my head back and scream shouts of praise to the Heavens. I probably looked like a stone-cold nut, but so what! I was going to praise like my life depended on it. I was aware of the stares at my growing belly. I was now thirteen weeks pregnant and glowing, something most in the church would scoff about. I was pregnant by a man that wasn't my husband and no longer wanted to be with me. Still, I counted it all as joy. God allowed me the privilege to carry life in my womb.

The church was on fire today. The sound of victory was being echoed all over the house as members went in for an old-fashioned hand clapping, foot stomping, praise break. I was pleasantly surprised to see even Bishop Fortune cut a step of his own. My eyes scanned the room for Nadira, who hadn't even stood up from her seat. She wore a look of disinterest as she sat in her chair on the pulpit, gazing out on the congregation. I prayed she wasn't slipping back into the place of mourning; she was finally coming around. I would be sure to see her when service was through, but for now I needed to press my way into praise and worship.

CHAPTER FORTY-SIX

Ring The Alarm

"He's so arrogant and bold, But she gon love that S$%& I know……I done put in a call, time to ring the alarm…..Cause you ain't never see a fire like the one I'ma cause."

Nadira

Service was finally ending and though present, I had missed the entire thing. I couldn't stop staring at the woman in the third-row thinking, *"What is this bitch doing here?* My armor bearer met me at the end of the pulpit and helped me down the stairs. It was time to greet the members of the congregation.

"I'll be good from here," I assured my armor bearer as I reached the front pew of the sanctuary.

I spotted Dani walking towards me and didn't want to make the mistake of having my armor bearer overhear anything that could be spread around the church as gossip.

"Afternoon, First Lady Fortune." She greeted wearing a sneaky smirk.

“Hello.” I spoke back, hoping our acquaintance would be brief.

“This is a beautiful church, and that message that your husband delivered was most moving. I take it that you’re one of those people who are in the church but not of it. Seeing as how you ignored our little understanding.” Dani said raising her eyebrow in my direction.

“This isn't a good the time nor the place for this.” I said, trying to dismiss her.

“Oh no, see when you’re dealing with my man after I told you to leave him alone… Is playing in my face. Therefore, any place I choose is the right place... Now, I think you better reevaluate your decision to play this game with me, Mrs. Fortune. That *Four Seasons* you like to creep at, is going to be the death of you or your marriage if you keep playing.” She warned.

I want to pop off but I couldn't create a scene, not here and definitely not now.

“You do remember what happened to Lot’s wife in the bible don't you? In case you don't, let me refresh your memory… She turned to go back to the same place that she had been warned to flee from and she turned into a pillar of salt. That's just what's going to happen to you. Stay out of Sodom, Lady Fortune. It ain't no place for a pretty little preacher’s wife. Do I make myself clear?” Dani said with her eyes squinted.

I wasn't about to appease her ass. I said nothing.

“Playing tough, are we? Let's just see what Hubby has to say about that. Oh, Bishop Fortune!” She called out, alerting Gregory who began walking in our direction.

“Good Afternoon, how are you?” Gregory spoke as he walked over and stood beside me.

My heart was beating a million miles per hour and I was sweating bullets.

“I was just speaking to your beautiful wife and I was wondering if the two of you could give my fiancé and I some counseling before we marry. Possibly, some insight on how to survive marriage without the ploys of infidelity as well.” She winked in my direction.

This bitch was crazy. I swear if I wasn't pregnant, I would beat her ass right here in this sanctuary.

“Sure, we could. Just make an appointment with my secretary when you’re ready.” Gregory said advised.

“Will do. I’ll be in touch.” Dani remarked, turning on her heels and walking out the back door of the sanctuary.

“She was interesting.” Gregory laughed a little as we walked together towards my office.

“That she was.” I replied, hoping he didn't see the slight panic that came over me a minute ago.

CHAPTER FORTY-SEVEN

Quickie

"I don't wanna be loved, I don't wanna be loved.... I just wanna quickie, No bite marks, no I scratches and no hickeys."

Sheila Denise

"Do you have everything?" I asked Vic as we walked down the stairs to the front door together.

It was very late and I needed a power nap before I made my way to the office in the morning.

"Yep." Vic spoke with an attitude.

"Alright, well I guess I'll see you again soon." I said nonchalantly as we reached the door.

I knew Vic was a little salty that I didn't allow him to spend the night tonight but I simply wasn't in the mood for a sleepover. Vic always seemed to confuse the nights that I allowed him to stay. So, I felt it was better to reestablish our boundaries.

"I'm not going to keep doing this with you, Sheila. I hope you know that." He said, as he stood in the doorway.

“Oh, and what exactly is it that you're not going to keep doing so I can be clear?” I asked cocking my head to one side.

I could already tell Vic was about to piss me off.

“I’m not going to just keep having sex with you and be turned out in the street like I’m a paid fun boy. If you don't want to be with me, don't expect to keep having sex with me.” Vic said sternly.

“Victor, do you think you're the only man in the world with a dick? I certainly hope not. I thought I made it clear to you that I am in no wise interested in a serious relationship right now. So, if you are dissatisfied with what it is I'm giving you… You have every right to move on. And, please know that I won't be mad at you in the least. Now, if you will excuse me from this conversation… It’s very late and I have to get to bed.” I said shutting the door in his face.

CHAPTER FORTY-EIGHT

Martimony

"It's hard temptation and all.....B&%$@! Trying to see if my relationship strong."*

Nadira

I wasn't myself, I was completely on edge. My phone rang all night until I turned it off. I had no idea who was worst, Keon or his psycho girlfriend. I scolded myself repeatedly as I realized I had messed up big time opening a door I wasn't sure how to shut. I woke up before Gregory this morning which was rare. He was definitely an early riser.

As I pulled myself away from the bed and into the bathroom, I grabbed my phone to bring along. I found it almost sickening that this is what my world had come to. I never wanted to be one of those people that kept secrets from their spouse. I had so many messages from Keon it was ridiculous. His girlfriend was on my ass, showing up in my office and now at the church while this dude was begging me to see him one more time.

I ignored the remainder of the text, throwing my phone into a basket on the shelf as I heard Gregory moving about in the bedroom. We had done too much to get back to where we were currently and I really didn't want to allow anything to come between that. But, keeping Dani's mouth shut and Keon away from me was becoming a full-time job.

CHAPTER FORTY-NINE

Love Just Ain't Enough

"Now I could never change you, I don't blame you.....Baby you don't have to take the fall.....Yes I might have hurt you but I did not desert you..... Maybe I just want to have it all."

Sheila

I watched the rain beat against the windshield for ten minutes before exiting the car. I dreaded today for my baby girl. I wasn't sure what the future would hold for her. As a mother, one of the scariest things in the world is knowing that you can teach your children right from wrong but you can't protect them from their own mistakes.

I took a deep breath and pulled the umbrella from the passenger side seat along with my *Celine* bag.

"Let me get that for you, Reds." Gregory said, as he walked up beside my car.

"Thanks. Good Morning," I smiled, walking close to Gregory.

His arm gripped me around the waist, to shield me from the rain as we walked to the doors.

"You look good, Reds. How are you feeling this morning?" He asked as we made our way through the metal detectors.

"Nervous." I sighed.

"Don't be. It's already been worked out for us. I prayed about it this morning, God let me know that he got us." Gregory encouraged.

"Thanks, Slick. Where's wifey this morning?" I asked politely as we walked side by side.

"She's in the office." He answered quickly.

"Are you two good?" I pried with my eyebrows raised.

"You know what this marriage thing is like, Reds. Marriage is like a roller coaster. You either throw your hands up and scream on the first decline. Or, you learn to enjoy all the twist and turns on the way to the next incline."

"*Humph...* Fair enough," I smiled at his analogy.

"I will tell you one thing though… You still ain't like the rest of them." Gregory said, confidently as we stood for the judge's entrance.

"Oh? And, how so?" I asked with my eyebrows raised, wondering what made him say that.

"No matter where we were on the roller coaster, you held on for the ride until the very end and even then, you were okay with going for another ride." Gregory remarked as the trial began.

Opening arguments began as my heart and mind wondered to a simpler time in our lives. I couldn't deny it; his words were true; I never wanted the ride to end no matter how bad it got

CHAPTER FIFTY

Anniversary

"Victoria will be no secret at the end of the day, It's our anniversary.... A small cup of tea to you and me it's our friend's anniversary."

Sheila

2011...

"He's the kind of guy that would say, Hey baby let's get away.... Let's go someplace huh.....Where I don't care He's the kind of guy that you give your everything.....You trust heart, share all of your love......Til death do you part." Hand in hand, we road down the mountain lined roads toward a destination unknown; grooving to the soulful sound of Aretha Franklin's voice that traveled through the car speakers.

Today, Gregory and I were celebrating another year of marriage. I looked over at the man who had owned my heart since I was but a teenager, realizing that I wouldn't trade not one in for the world.

I looked up just in time to see the red heart shaped signed that read, "You are entering the land of Love" an indication we had arrived at our surprise destination; Cove Haven resorts.

My heart fluttered a bit. This was the exact place we had celebrated our first wedding anniversary. I remember everything about that trip and all the magic it brought. I hoped that this trip brought, Gregory that same magic. Especially, after the last few years... Gregory and I could really use it.

"I'll be right back, Reds." Gregory kissed the back of my hand before he exited the car.

After a few minutes, he returned to the car with a huge bouquet of roses and the keys to our suite.

"Come on, my Queen. Let's go celebrate." Gregory opened my car door and kissed me on the forehead.

He gathered our luggage from the trunk before the two us headed inside. I had to admit when he opened the door to our suite, I was most impressed. Gregory and I hadn't had a romantic night in ages, it was nice to see him put up some fuss about me.

Gregory's next moves were ones that I wasn't expecting as he lifted me off my feet and held my back against the wall; pulling my Tahari sweater dress over my head. I became just a little bit self-conscious, everything was going through my head from the weight I had gained to whether I was still attractive to him. With one hand, Gregory unfastened his pants allowing them to drop down around his ankles while sucking on my breasts.

My thoughts were interrupted, the minute he slipped inside of me. It sent chills down my spine and the hairs on my arms began to stand up. I quickly could recall all the reasons why I had fell in love with him... Until, he let the next few words fall out of his mouth.

"You feel so good, Smooth." He moaned.

The whole room stopped. I was no longer aroused or in the mood to be intimate. Here I was, believing he was falling in love with me again. All the while, he was fantasizing about her while fucking me.

CHAPTER FIFTY-ONE

Second Chance

"Lord I need to feel the touch of your hand, You will for my life I want to understand.....Lord forgive me like only you can, For you're the God of a second chance."

Indiya

The courtroom was dead silent as I sat waiting for the judge to return with a decision.

I was fearful of the outcome. I had been praying for weeks that I wouldn't end up serving time behind this situation. Cam was being tried separately, and I suppose that was a good thing. When I got on the stand, I played dumb just as I was instructed. Even though part of my testimony was true, I didn't know about the drugs in the car.

"All rise." The court officer called out as the judge reentered the courtroom.

My hands began to shake as I looked up at the judge, who held a folder in her hand. I knew my fate laid within the content of that folder. I took a deep breath, finally looking behind me for the first time today. There was a brief moment of relief, as I looked back and saw my mom and dad sitting together. My mom wore no expression on her face while my dad nodded his head and mouthed the words 'you're going to be just fine.' I hoped he was correct.

"Indiya Chanel Fortune, will you please stand for the verdict." The court officer instructed.

I stood as I was told.

"Ms. Fortune, as you stand before me today… I see two things. The first, is a young lady who must become more aware of the company she keeps. The second, is someone who is being spared by the grace of God and the mercy of the court. It is the finding of the court that on today, Indiya Fortune has been found not guilty. court is adjourned." The judge banged the gavel and rose from the bench.

I felt every emotion possible in that moment. I hugged my attorney briefly as tears overflowed from my eyes. I turned to walk toward my parents, who were still seated in the same place they had been during the hearing.

My dad stood to hug me almost immediately, while my mom remained seated. I knew I owed her an apology. I grabbed hold of her hands as I bent down to whisper in her ears.

"I'm sorry, mom." I said, though my voice cracked mid-sentence.

She pulled me into an embrace and held me tightly."

"It's okay, baby." She whispered back in my ear, finally standing up from her seated position.

“Let's get out of here, little girl. This has been the first and the last time you visit this place until you pass the bar and try your first case.” She said, finally cracking a smile.

I held onto her hand as we walked outside, hoping to reassure her that I would never be coming back this way again.

CHAPTER FIFTY-TWO

Breaking Point

"Some women let you keep me in check.....Constantly disrespect, then show no regret.....Around here honey there's a limit to my love."

Keon

Danielle was going all out to prove that she was fed up. She did everything but walk out the door which I was just about ready for her to do. I sat on the edge of the bed texting away while she was acting like a mad woman all around me. Breaking shit, screaming and cursing. I knew my neighbors would be calling the police in a minute, if she kept it up.

"You want to keep playing with me, after I told your ass I wasn't having it no more. I guess you thought it was a damn joke when I told you the next time your ass cheated on me, I was going to hurt you and that bitch. Keep playing with me, Keon." She warned, knocking over the slew of pictures that sat on the night stand.

"Man, ain't nobody playing with you Danielle. Get the hell from in front of the T.V. while I'm trying to watch the news." I screamed back at her.

"Yeah, that's right watch the damn news. You and that stuck up whore you been creeping with are going to be headlining the news next. Let me catch you walking out some damn hotel with her again. It's all fun and games until somebody comes up missing." Dani wagged a knife in my direction.

"You better carry your ass in the kitchen and gut some fish with that knife. A nigga hungry and you talking about something coming up missing. The only thing that's missing around here is dinner. Why don't you make your paranoid ass useful and go make some food? If you spent more time pleasing me and less time conjuring shit up in your head, we might be alright." I snapped.

"I'm not cooking anything for you, cheater." Dani spat, rolling her eyes heard.

"You know what? That's cool, too." I brushed past her and grabbed my keys from the table.

"*I'll find something to eat, elsewhere.*" I thought as I slammed the door behind me.

CHAPTER FIFTY-THREE

My Little Secret

"I'm all caught up in this love affair baby, Speculation brings us stares.....All my friends are askin me about it......Still the truth can't be revealed."

Nadira

"It's quitting time for me, Mrs. Fortune. Did you need anything else before I go?" Janelle stood in my doorway, dressed in a *Burberry* Trench Coat.

Her handbag already hung over her shoulder. I could tell she was ready to go home. We had both shared an extremely long day of meetings, conference calls and briefings. Still, I wasn't ready to go home just yet.

"No, not at all. It's been a long day for the both of us. I'll be right behind you when I wrap up this report." I said with a warm smile.

"Don't work too hard." Janelle said as Keon waltzed into my office as if he owned the place.

"I didn't know you had another meeting this evening." Janelle looked over at Keon and then back at me.

"I didn't either." I replied, eyeing Keon.

"Do you need me to stay?" Janelle offered.

"No, love. We're good here, have a goodnight." I affirmed.

Janelle turned on her heels and walked out the door without another word as Keon invited himself to a seat in front of my desk.

"What are you doing here?" I addressed Keon, the minute the door shut.

"Since you ain't answering my calls, I figured I'd make my presence known." Keon announced.

"Yea, uh no… That's not going to work for me. The relationship that you and I shared is dead."

"You sure about that?" Keon walked up behind me, wrapping his arms around me as I pulled the blinds closed.

"Honey, if I wasn't sure… Your giant girlfriend sure helped settle my mind." I articulated, pushing his hands away.

"Damn, you don't miss Big Daddy?" Keon declared with his arms out to me.

I wanted to lie and say no but I couldn't. Things have been great with Gregory but I missed Keon's energy. In a motion that I couldn't explain, he had me on top of my desk with his head between my knees. I was trying with all my might to push him away, but the battle was lost the moment he slipped his hands inside my panties.

C H A P T E R   F I F T Y - F O U R

Needed Me

"I was good on my own just the way it was, that's the way it was..... You was good on the low for a faded f%$#, on some faded love.....S%$# what the f#@$ you complaining for....Feeling jaded huh? Used to trip off that s$#@ I was kicking to you.... Had some fun on the run though I'll give it to you......But baby don't get it twisted you was just another nigga on the hit list try a fix ya inner issues with a bad B&^%$.....Didn't they tell you I was a savage."

Sheila Denise

I sat on the edge of the bed trying to decipher the conversation I'd just had with, Quentin. My mind was boggled and confused as I tried to wrap my head around the news he just delivered to me. Tonight, he was celebrating two momentous occasions. The first, was his thirtieth birthday and the second was his engagement to his girlfriend of the last ten months. The latter was a shock to me. I shrugged off my thoughts and glanced down at the text he had sent a while ago, where he stated that he needed to see me.

"I couldn't refuse him my presence on his birthday, now could I?" I asked myself, as I smiled devilishly.

I walked into my walk-in closet, perusing the racks just a bit. I finally settled on a black leather *Alexander McQueen* pencil dress that fit like second skin. On my feet, I sported a pair of *Christian Louboutin* peep toe booties. I fingered through my hair that was loosely curled and smeared *Red Velvet Nars* lip stain on my lips. Tonight, I would remind Quentin of all the reasons why whomever he was marrying could never be me. Please, don't get it misconstrued. I wasn't jealous in the least, I could care less about who owned Q's heart, I didn't want that. I wanted that young dick that came attached to him.

I stepped out into the night air and climbed comfortably into my *Bentley GT* coupe. A smirk graced my face as I watched the diamonds in my *Rolex* dance under the night sky. This watch was a gift from Quentin, though I had a no gifts policy. He disobeyed it all the time, spoiling me. I arrived at the Mansion in Vorhees rather quickly, handing over my keys to the valet stationed outside.

There was a small crowd gathered under a sea of lights that shined brightly on the red carpet outside, along with plenty of media attention. In the center of that crowd, was the man of the hour and his fiancée; I presumed. I floated right through the middle of the crowd, gaining the stares of many onlookers as I sauntered past. I looked back over my shoulder to see Q staring at me, as he smiled for the cameras with his lady still glued to his arm.

I did as Quentin had asked and whispered my name into the ear of the hostess who stood near the entrance. Seconds later, I was being whisked away into a VIP area.

"Good evening. Can I get you a drink?" The waitress asked, as she approached the plush lone sofa where I sat.

"*Courvoisier*, please." I smiled slightly in her direction.

"Bring her the bottle of *Louis XIII* I put on reserve." Quentin demanded as he came over and took a seat beside me.

"You're killing that dress, ma." Q whispered in my ear.

His hand rubbed against my thigh and rested at the knee.

"Thanks. Happy Birthday," I removed the small gift box from my lap, placing it in his hands.

"You know there ain't a gift in the world I want more than you right?" Quentin said, steadily caressing my thigh.

"Oh yeah? What about your fiancée?" I asked in return, licking my lips just before swallowing a shot of *Louis XIII.*

Quentin shrugged his shoulders and rubbed his hands together trying to gather his words. I knew there really weren't any to be said. I took another shot, this time a double before standing to my feet and grabbing Quentin's hand.

"Where are we going?" he slurred, pulling off the black tuxedo jacket he wore.

I could tell he had quite a bit to drink but it was his birthday. I led him down a short hallway before stopping abruptly in front of the men's restroom. This was out of my element and something I had never done before but I had to make sure I gave him something to remember me by.

I grabbed hold of the *Ferragamo* belt Quentin wore to match his shoes, and pulled him into the handicap stall for space. There wasn't a soul in the bathroom besides us and I prayed it stayed that way. Though, thoughts of someone coming in and hearing us gave me a rush. I hiked up my dress and squatted down in front of him, pulling down his zipper with my teeth.

Q stood over me, his one hand neatly positioned on my shoulder and the other fingering through my hair. I was drawn to his scent, *Tom Ford Venetian Bergamont* covered every inch of him. I licked my *Nars* covered lips before guiding his erection inside. I couldn't help but moan as if I was devouring smooth rich *Godiva* chocolate. I deep throated Quentin until I choked. Still, I kept going. The effects of the alcohol were apparent, tonight. Oral sex wasn't my strong suit but you couldn't tell, the way Q was moaning and pulling my hair.

"Damn, you the best baby." Q moaned as his leg stiffened just a little.

"Come here." Q groaned, pulling me up from the floor.

He reached between my legs and ripped the panties I wore from in between them; I was turned all the way on. There was something about aggression that made me feel this way. Q took a seat on the toilet and pulled me over to him by my waist.

"Sit on it." He commanded, feeling my hardened nipples through my dress.

I didn't put up a fight, instead I backed my ass up and sat in his lap reverse cowgirl. I swung my hair to one side and looked back while moving up and down on his shaft. Q wrapped his arm around my waist before standing up from his seated position. He allowed his pants to fall to the floor completely while walking me over to the bar against the wall.

I bent over arching my back while Q slammed into me. For a minute, I became distracted by voices entering the bathroom. But, Q quickly snatched my attention back to the pleasure when he began stroking long and hard from behind. The noise and the notion that we had an audience added to my arousal.

"You know you my favorite, right?" Q moaned just as he came inside me.

I smirked and returned the favor.

In the words of Beyoncé, "*Damn that was so good I want to buy him a short set*." I thought.

I picked up the panties that were tossed to the side on the floor and stuffed them in Q's pocket. I kissed him passionately one time and grabbed my handbag that hung from the hook on the back of the door.

"Good Night, Quentin." I purred softly in his ear.

"Where are you going?" He asked, pulling me by my waist into him.

"Home, where I belong. Happy Birthday and congratulations." I said, throwing a kiss behind me.

I didn't care about the crowd of onlookers as I walked out of the stall. I was certain that stranger things had been seen in the men's room.

"Another closed chapter." I said aloud as I reached the valet stand. As much as I would miss Q, I was sure we would meet again in time.

C H A P T E R F I F T Y - F I V E

Lately

"Lately I've had the strangest feeling, with no vivid reason here to find.....Yet the thought of losing you's been hanging around my mind.....Far more frequently your wearing perfume With no special place to go......But when I ask will you be coming back soon....You don't know, never know...Well I'm a man of many wishes, hope my premonition misses."

Gregory

I wasn't sure whether I could call the feeling I got when my wife entered the room, discernment, intuition, or both. She was aloof, and distant as she mumbled a soft hello; placing her handbag in a chair.

"You alright?" I asked as I watched her begin prepping for dinner.

"I'm fine. How was your day?" She returned, never bothering to look back at me.

"It was pretty good. I thought you'd be in earlier tonight?" I said for reaction.

"I got caught up in the office. I apologize for not calling. I just wanted to get my work done and get home as soon as possible." She retorted as she began preparing the steaks on the cutting board.

My hands ran along her waist and into the flap where her dressed overlapped.

"What are you feeling for?" Smooth tensed up and looked back at me.

"Nothing at all." I answered.

The truth was, I wasn't looking for anything in particular. But, what I did know is my wife wore panties to the office today; that were now absent. I didn't want to make assumptions so I walked out of the kitchen and into the den instead. I couldn't allow the thoughts in my head to create something that was probably nothing at all.

Indiya

I cried a river of tears over the last few days. I received a letter from Cam telling me that he had been sentenced to five years in a federal detention center. Before he confirmed his sentence, I was sure I would be okay with whatever the outcome of his trial was. But, in the present moment I could tell you that was a lie. I felt like someone had died. I could barely eat or sleep. I spent my days and nights thinking about him, though I hadn't gotten the nerve or the words together to write him just yet.

Cam was the first guy to introduce me to real. I never loved another man the way I loved him, and though our relationship was a brief one; I appreciated everything that he taught me in the last few months.

I read over his letter again studying his words, "*Get back to living baby girl. Study hard and bring home that degree. Make me proud while I'm away and give me something to look forward to when I get home.*" A single tear fell from my eye as I tucked the letter back in the envelope.

"Hey, hey." Dij said as she tapped lightly on the door that was slightly ajar.

"Hey." I said, lifting my head from the pillow.

She and I were on speaking terms but nowhere near as close as we once were.

"What's good with you? You ain't been out this room since your boy got sent up." Dij said, flopping down on the bed bedside me.

"I'm pulling it together." I said, finally sitting up beside her.

"That's good to hear. I was starting to get worried about you. I thought I was going to have to come in here and drag you out of this bed." Dij half smiled, and rubbed my back a little.

"Nah, I'm good. I promise." I assured her.

"You sure there ain't nothing I can do to make you feel better?" She asked, still rubbing my back.

"Not really." I side eyed Khadijah just a little.

"Shit, I can think of somethings." Dij said, rubbing her hands together.

"Like what?" I said turning to her with my face balled up.

There wasn't another word echoed before Dij jammed her tongue down my throat. In my head, she had transformed into an octopus with eight hands roaming over me at the same time.

"Bitch are you crazy?" I screamed finally pinning her down as I sprang from the bed.

I hoped to God this girl was on a Molly, high off wet… Anything to justify kissing me.

"I'm sorry, Indiya." Khadijah said reaching out for my arm.

"Get out of my space, now!" I seethed.

Dij dropped her head and stood up from the bed.

"*Uggh.*" I couldn't believe Khadijah just tried me.

What the hell was she thinking? I slammed the bedroom door behind her and quickly packed an overnight bag, I had to get the hell out of this apartment before my ass caught a damn case. I was a lot of things but gay wasn't one.

CHAPTER FIFTY-SIX

Just Fine

"So I like what I see when I'm looking at me when I'm walking past the mirror, No stress through the night at the time in my life ain't worried bout if you feel it.....Got my head on straight I got my mind right I ain't gon let you kill it....You see I wouldn't change my life my life just fine."

Sheila

I looked in on Indiya on my way out the door.

She had come home late last night without much to say. She was visibly upset but at a loss for words, I guess. I was learning not to pry, she would talk when she was ready. A smile came over me as I opened the door and saw her resting peacefully. That same smile would carry me through as I began my day. I took the stairs quickly on the way to my car, as my phone rang. To my surprise it was, Gregory.

"Hello." I answered as I climbed inside.

“Good Morning, I didn't wake you, did I?” He asked, emphatically.

“Nope, I’m on my way out. To what do I owe the pleasure of this call?”

“I’m out as well doing some thinking and I wanted to ask you a question.” He revealed.

“Okay, shoot.” I said in anticipation of what he was about to say next.

“Now, be honest with me. When we were together, outside of me doing my thing; was there ever a time when I made you feel like you wanted to stray? Like maybe there was someone else better for you?” He asked taking me by surprise.

“My truth is this… When I was with you, I couldn't see past you. You were always the man for me. No matter how much running around you did or how mistreated I felt, I just couldn't seem to see myself with another guy. It wasn’t until I had to live without you that I learned to live without you.” I rationalized through the knot in my throat.

“So, are you saying you never found another man attractive while I was with you?”

“Whoa, simmer down now.” I chuckled a bit.

“What I’m saying is, when the view is perfect in front of you; you don't get distracted by what you see in the rear or the side view. The reality of life is that, it's perfectly okay to find another human being attractive. It's when we act on our attraction, that things get ruined. I never wanted to ruin us.” I said, before taking a breath.

“I've said it a million times and I’ll say it again, there is none like you, Reds.”

“You know what? Today, I’ll have to agree with you. And, here is a bonus… There isn't one in the world like you either, Slick.” I said as I pulled into a space outside Anita’s office.

“Have a good day, Reds.” Gregory said as I opened my car door.

“You as well.” I remarked as I exited my vehicle and headed inside the building.

“Well, isn't this beautiful… To see someone beaming brightly, today.” Anita complimented as I took a seat in my usual chair.

“Thank You, Darling. How are you?” I inquired, shutting down my phone so I could focus on my session.

“So, what's new? What's got you shining like a lamp, lady?” Anita asked, crossing her legs at the knee.

“It's a brand-new day.” I smiled.

“That it is. Do you care to elaborate?” Anita urged.

“Recently, I had to say goodbye to one of the men that I love, he turned thirty and told me that he's getting married soon. Then, there’s Vic whom I love. But he wants a deeper commitment and I’m not ready for that. And, then there is my ex-husband. Who just so happen to have called me on my way here today to ask me if I ever wanted to stray during our marriage.” I elaborated with enthusiasm.

“Wow. Let's start with the latter. Was there ever a time when you wanted to stray? Did you ever see yourself in the place you currently are, occupying and loving three men; in three different ways? And, if you could have your way, which of them would you choose? Would it be just one or all three combined?" Anita bubbled over with questions.

While I closed my eyes, and reached into the depths of my mind there was a chamber of kept secrets I was about to unveil.

CHAPTER FIFTY-SEVEN

I Don't Want To Know

"Gave you the best years of my life and I Gave you a woman who stood by your side, through all your ups and downs, Your rights and all your wrongs....And God knows there were wrongs I should've been long gone, but when I made you a promise for better or worse I said I'd Stand by your side, I swallowed my pride...And now your asking me to understand and I'm telling you I can't.....Why should I care about your feelings when you don't give a damn about mine."

Sheila Denise

2013...

I had consumed so much Hennessy, that I couldn't see straight. I swayed from side to side in the middle of the floor as Gladys Knights voice echoed every pain I felt in my heart. Just twenty -four hours ago, Gregory had me served with divorce papers and here he was putting the nail in the coffin when he showed up here tonight with a police escort to get the rest of his things. I watched him climb up and down the stairs, sweat pouring from his brow. He refused to look at me. I knew him long enough to know that he was embarrassed.

As bad as he wanted this divorce, he knew he was throwing away the best thing he ever had; to pursue something new. Who would have thought thirty years later, this is where my first love and I would find ourselves? Him moving on in a new direction while I was left to just find my way.

"Come dance with me for the last time, Slick." I called out as he reached the landing with his duffle bag slung over his shoulder.

The officer standing in the door looked at me as if I had ten heads and one of them was spinning in circles.

"Ma'am, it looks as if you have had a lot to drink tonight. Maybe he should be going." The second officer who was standing in the doorway, chimed in.

"It's cool fellas." Gregory convinced the officers. He dropped his duffle bag to the floor and walking over to me.

He wrapped one arm around my waist and intertwined his fingers with mine. Even though it was the last time, it felt the exact same way it did when he and I danced in the middle of the living room floor to oldies every Sunday evening since the day we said I do.

"Well I don't want to know, I couldn't care less about your feelings. Don't you know, you should've care more about mine. And I don't want to know, it really doesn't matter why you're leaving and you should know you're throwing away your life and I won't sympathize. You've hurt me for the last time, got no more

tears left to cry. Baby gave you three hearts One boy and one girl and a woman who loves you. We're sitting here falling apart. All through your ins and outs, your fears and your doubts....God knows there been doubts, but we've given you a home and you're just throwing it away baby. All for some girl born yesterday. And what about our children there is nothing to explain." Gladys continued to sing through the speakers.

"I'll always love you, Reds. I'm sorry I fell out of love with you." Gregory whispered in my ear as he loosened his grip around my waist. I watched a single tear fall from his eye just before he kissed me on the forehead. Without another word, he made his way to the door and disappeared seconds later. It didn't stop me from slow dragging in the middle of the floor though. I was certain that Gladys had wrote this hit just for me. I retrieved my bottle of Hennessy from the table and took a big swallow before singing aloud.

"Say goodbye to all the love and the memories, One last time, one good look at all the love that won't be in your life. Say goodbye I hope that you'll be happy. Don't look back, cause it'll be too late, I've gone on with my life. And I don't want to know I couldn't care less about your feelings. Oh don't you know? You should've cared more about mine." I belted before hurling the empty bottle into the wall. As the glass shattered, a million tears burst on the scene.

The actualization that Gregory had walked out of my life was finally present in my mind. I pulled myself together long enough to walk over to the coffee table where the Manila envelope sat and signed the paperwork that was delivered to me the day before. I would surrender his last name without any more fight, but in my heart of hearts I prayed that this wasn't the final goodbye.

CHAPTER FIFTY-EIGHT

God I Get It

"God, I get it… I'm a mess I admit it."

Nadira

I'd been sitting in the parking garage, in my car for the past thirty minutes unable to move. My thoughts were consuming me. How was I to fix what I screwed up so royally? Gregory, didn't speak on the fact that I came home with no panties a few nights ago. But, it was the words he didn't say that I could hear. I had failed him and I failed me. I told myself that last time with Keon, would be the last time.

"*How could I have gotten caught up so foolishly.*" I scolded myself.

I was doing things I would never do, for reasons I couldn't explain. I loved my husband, but I had an indescribable chemistry with another man. I wish I had a listening ear to reveal all of this too but once again, in my life I was at a crossroad where I knew no one would understand.

Tonight, I asked Keon to meet me for dinner. I had to end this thing face to face. I decided to drop him as a client as well. My marriage was on the line and no amount of money could compare to losing my family. Finally, I got up the nerve to pull away from the space I sat parked in. I began to pray hard that God would help me fix this awful mess I'd made; hoping soon I would feel better within.

Keon

“Hey, Beautiful.” I walked up behind, Nadira who was reading over the menu in her hands.

“Hey.” She spoke unenthused.

I took my seat at the table and tried to touch her hand but she pulled it back before I had a chance to.

“Wow. What did I do?” I inquired.

“It’s not you Keon, It’s me. I’m not going to try and hold back on this conversation because it’s time that we’ve had it, honestly. I messed up big time when I let you in. I made my marriage secondary. I should have never allowed our relationship to go beyond business. I’m sorry, Keon but as of today; I’m dropping you as a client. My firm will no longer advise or represent you. The relationship between you and I, is also through.” Nadira clarified.

I sat taken aback.

“Damn, just like that?” I sighed.

I thought for sure she and I were about to have a nice dinner together, obviously my thoughts were wrong.

“Here is the dissolution of contract. Our attorney’s will be in touch.” Nadira concluded.

I was unable to murmur another word to her, as she walked down the stairs and out of my immediate view.

Myka

I must've yawned for what felt like the hundredth time, sitting in the waiting room of the doctor's office.

It was funny because most were expecting me to be the patient. However, today I wasn't. I was here to support Nadira and learn the gender of my newest Godchild. I had already taken ownership, there was no question about that. I was overjoyed when she asked me to join her for her sonogram today.

How exciting would it be to see her and Gregory's baby made from love, on display? At twenty-three minutes after nine, Nadira walked into the doctor's office slaying per usual. Her hair was pulled back into a sleek ponytail and sunglasses adorned her face.

"Good Morning, Sugar Foot." I said as she took a seat beside me.

"Good Morning," Nadira responded in a low tone.

"Today's the day, aren't you excited?" I gushed aloud as the nurse called us to the back.

"Yes." She answered plainly.

Certainly not the response I was looking for, but it would do for now. She and I walked into the exam room that was already set up with an ultrasound machine.

"Are you ready to see your baby?" The nurse smiled, as Nadira prepared herself by laying on the exam table.

"I sure am." Nadira smiled finally.

The gel was applied to her stomach and seconds later, the baby appeared on the screen; heart beating strong.

"Alright, Mrs. Fortune. It looks like, it's a boy." The nurse announced excitedly.

"Yay." I exclaimed aloud.

Nadira grinned a bit, she had gotten her wish and I was certain that Gregory would be most ecstatic. After a short routine exam, Dira and I were free to go.

"How about an early lunch to celebrate baby boy?" I suggested as we reached the parking garage.

"Myka, I need to tell you something before we leave this parking lot. And, what I am about to tell you must stay in this parking lot." Nadira cautioned.

"Okay, what is it?" I stared her in the eye, already knowing something was bothering her.

"I had an affair, Myka. It's over now. I can't explain why I did it, Myka. It just happened." She confessed.

"He went from being just a client to the one I turned to while Gregory and I were separated. He was there on the nights I couldn't sleep. I ended it, Myka. I swear I did, but it's killing me." Dira continued.

I was speechless. Never in a million years did I think, this was what Dira was about to tell me. She and Gregory were so perfect together.

"You don't ever have to worry about me repeating a thing." I assured her as I watched tears stream down her face.

Who the hell was I to judge? From the looks of things, she was beating herself up enough.

CHAPTER FIFTY-NINE

Rumor Has It

"She, She ain't real.....She ain't gon be able to love you like I will.....She is a stranger, you and I have history or don't you remember.....Sure she's got it all, but baby is that really what you want…....Bless your soul, you've got your head in the clouds....She made a fool out of you and she's bringing you down."

Sheila Denise

The tension in the room was thick and the air was quite heavy. Yet, I was confident in what it was that I came to do this afternoon. I had been diligently reading a book entitled, "The Art of War" by *Lao Tzu*. There was one quote that stuck out to me and it read, "The journey of a thousand miles begins with one step."

However, what many fail to uncover is that one misstep in the journey could thwart the entire mission. That's why it's so important to pray, plan, and then execute. Today, as I sat at the table amongst the governing body of BOLD Brand; I was well prepared. I had prayed fervently and planned strategically, it was now time for me to execute.

"Good Morning, everyone." Nadira stood to greet the room. "First and foremost, thank you for your presence. As we begin this morning, I will draw your attention back to our last meeting in which we discussed BOLD Brand's IPO launch. Many of you had questions which caused the room to be divided and a consensus failed to be reached. On this morning, it is our goal to make a unanimous decision that will take BOLD Brand to the height and depth of greatness that we all know it can go. So, let's begin, shall we? I will start by opening up the floor for questions and comments." Nadira took her seat at the head of the table, while the room chattered.

"I'll go first." I stood.

I wasn't formally dressed like everyone else in the room. The destroyed jeans, T-shirt, along with the *Nina Ricci* blazer I wore; were certainly not boardroom material. But, they did suit me just fine.

"Good Morning, everyone. Shortly after the last meeting, Mrs. Fortune told me that the governing body of BOLD Brand was prepared to buy me out. And, I stand ready to make a graceful exit today if the executors of the brand are ready to make a substantial offer. If you want full control of my share of BOLD Brand, you will accept the number and the conditions I have prepared graciously." I handed Nadira the single slip of paper that I held in my hand and took my seat as I watched her open it.

I could tell her skin was crawling as she looked up at me with a scowl of disapproval. She quickly softened her face as I winked in her direction.

"Quiet in the room." Nadira instructed as she mulled over the number listed on the paper.

She whispered something briefly into Gregory's ear. I watched intently as the two of them stared at the paper in front of them. Five long minutes of silence followed, before Nadira looked up at me.

We accept." She said, shortly.

"In that case, I relinquish my seat and pray for BOLD Brands continued success." I conveyed from my seat before grabbing my YSL clutch and tucking it under my arm.

"I'll be expecting that in a certified check within the next seven days. Good day all," Cheerfully, I walked out the door to my car. I had accomplished exactly what I set out to do without breaking so much as a sweat and or a nail.

"Reds." Gregory called from the middle of the parking lot as I pulled away from my parking space.

I drove in his direction, pulling up beside him. I opened the car door and allowed my *Giuseppe Zanotti* Zebra skin bootie to hit the ground, one at a time.

"And, the band was playing as the ship went down." I proclaimed as I stepped into his embrace.

"What happen in there? Why did you sell your seat?" Gregory's brow furrowed as he questioned me.

"Baby, nothing last forever. And, at some point we have to take the way of escape that God has prepared for us." I shrugged.

"So… What's next for you, Reds?" Gregory asked, leaning up against my car.

"Travel the world… Start an investment group… Hell, I'm going to live life like it's platinum with that additional seven hundred and fifty mil BOLD Brand is about to drop into my bank account. And, there will be no shortage of adventure to follow with the five-million-dollar year severance either."

"You're a cold piece of work, Reds. Enjoy it." Gregory said, cracking a huge smile as he reopened my car door.

"Aye, Slick?" I called out as I settled back inside the car.

"You know there will always be a seat in the sun for you, don't you?"

"Thank you." Gregory grinned from ear to ear as he strolled back inside the church where the meeting was taking place.

Nadira

Sheila made out like a fat rat today and left smiling like a Cheshire Cat.

"*The nerve of this bitch.*" I pouted.

I was pissed that I allowed her to walk away with a year's earnings from BOLD Brand but it was what it was. I sat behind my desk tapping the *Mont Blanc* pen that I held in my hand against my datebook before me.

"Mrs. Fortune, you have a client here to see you." Janelle chimed over the intercom.

"Send them in Janelle." I responded exasperated.

Today, I had a meeting on foreign policy and trade with a group of international investors although I wanted to crawl into bed. I straightened the blazer I wore and sat up in the chair, crossing my legs at the knee; just before my baby boy gave me a subtle reminder that my body no longer belonged to me..

The double doors to my office flung open quickly and in walked Dani, carrying a large Manila envelope and wearing a grin as wide as the expressway. I swear I wanted to spew my lunch all over the paperwork on my desk.

"Good afternoon." I greeted before she had the chance to sit down.

"Mrs. Fortune, Mrs. Fortune." She sighed taking a seat.

"You look good with your unfaithful, hard-headed ass."

"Thanks." I smirked.

"Do you remember a while back you told me that you were a business woman?" Dani finished, as she threw the Manila envelope on the desk before me.

"I do." I confirmed, wondering where she was going with this.

"Well, Mrs. Fortune... I am too. In that envelope is the best investment, you'll make all year. Go on, take a look." She urged as I picked up the envelope and drew it closer to me.

The contents inside were enough to make me gag. There were panties that I had carelessly left behind and multiple pictures of Keon and I together in the bedroom, exposed in compromising positions. I inhaled deeply and exhaled as I laid the pictures down in front of me. I was sick to say the least.

"What is it that you want from me? Keon and I have severed all ties, Dani." I admitted, hoping it would be enough for her.

"See, that's the problem. You two should have never had any ties to begin with." She scoffed.

"Once again, I ask, what is it that you want from me?" I reasoned, trying to keep my cool.

"That depends... What is your marriage and your family worth? Three hundred thousand, maybe?" Dani shrugged coyly.

"Are you out of your god damn mind?" I said, raising my voice.

"Bitch, are you trying to blackmail me?" I stood from behind my desk and leaned in close to her.

"Darling, I'm not trying... It's being done. Now is your chance to accept it or reject it, the choice is yours. But, do understand the consequence of not accepting will be your husband knowing all your underhanded dealings. See, I think what you failed to realize is that I am not that old bitch who just let you take her man and ride off into the sunset." Dani spat.

"Get the hell out of my office before I call security." I warned.

"Not until I get what the hell I came for. Now, would you rather call the bank or a divorce attorney? Because, that's where you're headed when Gregory gets a hold of all of this." Dani said, cracking her neck from side to side.

I stared at her straight on with one eyebrow raised, I wasn't about to budge just yet.

"Oh, you must really think I'm sweet. That's okay, I have the golden ticket right here." Dani turned around and reached into her handbag and pulled out her iPad. After a few clicks, she found what she was looking for. She slid the iPad across the desk to me… The video playing, sickened me. Keon and I having sex in his bed a while back... My face must've turned burgundy as I stared down at the screen.

"You got it." I conceded. I was defeated.

I knew I couldn't fight any longer. This was bad and the odds were not in my favor.

"You'll have your check by the end of the week." I said in a defeated tone.

"That'll work." Dani said, as she walked toward the door.

I took a breath and picked up the phone to call Janelle.

"Yes, Mrs. Fortune?" Janelle answered cheerfully.

"Hi Janelle, I need you to call my accountant and have a check drawn up for a hundred and fifty thousand. Have it drawn and delivered in a certified check to my office by morning." I relayed.

"Got ya, love. I'll take care of it right away." Janelle replied.

"*Damn it, Dira 2-0.*" I reminded myself of the two losses I took today.

C H A P T E R   S I X T Y

Poison

"It's driving me out of mind, That's why it's hard for me to find.....Can't get it out of my head....Miss her, Kiss her, love her, wrong move your dead."

Keon

I woke up smiling until, my eyes open fully and I saw Dani sitting beside me in the bed wearing a lace negligee, and holding her little .22 in her hand.

"You must've been dreaming about your little whore huh? I just want to know was she worth your career?" Dani said, running the gun along my side.

I can't lie, I didn't condone violence on women but I wanted to hit this girl.

"What the hell is your problem?" I said sitting up beside her.

"You know what my problem is, Keon? I loved a sorry no good nigga while he was down and out, and when he got on… He forgot who was with him when he didn't have shit." Dani said through clenched teeth.

"You out here chasing women with husbands like you don't have a good woman at home. But, you know what? Karma's a bitch ain't it? You'll be back to needing me soon, especially since those checks are about to dry up." Dani smirked.

Dani was rubbing salt in an open wound, and it hurt like hell. After Nadira's firm dropped me, it was like a domino effect. I lost all the major endorsements they'd helped me to get, along with my spot on the team.

"Don't worry. Baby mama, gon always secure the bag for us."

"What the hell is wrong with your crazy ass?" I screamed.

"Nothing at all, baby. Just know, I got us." Dani wore a big old Kool-Aid smile as she walked out of the room.

My ass was shook.

"*That girl is real life crazy*." I thought, as I climbed out of bed the minute I heard the door slam.

C H A P T E R S I X T Y - O N E

Poison

"You're just like poison, Slowly moving through my system breaking all of my defenses with time.....You're just like poison and I don't get it how could something so deadly feel so right."

Nadira

"*Thank God for another day and another dollar."* I thought as I sat at my desk.

Yesterday, I left the office feeling like I had been robbed without a gun. Today, I was just thankful for another day.

"*Got to pay the cost to be the boss, I guess.*" I sighed at my own thoughts as I turned on the computer in my office.

"Good Morning, lucky lady. You have a delivery." Janelle announced, as she escorted the delivery guy who was carrying an enormous Bouquet of flowers into my office.

"You can sit those right over, there." I instructed as Janelle sat a box from Godiva in front of me.

I couldn't help but smile. I loved the mere thought that someone had thought of me.

"How sweet is that, literally." Janelle winked, as I pulled the top off the chocolate covered strawberries.

I wasted no time biting into one.

"Enjoy lady." Janelle smiled as she backed up out the door.

I stood from behind my desk and walked over to the other side of the room where the flowers sat. I immediately reached for the card, still smiling as I ate the chocolate covered strawberry that was in the other hand.

"*Can't trust a big butt and a smile that girl is POISON. Literally.*" The card read.

I carried the card back to my desk with me, prepared to call my husband and thank him for the kind gesture when I was struck by an immediate pain in my abdomen.

"*What in the hell?*" I thought, as I was hit by another pain that rocked me in my seat.

As minutes passed, the pains only grew in power and frequency. I hadn't experienced pain like this in my life, outside of child birth and it was much too early for that. I stood to my feet despite the weak feeling that had overtaken me. I walked to the bathroom while holding onto the wall for stability. Hot tears began to roll down my face as I finally reached the bathroom and sat on the toilet. There was so much blood, I felt faint.

"God, no this can't be!" I cried aloud.

I tried my hardest in the seconds that followed to gather myself but it was impossible. My body felt immobilized as if I couldn't move at all. My limbs were going numb as more blood poured from between my legs. My scream was stifled by thoughts of one of my partners coming in here and finding me with my pants around my ankles. I dropped onto my knees and crawled out of the stall and over to the phone on the wall.

My heartbeat was slowing.

"Yes, Mrs. Fortune?" Janelle answered in a perky tone.

"Janelle, come into the bathroom. I need you." were the last words I remember before everything around me faded to back and my consciousness became no more.

CHAPTER SIXTY-TWO

Help

"I need a life line right now....911 won't do, My back's against the wall now......Done all I could do.....I prayed every prayer and went to every service......Like I know how....Just a ship without a sail.....I'm lost without your help."

Myka

Sheer worry and panic engulfed me as I listened closely to Gregory's voice on the phone. He had called to tell me that Nadira had been rushed to the hospital. He didn't know the details except the fact that she had lost a tremendous amount of blood and was found unconscious in the bathroom in her office. I rode to the hospital like a bat out of hell neglecting the fact that I had Heaven in the back seat, praying all the way there.

When I arrived at the hospital, I half parked my car in the first space I saw and grabbed the ticket as I exited the garage. My only mission was to get to the side of my best friend and find out what had gone wrong.

"God, you are the supplier of all of our needs and the healer of all of our infirmities. Father, I pray that you would send your healing angels now. In Jesus name, I pray. Amen." I prayed silently as I finally reached the waiting room with Heaven.

"Hey." I greeted not knowing what else to say as I took a seat beside Gregory.

His face showed signs of worry and fear as he picked Heaven up onto his lap. Janelle sat a few seats over, her eyes glassy and filled with tears.

"I'm sorry, Myka. I don't know much yet. They rushed her into surgery before I got here.

"Let's just keep praying." I tried to encourage him.

Though, I was feeling helpless myself. Heaven was squirming around in his arms, trying to get free so she could run around like the busy little three-year-old she was and the frustration was evident in his face.

"I'll take her," I finally said after a few minutes more of watching her squirm.

Just as I stood to walk Heaven over to the vending machines, two men dressed in suits who identified themselves as detectives and a doctor approached us. I looked over at Gregory, who had signs of many questions on his face.

"Mr. Fortune, I am Dr. Presley one of the treating physicians on your wife's case this afternoon. Your wife is still in surgery. Myself, along with these two detectives have some questions and need a bit of information from you. It seems your wife was poisoned. Do you have any idea of what she may have consumed today?" The doctor asked.

Gregory looked puzzled, he scratched his heads as he'd trying to bring something to his recollection.

"I'm sorry. My wife was in her office since eight a.m. The young lady to my right may have some idea if she had breakfast or ate anything today." Gregory said, looking over at Janelle with pleading eyes to help with information.

Janelle stood up and walked closer to where Gregory and I sat.

"Janelle, you work in the office with Mrs. Fortune?" one of the detectives stepped up and asked.

"Yes, I am her Administrative assistant." Janelle answered proudly.

"Can you recall if Mrs. Fortune consumed anything this morning?" The detective asked Janelle as he scribbled on the notepad, in his hands.

"The only thing I can recall her eating are chocolate covered strawberries that arrived a few hours ago along with flowers." Janelle explained.

"Did Mrs. Fortune become immediately ill to your knowledge?" The other detective asked almost immediately.

"It was about ten minutes after I left her office, she called me from the bathroom." Janelle answered.

"Mr. Fortune, did you send your wife a delivery this morning?" One of the detectives questioned.

"No, I didn't." Gregory answered perplexed.

"Janelle, do you recall Mrs. Fortune saying who the delivery came from or opening the card while you were present?" the other detective quickly asked.

"No, I'm sorry I don't. I left to show the delivery guy out after bringing the two packages in." Janelle answered shyly.

"Mr. Fortune, we are working diligently to find out what happened in your wife's office today. If we have any more questions, we will be in touch and if any of you can remember or recall anything that might be useful in this case; please don't hesitate to call us." The detectives handed out each of their cards before they began to converse with one another.

The air in the room had grown thick and tense. I looked over and could tell instantaneously that the wheels were turning in Gregory's head. He was probably wondering much like I was who the hell sent Dira flowers and chocolate covered strawberries, and who the hell would want to poison her?

CHAPTER SIXTY-THREE

Tonight Is The Night

"Tonight is the night, That you make me a woman....Mmm, You said you'd be gentle with me and I hope you will, Mmm, mmm"

Indiya

"Well, that's the last of it baby girl. Let's get on out of here." My mom said with a smile.

She was in a pleasantly good mood today which could be rare. Sheila was hard to read at times, you never knew exactly what mood she was in if you were to judge by the resting bitch face she often displayed. I moved out of my apartment on campus, today by choice. I couldn't take the thought of ever being put in such an awkward position by my best friend ever again. Don't get me wrong. I had nothing against anyone's sexual preference, I just didn't dig when others forced their preference on me.

I climbed into the passenger seat of my mom's *Bentley* as we watched the mover's truck head on down the street. It was her idea to hire movers rather than just do it ourselves, but God forbid Sheila Denise break a nail. My mom turned up the music in the car, she was in a zone as she sang every word of the song playing with passion. In my head, I was quite sure I was much too young to hear my mom singing the lyrics that she echoed but it felt good to see her in such a good place.

"Yeah, I wanna thank your love, because you make me feel good. And I love you baby. I love you and I know it and I ain't too proud to go show it, Cause I love you baby." My mom sang aloud, swinging her flowing hair from side to side.

"Yessss, girl!" I commented, looking over at her as she grooved at the traffic light.

"Hush." She smiled.

"So, who are you singing this little song all hard for girl?" I meddled a little, knowing I'd probably never get an answer.

"Some songs just remind us of happier times, that's all." She shrugged girlishly.

"Well Sheila, take me to that place honey because you were in a zone." I clapped.

"You were made in that happy place." She smiled, sticking her tongue out at me.

"Yuck. Okay never mind girl, just drive." I laughed as I reached into my book bag and pulled out my phone.

"Oh my God!" I screamed aloud, looking down at the multitude of text from my dad.

I was so busy packing and moving that I hadn't checked my phone in a few hours.

"What's the matter?" My mom asked calmly.

"Dira, is in the hospital. She had to have an emergency surgery, someone poisoned her." I rattled.

"Okay, calm down Indy. Pick up the phone and call your father." She instructed.

I took a breath and pulled the phone to my ear after dialing his number, he quickly answered. He gave me few details outside of the matter being very serious. That was enough for my mom to hit a U-turn and head in the direction of the hospital almost immediately.

Sheila

I was pulled in a direction I wasn't ready for. When Indiya and I arrived at the hospital, the pain and concern that lined each face was evident. I almost felt like a fish out of water as I greeted everyone.

"*Maybe I should have allowed Indiya to come here, alone.*" I thought to myself, as I took a seat beside her.

Gregory was pacing the floor of the waiting room while trying to remain calm. I knew by the look on his face, he was worried out of his mind. Still, I sat in the corner and began to pray instead of speaking.

Indiya's head rested on my shoulder while little Heaven made her way onto my lap and was now fast asleep. Hours had passed since Indiya and I had arrived, when the doctors finally came to speak to Gregory.

"Mr. Fortune." One of the doctors greeted, as he finally got close enough to speak to Gregory.

"We have come to speak to you about your wife's condition, would you like to speak in private?" The other doctor asked.

"No, everyone here is family." Gregory stated firmly, as he took a seat beside me.

"Okay, that's good to know. There is both good news and bad news. Unfortunately, your wife ingested something that was laced with Cytotec. This medication is typically prescribed for stomach ulcers. This medication however, is also known to cause spontaneous abortion. Mr. Fortune, we were unable to save your son. Your wife has been placed in a medically induced coma until her condition stabilizes. We will allow you to see her briefly but she needs to rest." The doctor concluded.

I watched as tears fell from Gregory's eyes. No one moved immediately to comfort him. Everyone in the room seemed to be dealing with hurt and shock of their own.

"Go see her, Slick." I said with my hand on his shoulder.

I urged Indiya to go in with her dad. Myka and the other young lady present, walked behind them as I sat out in the waiting room with Heaven on my lap. I was wrecking my brain trying to understand just what happened today and why anyone would want to poison her.

"*Was this an accident? God, watch over this family.*" I prayed.

A few minutes later, Indiya rejoined me. I reached out and pulled her into my embrace. Her body shook as tears ran heavily down her face. Myka returned to the waiting room equally as devastated. I wasn't sure what they saw down the hall, but the expressions on their faces said it all.

Myka

"God, I know you make no mistakes. But this all seems so unfair to me. Haven't we experienced enough tragedy and loss? How can we bear another thing? When do you put an end to all of our suffering?" I hated to question God but I needed answers with this one.

I didn't understand how this came to be. I just spoke to Dira last night and everything was fine. And, now I walk into a room to see her after she'd been poisoned. She was hooked up to so many machines, and even suffered the loss of her baby without knowing a thing.

I sat in the waiting room beside Sheila and a sobbing Indiya, Janelle was too shaken up to even come back into the waiting room. Some of Dira's partners and her mother had arrived, and everyone had questions.

"Myka, I am going to get out of here. I'll be praying for you all." Sheila said touching my shoulder as more and more bodies filled the room.

"No, you shouldn't go." I said grabbing hold of her hand.

"Walk with me, love." She said with my hand still tucked in hers.

I slowly walked out of the waiting room with her while onlookers stared. She gently placed Heaven in my arms as we made it to the elevator.

"Myka, I know right now is a sensitive time and I am most certainly praying for the best outcome. However, you saw all those stares back there. I couldn't possibly stay and give people more to talk about than a speedy recovery and well wishes for Nadira. I will be there if you or Gregory should need me." She gave my hand one last squeeze before guiding Indiya onto the elevator with her.

I respected Sheila. There was a time when I didn't like her, but I sure had to respect her. That was a boss move she just made despite all the negative things that have happened in the past. I returned to the family waiting room and was met by the same faces who were here before and lots of tears.

I fought against the urge to get choked up, by taking a deep breath and rubbing my hand against a sleeping Heaven's face. She needed me to be her strength even though she had no clue about what was going on around her.

CHAPTER SIXTY-FOUR

Love Em' Aee

"Why can't they understand, sex is irrelevant.....Just a game in my head that I'm playing and I'm winning.....Oh I broke another heart today...Oh and I didn't care I just walked away."

Sheila Denise

Today, had been an exhausting one indeed. Indiya and I had finally settled in at home. Needless to say, she was hurting for Nadira. I made it my business to hit my knees and pray for Gregory, Nadira, and everyone surrounding them the moment I walked in the door. As soon as I laid across the bed to catch my breath, my telephone was ringing.

Annoyed, I sat up and reached over to the night stand to grab it.

"Hello." I answered before looking at the caller I.D. display.

"Hey Baby." Vic replied quickly.

"*Damn it! I really should have shut this thing off.*" I sighed.

I was simply not in the mood for conversation tonight.

"What's up?" I asked as pleasant as I could.

"Open the door." He instructed.

"Here the hell we go with the pop up visits." I slid my feet in the slippers that sat beside my bed and made my way downstairs.

"Yes." I huffed as I pulled open the door, resting my back against the frame.

I eased up when I noticed the gifts and flowers in his hands, moving to the side so he could come in.

"What's the matter, babe? Aren't you happy to see me?" Vic asked, pulling me into him by my waist.

"I didn't expect to see you is all." I said, reaching for the flowers he was handing me.

"I didn't know I needed an appointment to check on you or bring you flowers, Sheila. I miss you. The least you can do is show me some affection." Vic pretended to pouted.

I began filling a vase with water at the kitchen sink, while Vic found his way behind me. His arms wrapped around my waist and his lips pressed against the back of my neck. I side-stepped him, placing the flowers on the counter.

"You make it hard to love you, baby. It's like I can't satisfy you no matter how hard I try, Sheila. When I was still married to my wife, you couldn't get wait for me to make a move and get divorced. The moment she passed, and I became a free man; it's like you don't even want me anymore. What's with that?" Vic asked furiously.

"Vic, today was a very long and draining day. If you had called before you visited me, you may have known that. I'm just truly not up for company. If you don’t mind, I’d actually like to just take a bath and go to bed.” I announced as I led the way back to the front door. Victor didn't say another word instead he followed me defeatedly toward the front door.

“I came here to give you something. I’ll just leave it with you instead.” Vic placed a large envelope in my hands as he stepped further out of the door.

“Have a good night, Sheila.” I closed the door behind him, wondering what the envelope in my hands contained.

But, what I wanted more was a stiff drink. I grabbed my Jacket from the coat rack along with my handbag and keys, as I inched toward the door.

“Indiya, I’m going out.” I called up the stairs.

I paused for a minute awaiting a response, when none came I knew she was fast asleep and probably would be for hours.

CHAPTER SIXTY-FIVE

Love T.K.O

"Tried to take control of the love, Love took control of me……Cause you lose all thoughts and sense of time and have a change of mind…..Takin the bumps and bruises of a two-time loser….Tryin to hold on, faith is gone…It's just another sad song."

Gregory

"*How you get her is how you'll lose her, Gregory.*" In the back of my mind, I could hear the voice of my ex-wife warning me.

My heart was sick that I had not taken heed. As if it weren't painful enough having to watch my wife hooked up to multiple machines after being poisoned and losing our son, I came across the most devastating blow while trying to silence some of the noise so I could sleep. All the visitors had gone their separate ways as visiting hours ended, leaving an unconscious Nadira and me.

Her iPhone began to vibrate for the twentieth time. So, I walked over to the table tray where it sat; in effort to silence it but my heart told me otherwise. I unlocked it and across came the most salacious video I have seen on a cell phone to date. My wife engaged in sex with a man that wasn't me.

It sickened me to my soul as I replayed it, trying to understand what I did to deserve such a thing. The video should've been enough but my heart was full of curiosity. I kept thumbing through until I found more evidence of her infidelity. Text messages, pictures and even a video she sent him of herself masturbating. I almost wanted to call for medical attention for myself as I sat there with my head in my hands and my heart bleeding.

I quickly knocked away the lone tear that sat on my cheek. I was insulted, humiliated, and outright disrespected. I banged my closed fist against the arm of the chair, enraged. Here I was, doing everything in my power to be a better man than I used to be and my wife was playing me. To cheat is one thing, but she was carrying my baby.

"*Did that child even belong to me*?" I was flooded with thoughts as I stood to walk out of the room.

I needed some air, and as much as I hated to leave my wife alone; what I hated that much more was the knowledge she was cheating on me.

What was I supposed to do now? Ignore what I knew and pretend like everything was okay? The way I was feeling right now, I was liable to kill her before she woke out of her coma. I knew from the cynical thoughts I was having, I had to step away. I pulled out my phone and texted the one person I knew I could trust to lead me back to a logical place.

Sheila Denise

After two drinks at an old, rundown hole in the wall; I began to ride around aimlessly.

My thoughts flowed into the night air as I finally drove into a parking space on Kelly Drive. I reached in my handbag and pulled out the envelope that Vic had given me. Inside, was a flight itinerary for Paris. And, a note on a post-it that read "*Come and go with me.*"

I felt a wee bit of conviction for the way I had treated him today. I knew this was a sign that Vic had landed the contract he was working on internationally. My phone sounded beside me. I reached for it and read the text on the screen which had my immediate attention. Quickly, I put the car in reverse and headed in a direction opposite of my plans to nowhere.

Fifteen short minutes later, I arrived at University of Penn Hospital and parked my car with the valet. I walked inside and up to the fourth floor without so much as a question from the staff there. I found just the person I had come to rescue, sitting in the same place he occupied earlier in the day. His head hung low and his shoulders were slumped. I prayed he wasn't about to tell me the worst as I approached.

"Hey, Slick." I said taking a seat beside him.

"Thanks for coming." He sighed. His huge hand rested on my leg.

"You said you needed me, what can I do for you baby?" I asked calmly.

"I have to get out of here for a minute." He said with his head still bowed, his eyes never met with mine.

"What's wrong, Slick?" I asked lifting his head with my finger and forcing him to look at me.

His next action was one I couldn't be prepared for. He threw the iPhone he held in his hand, against the wall; shattering the screen.

He looked up and spoke.

"My wife is cheating on me." His words hit my chest like a 400lb weight.

I wasn't quite ready for what he just said to me.

"Let's get out of here." I whispered as a guard peeked his head in the room to see if everything was okay.

Gregory

I didn't question where we were going as Sheila drove along.

In that moment, it didn't matter to me at all. I just wanted to go somewhere and lay down my head and my cares for as long as I could. My heart was crushed in a million pieces and my male ego had been defeated. I didn't know it was possible as a man, to feel the kind of hurt I was experiencing. I guess that's the thing about tables, when they turn; you never know how you're going to be effected.

I stepped out of the car first and walked around to open her door. Of course, she had already opened it on her own.

“Close that door, Reds.” I smiled just a little.

She looked up at me puzzled, before closing the door.

“It's been such a long time since someone did that for me, I almost forgot what it was like to be in the presence of a gentleman.” Sheila said, nudging me as we walked up on the doorstep.

She placed the code in the keypad and the door opened, allowing us entry.

“You should always be treated like a lady, Reds. You have never been anything less.” I complimented, as I stepped inside the foyer.

Sheila smiled modestly as she turned the lights on dim.

“Indiya, is upstairs sleeping. So, keep it down Sir and make yourself at home.” She teased.

I was enthralled by how much like home it felt inside. Nadira and I shared a home equally as beautiful, but the feeling wasn't quite the same. Sheila was a real woman's woman. I could smell the scent of her favorite candle burning and everything was neat and in its proper place. There wasn't one dust bunny in sight. Most importantly, I knew that her home had been cleaned by her own hands; there were no maids or chefs around.

Sheila was domesticated and sophisticated, she embodied woman in every sense of the word. Our children were raised by her, and not taken care of by a nanny. My meals were prepared by her, and not a chef or a fancy restaurant. She did everything to make our house a home.

"*Damn, I wish I had known back then what I know now.*" I thought silently as Sheila lit the fireplace before walking toward the doorway.

"Can I have a few minutes?" She asked softly.

"Sure, you can." I said as I poked around the candy dish on the table.

I watched as she disappeared up the floating staircase. I rubbed my hands together before sliding to the edge of the seat to scope out the rest of the room. My heart grew warm as I looked around. Although, I painfully tried to erase every memory of my ex-wife when I started my new life; it was humbling to see that she hadn't done the same with me. There were pictures of our family that adorned the room. First Christmas, birthdays and even our wedding day.

"You never forget the happy times," Sheila said as she rejoined me in the room.

She had shed the outfit she wore earlier and smelled refreshed like her favorite perfume, *Chanel No.5.* She wore a simple long black dress that did little to hide her curves, and her hair was swept into a bun instead of hanging long as it did earlier in the day.

“I see you never did.” I smiled back.

“How about some tea, Slick?” She offered as she walked toward the kitchen.

“Got anything stronger?” I joked, although I was serious.

“*Johnny Walker Blue Label*” She said, pulling out the brand-new box that held the Scotch whiskey.

“I'll take it with my tea.” I agreed.

“Coming right up,” Sheila almost sang as she grabbed a mug from the cabinet.

CHAPTER SIXTY-SIX

If I Was Your Woman

"If I were your woman and you were my man.....You'd have no other woman....You'd be weak as a lamb...If you had the strength to walk out that door.....My love would overrule my sense and I'd call you back for more."

Sheila Denise

"If I were your woman, If you were my woman. If I were your woman. If you were my and you were my man." I sat tapping my fingers against my thigh grooving as Gladys voice flowed through the speaker.

She was the one songstress, Gregory and I could agree on. Gladys and I had a personal relationship. I swore by her music, she got me through a lot of nights when I should have lost my damn mind. Gregory sat on the other end of the sofa equally enchanted by the music as he drank the content of the mug in his hand.

"How's your tea, Slick?" I asked, looking over at him.

"It's helping." He answered suavely

"I'm sorry that I don't have any real remedy for your broken heart, except time. I mean they say it heals all wounds."

"Yea, but what about the wounds that leave a scar?" Gregory asked boldly.

"They remind you that you if you survived that hurt, you can survive anything." I shrugged lightly.

Gregory leaned forward and sat his mug on the table in front of him before walking over and standing in front of me.

"What are you doing Slick?" I asked as he reached out for my hand.

"When was the last time you danced with someone?" he asked.

Again, I just shrugged. I couldn't answer that with the truth. The last time I danced with someone, this negro was leaving me. He held my hand and walked me over to the *Bose*` stereo. He hit one button, replaying the song from the beginning.

"That Johnny Walker must've kicked in." I smirked at my thoughts.

"Dance with me, Reds." He whispered in my ear.

I obliged his request as he pulled me tightly, so tightly I could feel his chest beating against mine. This place felt all too familiar. Tears ran down my face as we swayed in sync with the music.

"Sing to me, baby." He spoke in my ear.

"*Yeah life is so crazy, and love is unkind, because she came first darling. Will she hang in your mind? You're a part of me and you don't even know it. I'm what you need and too afraid to show it. If I were your woman.*" I sang along with Gladys through my tears.

"I never stopped loving you, Reds." He admitted as his hands traveled down my waist and rested on the round of my hips just before our lips met.

His tongue slipped inside of my mouth, the taste of Johnny walked danced on my tongue and my heart pounded in my chest like the first time we kissed. I closed my eyes as tears ran even heavier down my face. In my head, replayed the words.

"You're a part of me and you don't even know it, I'm what you need and too afraid to show it."

Gregory swept me off my feet and carried me over to the wall. My dress now rested at my thigh and his hands roamed freely underneath it. I swear there was a puddle of wetness between my legs. If he placed his face down there, he would probably drown. He kissed me repeatedly, creating an even more intense feeling between the two of us. My heart raced and my breathing pattern changed.

I couldn't stop the steady stream of tears, though Gregory tried to brush them away with his lips; kissing the exact spots where they fell. I missed everything about the man that held me in his arms. As I inhaled his scent, I realized that this is what I was looking for over the past three years in Quentin and Vic alike. No one could replace, Slick.

"I missed you, Reds." He continued to run his hands down my spine.

Our bodies remained perfectly intertwined as one. Without so much as another word, his pants fell to his ankles and he entered me. Chills ran down my spine and my hands cupped the side of his face as I kissed him passionately. My eyes were closed and my legs rested firmly around his waist while he explored my sacred place, a place he hadn't visited for many moons.

“Hmm. I missed you too, Slick.” I finally allowed myself to say.

Those words did something to Gregory. He lowered me from the wall, spinning around quickly. He placed my hands on the wall above my head and helped me to bend over just enough for him to enter from behind.

“Damn it, Slick.” I managed to scream as he began sexing me from the back.

For a guy of a certain age, I had to say Gregory was giving my old ass a work out.

“You missed Daddy?” He asked over my shoulder.

The idea of calling any man daddy other than my daddy was utterly ridiculous in my head.

“Yessss...” I purred as Gregory continued to long stroke me from behind.

He gripped me around the waist and began walking toward the sofa, our bodies never disconnected until he took a seat, leaving me to straddle him. His hands felt there way to my breasts, discarding the dress I wore.

“Slow down baby, I want this moment to last forever.” Gregory's hands moved down to my hips controlling my body as I rose up and down gently, my walls gripping him each time.

The pleasure was obvious as I looked at the glare in his eyes. His mouth made its way to my breast as he began to suck like a new born baby.

“Don't stop, baby.” I hissed as I continued to rock back and forth on top of him.

“Cum with me, baby.” Gregory panted.

I threw my head back as my eyes rolled in the direction of the ceiling. I was certain this was the most pleasure I had felt in a very long time. Gregory's body stiffened as he released his fluid inside of me and I allowed myself the freedom to let go of the orgasm that had been building. Out the corner of my eye, I caught a glimpse of the one sight that could sour my mood… Indiya, who stood in the doorway momentarily before disappearing as our eyes met.

Gregory regained my attention, kissing me passionately on the neck while he continued to pant heavily.

Indiya

"What in the hell did I just see?" I scurried up the stairs to my room feeling a rush of emotion.

I felt everything from wanting to rip my eyes out of my head to happiness, to sadness as thought of how this could end. I wanted to be happy. This was all I have wanted for years, is to see my parents back together again. But could they ever really be back together? Was I dreaming?

"Bitch, you must have a damn fever! There was no way in the world I had just witnessed what I think I did. Not Sheila Denise and Gregory David?" I finished aloud.

If anyone would have walked in on this conversation, I'm sure my ass would have been diagnosed with a mental illness. I didn't give a damn that there wasn't a soul in the room to hear me or to help me sort out the details of all the craziness and noise going on in my head.

I could hear footsteps coming up the stairs. I dove into the bed as if I were still ten years old and listening outside of my parent's door. Curiosity was getting the best of me. I wondered if my dad had gone back the hospital to be by Nadira's side? Or if him and my mom were about to move along to round two. Whatever was about to happen was really none of my damn business, I resolved as I laid my head down on the pillow.

I needed to get some sleep. This was all too much for me. Hopefully, when I woke up in the morning; I would be met with the reality that everything I thought I saw was just a dream.

CHAPTER SIXTY-SEVEN

Hard To Do

"Cause what ya' gon do when I put this pretty thang on you....I usually don't do this but I'll do it for you....Oh' baby cause missing you is way too hard to do....I'd rather be f#@%&$ you....Do you mind if I give your love, Cause I just wanna give you love....Won't you tell me if I'm doing too much......Missing you is way too hard to do."*

Sheila Denise

I lay in the bed, wide awake.

Gregory lie sleeping behind me, his arm wrapped tightly around my waist as he held me close to his chest. I was riding a high that I didn't want to come down from. I peeked up at him as he slept as peaceful as a baby. I caressed his shoulder with my hand. I wanted him to wake up, although I knew that he probably needed to rest after the day he had. After a second touch, his eyes finally opened.

“Why you still up, Reds?” Gregory spoke in a low tone just before kissing my forehead.

“Can't sleep.” I answered softly.

“What's the matter?” Gregory pulled me on top of him until I sat up straddling him in the bed.

I swear he had to be feeling the same way I was, it was evident in the instant erection he got when I rested on him.

“Just thinking, that’s all.” I conveyed innocently.

“If I told you ten million times that I missed you, it still wouldn't be enough. My heart probably wouldn't be so damaged if I left it in the hands of the one who truly cared for it.” Gregory spoke with conviction.

“I just want your heart to be whole, whether it's here with me or a million miles away.” I said as Gregory planted kisses on my bare stomach and breast.

“Tell me you missed me, Reds.” Gregory whispered in my ear as his erection found its way inside of me.

My body shudder for a second, I bit my lip temporarily unable to utter a word.

“Missing you is way too hard to do. I rather be fucking you.” I sang in his ear.

Gregory grinned from ear to ear as we entered round two.

Keon

I was wrecking my brain, trying to figure out where in the hell Nadira could be. I needed to talk to her. My life was really in shambles since she walked away. I had no work and no endorsements, which meant no money coming in. Worst of all, I didn't have her. What we had wasn't long- standing but it was real, At least, that's how I felt. I called and texted her at least thirty times since I woke up this morning and got nothing in return. I couldn't go for that.

I purposed in my heart that she was going to see me and talk to me today, whether she liked it or not. I rode the elevator upstairs. My hands were tucked inside my sweats, as I was trying to hide my nervousness. When I stepped off the elevator, the atmosphere in the office was different. There were people in suits gathered around Janelle's desk, talking. They all turned around to look at me as I slowly approached Janelle's desk also. Janelle stood as soon as she saw me standing there, amongst the suits in the room.

"Hey, Mr. Walsh." Janelle said as she walked around the desk.

"Let's go into the conference room, to speak." She said, pulling me away from the small crowd.

"What's up. Where's Mrs. Fortune, this morning?" I asked as we marched past her office.

"Shh. Keep your voice down. Everyone is pretty shaken up around here." She said, as she opened the door to a small private conference room.

"Shook Up? What are you talking about? What happened?" I was piling more and more questions on Janelle by the second.

"Someone tried to poison Mrs. Fortune yesterday." Janelle whispered through tears.

"What the hell do you mean poison her? Is she, okay?" My voice elevated as I began pacing the room.

"Listen, that's all I know." Janelle said wiping the tears from her face.

The small conference room became a scene straight out of a movie in the next second. Police officers, Reporters and Detectives and dark suits filed in the room.

"Keon Walsh?" One of the detectives spoke up finally.

"Yea." I answered, looking back at him.

"We have a warrant for your arrest."

Immediately, one of the officers who was way too arrest happy if you ask me; pulled out his cuffs and stepped behind me.

"*Yo, what the hell was going on? I hope they don't think I poisoned her.*" I kept my thoughts to myself.

I had learned enough growing up to know, not to resist and say nothing. My lawyer would do the talking.

.

Gregory

When I rolled over in the bed after eleven a.m., it was empty. I could hear the shower running in the bathroom.

My daughter Heaven was weighing heavily on my heart this morning, I missed her. I rolled on my side and grabbed my pants from the side of the bed. I pulled out my phone to see a slew of calls and text that had been missed during my slumber. I placed the phone to my ear to call Myka before returning any of the other calls in my call log.

"Hey Bishop. How are you holding up?" She asked the moment she answered the phone.

"I'm alright. How are you and my baby girl?" I asked as Sheila walked into the room.

I couldn't help but watch her out the corner of my eye. The red silk robe she wore was almost like a magnet. I was drawn to her like never before.

"Baby girl, is her usual energetic self. We will see you at the hospital a little later today, right?" Myka asked.

"For sure." I answered quickly, hoping to bring our conversation to a close.

"Okay, I will talk to you soon." Myka ended our call.

I checked over a few messages before turning my attention to Sheila.

"You want some breakfast, love?" She asked kindly.

“You don't get have to go through any more trouble for me. You have done more than enough.” I said as I sat up on the side of the bed.

“No trouble at all. I ran you some bath water. And, grabbed you some things this morning. I’ll be down stairs making you something to eat.” She winked before leaving the room.

I walked into the bathroom, amazed that she had drawn a bath and everything that I needed for the day was inside of the Macy's shopping bags that sat on the ottoman. I climbed inside the tub of warm sudsy water and closed my eyes. Instantly, trying to pull my mind together. My heart was in one place and my head was still at the hospital with my wife. I was mad as hell that I had been betrayed by her, and plagued by the loss of my son.

“*His ways are past finding out.*” I reminded myself as I shook away my thoughts in efforts of stealing a moment of peace.

CHAPTER SIXTY-EIGHT

Back Down Memory Lane

"I see us standing there such a happy pair, Love beyond compare.....Look-a-there, look-a-there...The way you held me...no one could tell...the love would die....why oh why....Did I have this photograph....Thought I had forgot the past.....But now I'm slippin'fast....Back down Memory Lane."

Sheila Denise

Porgies, grits, wheat toast with strawberry jam, and a tall glass of orange juice were prepared then sat at the head of the table; awaiting Gregory. I would prepare this exact same meal, at least once a week for breakfast. It was his favorite meal, and I enjoyed making it. I pulled off the apron I wore, to run up the stairs to check on him. As I walked down the hall, I ran into him a lot faster than I anticipated. He was standing in the den, staring at the pictures on the wall. When he turned around to face me, there were tears in his eyes.

"You know Slick, I remember a few years ago when I moved into this home; I really wanted to burn every picture you and I ever took. But, my therapist enlightened me on something. She said to me, "*Sheila, you could set fire to the house you lived in, the cars you drove, and rip all the pictures into tiny pieces; and it still wouldn't rid you of the memories.*" So, every now and again… I reminisce and go down memory lane, the only difference is I can now do it free from the pain, because I was able to forgive and release it." I said stepping in closer to where he stood. He opened his arms to receive me.

"I preach forgiveness often, but I never knew what it really means to forgive until I looked at you last night. Thank you, for forgiving me and loving me enough to open your heart and your home to me." Gregory said kissing me on the forehead.

There was something so special to me about forehead kisses, they always seemed to make me melt. I pulled back from Gregory's embrace and took him by the hand, leading the way to the dining room.

"Ain't a woman alive that could take your place, Reds." Gregory said, in between chews the moment he took his seat.

I sat in the chair beside him, looking through the newspaper as he ate. I didn't really have an appetite at all.

Gregory sighed, looking up from his phone.

"I have to go down to the police station in a little bit.

"You'll be fine. You have nothing to hide." I encouraged.

"How can you do that every time?" he asked with a grin.

"Do what?" I questioned, looking over at him strangely.

"Turn my mountains into mole hills." He laughed.

"It's just what I do. Now, eat your breakfast. You have a long day ahead." I smiled before standing up to leave the table.

I too had some task to get to. Including, having a little lunch date with my daughter to discuss what she saw last night.

The doorbell sounded as Gregory finished his meal.

"*Who in the hell would be at my damn door anyway?*" I thought as I looked through the side window pane to see, Sha.

I took a deep breath and swung open the door. Wasn't no sense in hiding what was going on, I'd only tell her ass a littler later any way.

"Good Morning." I greeted casually.

"Took your ass long enough." She huffed, the moment her feet touched the indoor welcome mat.

"Aren't you in a delightful mood." I rolled my eyes playfully.

Gregory stepped into both of our view, creating quite an awkwardness amongst the three of us.

"Morning, Slick." Sha said with raised eyebrows.

"Good Morning Sha. Sheila, I must get on out of here. My ride should be outside." He informed me, kissing me on the cheek.

I nodded to let him know I heard him as I opened the front door for him.

"Ooh, Honey! You better spill all that tea. And, don't try to give me that decaf fixated version either because that glow on you; let's me know that man wasn't just here to drop off alimony." Sha said, making herself comfortable in the sitting room.

"Sha, I have errands to run and business to tend to." I stood in the doorway of the family room, praying that she would get the hint that I didn't want to explain my rendezvous with Gregory to her or anyone else for that matter.

"Oh. Well, I guess that means I am going along for the ride because ain't no way I'm letting you escape without giving me the details." Sha hopped up off the sofa and followed me over to the front door. She didn't say another word. I could tell she was waiting for all the juicy details which would make for one hell of a car ride.

CHAPTER SIXTY-NINE

Power In The Blood

"There is power, power, wonder working power……In the blood of the Lamb……There is power, power, wonder working power in the precious blood of the lamb……..Would you be free from your passion and pride…..There is power in the blood, power in the blood….Come for a cleansing to Calvary's tide….There's wonderful power in the blood."

Myka

Life is funny.

The moment I begin to battle my own demons and issues, God always places me right in the midst of another with issues that seem to trump mine. As I sat beside Nadira's bedside, my spirit was overwhelmed with the need to pray. I had no idea how my best friend ended up in this position or who could be so malicious. But, what I did know is that God had been merciful in sparing her life

There was something not right about this situation that had been troubling me all night long as I slept. And, discernment told me it had everything to do with the little secret that Nadira revealed to me just a few weeks ago. I fixed the covers that lay atop of her and stroked her hair as she lay peacefully in the bed. The tubes and the monitors everywhere were quite disturbing, still I did everything I could to make sure that Nadira was comfortable and that the room was inhabitable when she woke up.

I spun around at the sound of a familiar voice as Gregory walked through the doorway.

"Hey, Bishop. How are you holding up?" I asked, seeing the pain in his eyes.

"Hey Myka, I'm alright." Gregory answered, as he took a seat beside Nadira's bedside.

"Well, I'm going to be getting out of here in a few. I'll pick Heaven up from the Nanny on my way home as well." I said anxiously.

I walked over and kissed Nadira on the forehead before grabbing my handbag from the chair.

"Myka, just tell me one thing." Gregory stopped me in my tracks.

"Did you know?" Gregory asked staring me in the eyes.

Although, he didn't speak of it directly; I knew just what he was referring to. I choked up as I tried to answer. "I. I'm sorry It's really not my place." I answered empathetically before disappearing out the door.

CHAPTER SEVENTY

After The Pain

"Yeah, I know you're laughing those of you who heard 'Pain'....Yeah you're right I sure did I said I'd said I'd never take him back again......Well It's a woman's prerogative to change her mind isn't it? But we do it all the time..... You probably done the same thing too.... It's just that you know me and I don't know....You know time has taught me that having a little piece of man is better than having no man at all.....So Imma just take what I got and work with it."

Sheila Denise

I was sitting across the table from my now adult daughter.

Although, I often treated her like my little girl because that's who she would always be in my heart. I could tell by the way that she was fidgeting in her seat, she had a lot on her mind that she wanted to say to me. And, understandably so… She did witness her divorced parents having sex while her step mother lie in the hospital after being poisoned.

"Do you know what you want to order?" I asked as I placed the menu on the table in front of me.

I removed my eyeglasses and replaced them inside the case, in my handbag.

"Uh, I think so." Indiya answered coyly.

"Are you okay?" I asked watching as she shifted around in her seat.

Her eyes bounced from sight to sight but never made contact with mine. Usually, this would annoy me but today I was clear on why she couldn't look at me. We placed our orders just before I took a deep breath, it was time for me to cut right to it.

"Indiya, I don't know if there is an easy way to explain what you saw last night. Everything about that situation is complicated. And, you have been a part of a very complicated adult world for the past thirteen years of your life. For that, I apologize. I love your father, I always have and I always will. My intentions were to be his shoulder last night, everything else sort of happened. And, as much as I would love to apologize for it... While I am genuinely apologetic that you had to see it, I'm not sorry." I shrugged lightly, praying she could understand my plight.

"Mom, I know that you love my dad. And, while I love the both of you equally but different, I am concerned for you. I remember you telling me three years ago, "*Indiya, if a nigga ain't capable of caring for your heart, he ain't got no business caring for your kitty*." My dad is a man, whom I would never reduce to being just some nigga, but he does have those tendencies." Indiya giggled nervously before continuing.

"I just don't want to see you hurting again. If he truly loves you, he should respect you enough to leave you to the fabulous life you've been living until he's ready to commit to you one hundred percent." Indiya finished.

I had to give it to this little girl, she was smart indeed and it was a beautiful thing to see that she had been listening to me all along.

"You know what? Little girl, you are right. But, I think there maybe one thing that Mommy forgot to mention and that is the heart wants what the heart wants even if it's poisonous." I took a drink of the Chardonnay in my glass and shrugged just a bit.

I didn't have a logical explanation for this one. All I knew is, it felt good. And, lately that was what governed my decisions in the current. When it no longer felt good, I would relinquish it. Oh, but honey until that time came I was going to ride this here wave until the wheels fell off.

CHAPTER SEVENTY-ONE

For Free

"I always wonder if you ask yourself, Is it just me? Is it just me? Is this sex so good I shouldn't have to f$#@ for free???"

Keon

I sat in the dark in my living room, staring out the bay window as my jaw flexed and my chest pumped up and down.

My fist was clenched just as tight as my mouth. I was heated to say the least. I had spent seventy-two hours in jail, and been charged with attempted murder. You would think that I felt some relief when the guard called my name this morning saying that I had made bail, but I didn't. I knew I was liable to commit a murder once I was released. I didn't have shit to do with Nadira being poisoned but I was almost certain I knew who did.

"What the fuck did you do, Dani?" I screamed between clenched teeth.

She was running around here for the last three hours since I had been home acting like all was right in the world.

"Quiet down, baby. I'm right here, there is no need to yell." Dani smiled as she walked over and sat in my lap.

I pushed her ass to the floor with all my might.

"What do you think, this shit is a game? I seethed with anger.

"Absolutely not, Keon. Who do you think hired you a lawyer or paid the hundred-thousand-dollar cash bail?" She sneered.

"Where the fuck did you get a hundred large in cash from?" I objected immediately.

"Well, while you were out here fucking for free, I saw your rich little girlfriend as a payday. So, I cashed the in. Now, say Thank You." Dani cackled, sticking her tongue out childishly.

All the blood in my body was rushing to my head.

"You dumb ass bitch, this is my life you're playing with. Now, tell me what did you do?" I screamed with my hands wrapped around Danielle's neck.

I released her quickly as I watched her vein begin to pop out in her forehead and her eyes bulge.

"You know I like it rough..." Dani teased licking her lips.

I watched enraged, as her hand searched through her bag for what I prayed wasn't a gun. She pulled out two receipts and placed them in my hands with the sneaky smile still plastered across her face.

"What the hell is this shit?" I said looking down at what was in my hands.

"You asked what did I do, I thought I'd show you what we did." She said adding extra emphasis on the we.

The smirk on Dani's face grew larger as my eyes widened looking down at the papers she had placed in my hand. I still didn't get it, what the hell did this bitch mean?

"Now, in case you can't conceive what I'm trying to convey because you're too busy worried about the bitch who should be good and dead by now, let me explain. You sent her the flowers and the chocolate covered poisoned berries too. See, that's your card information right there." She pointed out, grinning from ear to ear.

This bitch was psycho.

"But, this can all go away if you go along with my plans." Dani squealed, rubbing her hands together as if she had some big pay day coming.

I didn't say a word, I took a seat on the edge of the sofa instead. This bitch had me by the balls. I couldn't think fast and/or logically. If I didn't go along with her, I would probably ruin my own damn life. And, if I did go along with her; I would still probably ruin my life. Either way, I was screwed.

C H A P T E R S E V E N T Y - T W O

I Care

"You see these tears falling down to my ears, I swear you like when I'm in pain……I try to tell you all my fears….You still don't care….That's okay."

Myka

No matter how strong a woman pretends to be, we all have a breaking point and today I'd reached mine.

I walked down the hall holding the flowers I had just purchased from the gift shop. As I approached the nurse's station, I felt like the entire room was in slow motion. There stood Sean, in the face of one of the nurse's; looking quite friendly and comfortable as he played with her curls and whispered in her ear.

My heart ached with a pain I couldn't begin to explain. Here was the moment he warned me about, where I'd watched him do with someone else what he was trying to do with me.

I stood frozen in thought, unable to move amidst the puddle of water and broken glass around me. The attention of everyone on the floor was now directed towards me. Sean wore a smile of victory as he looked over at me. In fact, I swore the bastard was laughing as he approached me.

"Looks like you made a little mess here. Are you okay?" Sean asked as he bent down to begin to pick up the glass before my feet.

I couldn't find the words to say so I just stared down at him as the nurse he was getting close to a moment ago, approached the two of us.

"Miss, are you okay?" She asked touching my arm.

I stood there, still in shock. My tongue felt as if it was glued to the roof of my mouth.

"Um, yeah. I'm okay." I finally managed to say.

"Let me call housekeeping." The nurse sauntered over to the phone and placed the receiver to her ear.

Sean gathered some paper towel and began drying up some of the water around me. I tried to bend down to help him but it was damn near impossible to bend over in this state.

"Don't worry about that, you shouldn't be bending." Sean said, finally softening his approached toward me.

"Thanks. I'm sorry about this mess, my nerves are all over the place." I confessed.

"Are you okay? What's going on?' Sean asked becoming concerned.

"Sean, do you know her?" The nurse asked with an attitude, as she rejoined he and I by the elevator.

"Yes, this is Myka. My child's mother, actually." He said as the elevator opened.

The nurse was left with her mouth hanging agape.

"Myka, let's take a walk so we can talk." Sean invited, holding the elevator doors open for me.

CHAPTER SEVENTY-THREE

Mr. Pitiful

" Mr. Pitiful.... That's my name now.....They call me Mr. Pitiful, that's how I got my name... "

Gregory

Back at my wife's bed side I sat, and then I stood even paced the floor. I was wearing the floor out, walking and calling on the Lord to walk by the room and send Nadira a special touch that would pull her out of her condition; that all the doctors described as critical. It was a devastating feeling trying to cope with the thought that I had lost a son. A son that I never even got the opportunity to hold.

"Mr. Fortune, we are just going to change Mrs. Fortune's dressings." The nurse informed me, as she walked into the room wheeling a cart accompanied by another nurse.

"I'll take a little walk." I said standing from my chair quickly.

I couldn't handle the bare sight of my wife's wounds. Not that I was a squeamish man, I just hated the thought of the pain and agony

I knew she would be feeling once she woke up to our present nightmare.

I rode the elevator to the ground floor of the hospital and threw on my sport coat as I stepped out into the night air, which was chilly and damp. I reached into my pocket and grabbed my cell phone to check on Heaven. I knew she was in good hands since Marta dropped her off with her big sister. Still, I felt it was only right I that check on her.

"Hi Dad." Indiya answered after a few rings.

"Hey, baby girl. How are you?" I answered, as I found a little corner to occupy.

"I'm good, dad. How are you holding up? How's Nadira?" Indiya asked anxiously.

"I'm okay, baby girl. Still not much change in Nadira's condition. How is Heaven? Is she giving you a run for your money yet?" I asked.

"Never. She's down the hall in the room with, Mom. I can get her if you want to speak to her." Indiya offered.

"Sure, that would be good." I stood by while I listened to Indiya travel down the hall and knock on her mother's bedroom door.

Sheila

“Come in.” I called out after a slight tap on the door.

I lay with my back rested against the mass of pillows behind me, too afraid to move for fear of waking Heaven; who was sound asleep on my chest. She was quite active but that was to be expected for a toddler who was full of life and energy.

A second after I called out to the door, Indiya walked into my bedroom with a slight smile and her phone held in her hand. She extended her hand, placing her phone in mine.

“Dad, wanted to speak to Heaven. I guess you can tell him that she's asleep.” She shrugged a little while wearing a grin as she backed out of the room shutting the door behind her.

“Hey.” I spoke into the phone, still staring at the door wondering why Indiya hadn't just told him Heaven was asleep.

“Hey. I didn't wake you, did I?” Gregory spoke sincerely.

“Nope, not at all. We aren't all as fortunate as little Miss Heaven who is peacefully sleeping.” I laughed a little.

“Yeah, sleep don't come as easy for me either.” Gregory laughed in return.

“How are you?”

“I’m alright, Thanks for asking.” Gregory returned.

The sound of his voice told me that he was lying.

“Well, your little Princess is in good hands. And, I am here if you should need me.” I offered.

“Thanks, I appreciate you.” Gregory said sweetly just before hanging up the phone.

I placed Indiya's phone on the nightstand and hit the lights. I was exhausted and in need of rest; I figured I'd take full advantage of the moment.

CHAPTER SEVENTY-FOUR

Blame It On Me

"Blame it on me, say it's my fault…….Say that I left you outside with a broken heart, I really don't care… I ain't crying no more….Say I'm a liar, a cheater say anything that you want."

Nadira Sy'Mone

"Mrs. Fortune? Mrs. Fortune, do you know where you are? Can you speak? Mrs. Fortune? Mrs. Fortune? She's awake." The voices around me spoke loud and clear, still I couldn't seem to stop staring at the glaring light that shined just above my head.

I was lost, trying to understand just why the hell I was laying here surrounded by people wearing scrubs.

"*Where in the hell was my husband? My mother? Hell, my damn friends? Why was I alone?*"

"Mrs. Fortune if you can hear me please follow the light." Someone spoke from beside me as yet another bright light was shined in my eyes. I pushed away that hand that flickered the light above my head, turning my head slowly in the direction it came from.

"She's awake! She's awake!" Another nurse shouted.

"*What the hell is wrong with these people?*" I wondered as I tried to get out of the bed... Only to be quickly restrained.

I wanted to stand. I wanted to see something or someone familiar. Instinctively, my hand ran down the gown I wore and over my stomach.

"*Something wasn't right. My baby isn't there?*"

"Where is my baby?" I screamed, alarming everyone in the room.

The nurses and doctors did what they could to restrain me but I was fighting like hell and wanted answers.

"Tell me where my baby is?" I cried aloud.

"Mrs. Fortune, I'm sorry. The baby didn't make it." The doctor finally stepped up and said.

Those words hit me like a boulder.

"*What did he mean my baby didn't make it? What in the hell happened to my baby?*" I cried loudly.

"We did everything we could. We are sorry that we were unable to save him. His lungs and heart were not developed enough to survive." He went on to explain.

"No, give me my damn baby back!" I flipped over the tray table in front of me, in a fit of rage.

Someone was going to bring me my god damn baby. During my commotion, in walked Gees carrying coffee in one hand and the *Daily Newspaper* under the other. His eyes widened at the sight of me.

“Smooth.” He said stepping closer to me. He tried to reach out and hug me but I refused.

“*Where the hell had this nigga been in my time of need anyway?*”

“Smooth, calm down.” Gregory stepped between the doctor and me.

“No, I want my baby! Where is my baby, Gregory?” I cried while pounding my fist wildly against his chest.

“Calm down.” Gregory said assertively, grabbing hold of my wrist.

His words fell on deaf ears as I did everything to pry myself from his grip.

“You were supposed to protect me! You weren't even here for me. Give me my son, Gregory!” I cried.

My eyes were so full of tears, I could barely see.

“I was supposed to protect you? How could I protect you when you were lying to me? How could I protect you when you were out here cheating? You were supposed to house and protect our son. You're the reason that he's not here with us. You're the reason that I’ll never get to know him. You want someone to blame? Look at this and see just who's to blame. That's your little boyfriend on the cover story, not me.” Gregory threw the *Daily Newspaper* he held in his arms into my lap.

On the cover, was Keon in handcuffs surrounded by police. The headline read, “She’s just like Poison” and underneath read ‘*Prominent VP of Shipman and Thales in critical condition after being poisoned at the hands of her Pro NFL lover.*’

Gees stood before me, his jaws flexing and eyes red with anger. I could do nothing but sit back while tears poured from my eyes.

"*What did I do to my damn family?*"

"Lie back and allow the doctors and nurses to care for you as they have been for the last five days." Gees said as he stepped in a little closer to me.

I had no choice but to comply. I was embarrassed, I had been exposed. And, worst of all… Though it was in my nature to be a fixer, I had no clue how or if I could fix this at all.

CHAPTER SEVENTY-FIVE

Hello

"It was many years ago, baby when you stole my cool……Cause you had me at Hello,,,,,Hello…..Hello oh oh oh oh oh"

Sheila Denise

My ringing phone woke me out of my sleep. I looked to my left where Heaven still slept just as peacefully as the minute I laid her down.

"Hello." I spoke into the phone just above a whisper.

" Hey, I'm outside. Can you open the door for me?" Gregory spoke into the receiver.

"Yes, just a minute." I complied.

I hopped up from the bed and into the mirror. I fingered through my disheveled hair and ran down the stairs. I hated to be caught off guard but I couldn't leave Gregory standing in the cold much longer. At the door, Gregory stood with his back pressed against one of the large columns outside.

“You alright?” I asked, noticing the broken look on his face. He offered me a small head nod rather than saying anything as we stepped inside the house.

“Baby girl is upstairs in the bed.” I informed him as he and I walked into the kitchen.

The moment we reached the kitchen, Gregory sat the newspaper with a picture of Keon and a smaller picture of Nadira on the counter. My eyes roamed the headline and suddenly there was a twinge of sadness that overtook me. I cared deeply for my ex-husband and as terrible as he had been to me in the past, I still couldn't separate myself from caring about his heart.

“I’m sorry, Slick.” I rubbed his shoulder and sat a cup of tea in front of him.

Gregory’s arm wrapped around my waist as he pulled me closer to him.

“It’s alright. I guess this is my karma, right?” Gregory asked before taking a drink of the tea in front of him.

“Baby, I wouldn't wish that kind of karma on my worst enemy. Physical pain ain't even enough to compare to the pain of heartbreak. Hell, broken bones may heal faster.” I shook my head at the mere thought.

“You got that right.” A tear fell from Gregory's eyes, he brushed it away quickly.

I stood glued to his side not saying anything, yet not wanting to move. I could feel his heartbreak the closer I got to him. Instinctively, I wrapped my arm around his back. I knew nothing better than to comfort one in need.

“Tell me something good baby,” Gregory whispered to me.

“At, Reggie Watson’s Dollar Party you had me at, ‘Hello’ and even in 2013 when you said goodbye; you still earned a piece of my soul.” I kissed his cheek just before he stood to his feet.

Together, we walked down the hall toward the stairs.

“I love you, Reds. Our girls deserve a world of simplicity and I hate to continue to complicate things. So, I’ll stay down here tonight.” Gregory said kissing me on the forehead.

“I’ll bring you a blanket.” I agreed.

I too didn't want to complicate things at least not for our children's sake.

CHAPTER SEVENTY-SIX

Stupid Girl

"Men roam the world looking for us, someone they can f#$% around with......Make us really trust them and we never have a clue.....We never see it coming, Train wreck headed for us....But we never think of running.... So which one are you, Because I know who I am..... And you have to choose to use your head or be a stupid girl....What will it be? Don't wanna end up with me-e-e-e.....So use your head, don't be a stupid gi-i-rlll."

Nadira Sy'Mone

The effects of the narcotic pain medicine the nurse had just given me, were kicking in full throttle.

I felt no pain, yet all the pain in the world. My heart was aching in a way that was unreal. How did I allow my little boy to get caught up in my adult world? There was no apology big enough to soothe Gregory's heart and how could I blame him. I had done the one thing to him that I asked him not to do to me; I betrayed him.

I wanted to close my eyes and sleep. But, there was pain in my dreams too, they'd become nightmares. I kept looking at the *Daily News* wondering if it were true. I knew Keon was hurt when I ended our relationship, I just never thought he'd want this kind of revenge. My cloud of thoughts was interrupted by the sight of Myka slipping into the room. With fresh sunflowers in her hands, she kissed my forehead and smiled.

"Hi there." Myka gushed.

Today, was the first day she visited while I was remotely conscious. After my breakdown yesterday, the nurse made sure to let me know that I'd had lots of company while I was unconscious.

"Hey." I spoke from my haze, my eyes fixed on the newspaper in front of me.

"Dira, let's move this out of the way and focus solely on your healing. You shouldn't be agonizing or even entertaining what they are saying." Myka snatched the newspaper from the table tray and tucked it away in the corner of the room.

"I know this is going to sound like a bunch of words right now. But, God will get the glory even out of this." Myka encouraged.

I nodded my head in agreement. My medicine had fully overtaken me. I finally closed my eyes and allowed myself to drift off to sleep.

CHAPTER SEVENTY-SEVEN

Money Make Me Cum

"Something come up short...she'll point it out....She will catch a flight, she'll run a route....We got grams in this Bi&%, girl come and get you some, Money make me come, Money, Money make me come."*

Indiya

I was blessed as a child not having to want for much.

My parents didn't really skip a beat when it came to my needs now, either. However, being with Cam showed me money on a level that I wasn't even aware existed… Fast money, that is. I now had an insatiable desire for paper, Dinero, cheddar, Guap or whatever you choose to call it. I wanted it, and in my head… No 9-5 was about to give it to me.

However, I took a part time job as a receptionist to satisfy my mother who urged me to get a job. Looking around the small office, disgusted me. The senior employees made my skin crawl on the daily. They were bitter, miserable old bitties that pecked like hens trapped in a chicken coop. The coop, being this dead end ass job. I would probably be equally as miserable if I never tapped into my life's potential. These old heifers couldn't stand my ass, I guess I reminded them of what they should have been once upon a time.

Today however, I was bothered to my core with office politics and this little ass check I was collecting.

"Uh, Indiya? I'm going to need you to file these and make callbacks before you go, today." The lead clerk instructed as she came over and dropped a mountain of files on my desk with a note on top.

This chick had lost her damn mind. It was already 2:38p.m, meaning I had twenty-two minutes left in my day...

"Yeah, about that… Filing isn't what I get paid to do. That is two steps above my pay grade, or in short; that's going to be a no for me." I returned, placing my notepad and water bottle in my *Louis Vuitton* Never-full tote bag.

"Excuse me?" She spun around quickly on her cheap heels, causing all the old bitties in the room to stop and stare.

I wasn't the least bit effected by her demeanor.

"Sweetheart, if you want your little job… I suggest you get up off your behind and do as I asked. See, you might make the rules on campus or even at Mommy and Daddy's house but here you will operate by my rules. And, I said get to filing." She barked.

"Bitch, kill yourself. See, this maybe the end for your uneducated, cheap shoe, synthetic hair wearing ass. But, it damn sure isn't for me. While your scraping the bottom of the barrel, trying to get ahead in life with your tired middle-aged ass; I have barely scratched the surface and am just getting started. It would be a lot harder for you to get a job out here than it would be for me. Now, you file them folders bitch. I quit!" I flipped her ass the bird before rising up from my chair and walking toward the door.

"Oh, and another thing… All you, miserable gossiping ass whores can kiss my ass." I announced as I proceeded to open the front door.

"*Damn that felt good.*" I thought on my way to my car.

I had been thinking this thing through for weeks and though some would call me crazy, I knew what my next move had to be. I was about to boss up on a level that was altogether different. Cam introduced me to the game, but I was about to I reintroduce myself. If my stepmother had taught me nothing else, she taught me that you're not actually a boss until you can call the shots. I was no longer going to be the girl that ran the routes.

I was about to call the shots and no one would ever suspect a thing… After all, I was just a naïve little preacher's kid.

CHAPTER SEVENTY-EIGHT

Each Tear

"No Mistake, No Heartbreak can take away what you're meant to be……We can't change the things that we done in the past."

Nadira

Eleven days had passed and I was finally being released from the hospital.

I missed my daughter sorely. And, mentally the hospital was more draining for me then the confines of my home or at least it seemed that way. I was apprehensive about going home today. So apprehensive in fact, that I told Gregory he didn't have to pick me up.

"Hey, Lady." Emilio peeked his head in the room as I gathered the last of my things from my hospital stay.

"Hi, Emilio." I spoke softly.

"You ready to rock and roll?" He jeered, picking up my belongings to carry.

I took a seat in the wheelchair as my nurse came to wheel me downstairs. It had been quite a long stay and I had gotten to know many of the nurses who provided care to me daily.

"I was almost certain that Mr. Fortune would be here today." Emilio said helping me inside the SUV.

"He's home with Heaven, today." I replied, hoping he didn't question me any further.

Emilio was quiet for a second as he began driving to my home. I watched as he looked up in the rearview mirror, knowing he had something to say.

"You know, Mrs. Fortune… Every marriage goes through a storm. Only the strong couples survive the storm." He advised.

The remainder of my ride was silent. There were no words in the English language to articulate my feelings today.

CHAPTER SEVENTY-NINE

No Limit

"You know you fine....Baby you know that you fine....I'm just try a make you....Tryna make you mine. Yeah I'm Tryna make you mine... Put a tingle in your spine, We got a vibe.....we got a wave you should ride on it.....All the places I could take."

Keon

One Month Later....

"*Sheesh... Damn! This lil sexy motherfucker gon be the death of me.*" I dug one hand into my pocket as I walked toward the car.

She stood posted up against the hood, dressed in all black everything. Her natural hair pressed to perfection, framing her face just the way I liked it and her body looked amazing. It was the first time I saw her in months not sporting a belly full of baby. She wore a *Black Isabel Murant* motorcycle jacket with sequin sleeves, a black jumpsuit that laid firmly against her body. I looked both ways, dodging cars and possibly Dani's psycho ass watching me.

"Hey." I spoke as I got closer to her.

She offered nothing but a head nod my way as she pulled an oversized pair of black frames onto her face. I tried to reach in for a hug but she instantly pulled away.

"Listen, I'm not trying to take up a lot of your time. I just need you to know that I'm not the monster that they're trying to say I am. I would never hurt you in that way. I love you and you know that." I pled.

Her head hung low to the ground and as she wiped her eyes underneath her glasses, I knew she was crying. My heart started aching. I couldn't take seeing her this way.

"I lost my baby." She managed to say though her voice was broken.

"I know and I'm sorry. I hate that this happened to you. I swear I would kill whoever if I knew who did this to you. I love you baby, I swear I do." I breathed.

Nadira pushed her glasses to the top of her head. Something finally softened in her face. I hoped in my heart that she was open enough to hear what I was about to say next.

"Listen, I'm not going to hold you up much longer. But, I'm begging and pleading with you to drop the charges. Don't let this go to court. If you don't show up, the state's attorney will have no choice but to declare a mistrial in this case. That conviction could ruin my life. I already don't have much. Please don't take what I have left, away from me." I begged with tears in my eyes.

I was putting my acting skills on a bit, but I meant what I was saying. If she went through with the charges it could mean a heavy prison sentence for me.

Nadira walked around her car and opened the driver's side door. She had yet to say a word to me.

"So, you're not going to say nothing to me?" I shouted with my hands up in the air.

Nadira's only reply was tires screeching as she pulled out of her parking space.

CHAPTER EIGHTY

Cause I Love You

"Baby I'm thinking of you tryin' to be more of a man for you....And I don't have much riches But we gon see it through, cause I love you.....Ho......Some men need lots of women, For their passions to feel, But I only want you girls, If it's in, If it's in, If it's in God's will.....Cause I, cause I love you."

Gregory

"Aye, Babe. I'm home." I called up the stairs the moment I entered the house.

I stood at the bottom of the stairs, peering upward waiting for Nadira to appear. After a few seconds, I called out again… still there was no answer. I took the stairs two at a time on the way up to the bedroom to check on her. In my mind, I figured she was probably fast asleep. She had been spending a lot of time in the bed since being released from the hospital.

"Aye babe." I said as I stepped into the bedroom.

The room was pitch black. The only light that showed in the room, came from the clock on the nightstand. I hit the light on the wall, and to my surprise; the room was empty. The bed was neatly made and there was no sign of Nadira or my baby girl. I sat down on the edge of the bed and pulled out my cell phone. I dialed Nadira, immediately.

My call went straight to voicemail. I hung up and dialed her again. After calling three times in a row, I decided to give it a rest. I guess she would call or come home when she was ready. I loosened the tie that I wore around my neck and found my way back down the stairs. I walked in the den and took a seat behind the desk. I had a lot on my mind… The state of my marriage, my Sunday morning sermon and *Her,* Sheila Denise.

All my thoughts seemed to run together as the doorbell chimed.

"Good Evening, Bishop. Sorry to disturb you at home. I was hoping that I could possibly speak to you and First Lady." She spoke softly.

"I'm sorry my wife isn't in. I would be happy to give you the names and numbers to some of our ministry staff that may be able to assist. You can also call my secretary and set up an appointment for, Sunday." I said, wrecking my brain to remember her name.

"Oh," She added with devilish grin.

"You know what? Sunday would be great. I'll see you then." She said, turning on her heels before I could say another word.

"Strange woman." I said aloud while retrieving my keys from the den.

Sheila Denise

Tonight, I had plans and they involved only Sheila Denise.

Lately, I had been overly consumed by things that really didn't serve me. I no longer wanted to wait for a man to take me out to dinner, I wanted to become content with doing me once again. That was my plan, before I pulled open my front door to find Gregory standing there with roses awaiting me.

"Good evening." I spoke, looking up at him strangely.

I wondered to what I owed the pleasure of this surprise visit.

"Hey. Looks like you were on your way out. I'm sorry to get in your way." He said, handing the roses to me.

I took them from his hand and moved to the side, allowing him to enter the doorway. I inhaled a whiff of his *Yves Saint Laurent* cologne and had to remind my kitty not today. He was dressed casually, not the Gregory I was used to seeing. He wore all black everything and on his left hand… He lacked one essential thing, his wedding ring.

"I was on my way to dinner." I informed him.

"Let's go." He invited, stepping forward toward the door and pulling it slightly ajar.

My hand moved above his, closing the door he'd just opened.

"Darling, much like what happens in Vegas stays in Vegas, what happens here in my home is strictly between you and me. I apologize, but I am not bold nor brass enough to be seen with you; out on the town. I honor the sanctity of marriage, Gregory. Now, get comfortable and I will make us some dinner."

Within seconds, I had removed my coat and was on my way to the kitchen to prepare a meal for the two of us. Gregory made his way to the family room and turned on Sports Center.

CHAPTER EIGHTY-ONE

Do You Mind

"Yo, he ain't messing with no average chick, pop, pop.....He got Nicki, He know that he hit the Jackpot. Every baller tryna score, check them shot clocks…….But I hit em' with them Bron/Igoudala blocks. Eat the cake, Suck on my toes, Yes. Hitting them home runs, I be like GO Mets. I want a dude that still kiss me when I'm mad.....Type to cop me diamonds he can miss me with them bags."

Nadira

"You got a death wish huh, High Maintenance? You know what? It's always you bourgeois' bitches that think y'all above the damn law." She spat angrily.

The lump in my throat, grew in size as I tried my best to show no fear. The barrel of the twenty-two was pressed firmly against my bottom lip. Fresh blood coated my arms and ran down my leg as Keon lie beside me, twitching and bleeding. The gargling sound he made let me know that he was close to death. And, help wasn't coming for either of us.

"See, that's what happens when you get caught up with Romeo. You must've thought this love affair was going to end like the last one where you just ran off with someone else's lover. I told you on day one that it wasn't gon' be that easy, Sis. Now, look at you... Lying next to your nigga while he bleeds out. All that education and, you're a dummy. Kiss your man good bye." She snapped.

The room went dark while the sound of the bullet that ripped from her gun, filled the room.

My eyes fluttered opened and I quickly scanned the room. It was so quiet, you could hear my heart beating fast through my chest. Gregory was snoring lightly on the other side of the bed. I wanted to crawl into his arms but I was afraid of being rejected. He and I, had yet to speak a word about our marriage. We barely spoke to one another at all, since I had been released from the hospital.

I was grateful, though. Gregory didn't make things tense and/or uncomfortable. He was genuine in his concern for my healing. He went to all my doctor's appointments and assisted around the house. But, I could tell things were just not the same in his head nor his heart.

CHAPTER EIGHTY-TWO

Is Your All On The Altar

"You have longed for sweet peace and for favor to increase……You have earnestly, so fervently, oh,oh you really prayed...Oh yes you have.....But you cannot find rest, nor be perfectly blessed....Until all on the altar, until it's laid."

Sheila

The moment the sanctuary doors opened, the melodic sounds of praise and worship hit my core.

It had been almost three years since I attended an actual church service. Chills ran down my spine and the hairs on the back of my neck stood at perfect attention as I excused myself into the row where my mother sat proudly. She acknowledged my presence with a graceful head nod and smile. I sat back in my seat as my ears perked up immediately. Inside, I felt like the gates of my soul opened. The tears building in the corner of my eyes were evidence that God had done just what I asked him to do, and met me at the door.

The lead soloist was instrumental in ministering to my heart as she opened her mouth, allowing the words to *Yolanda Adams* "Is Your All on The Altar" to flow from her lips. I wanted to fight the onset of tears but I could no longer resist. When they burst on the scene, they came full force. The spirit flooded the room as the souls around me stood, crying out to God. There were echoes of hurt, pain, and conviction all around me. The wailing and weeping around me told me, that many felt the same kind of conflict internally that I felt on this day.

Pastor Warren took to the pulpit as the sound of worship continued. He invited the congregation to stand to their feet and lift their hands in worship. I stood to my feet, my locking eyes with Lady Kelis Warren, wife of Pastor Brian A. Warren Jr.; also, my beloved friend of the last thirty-three years. She was one woman that I trusted with all of me. She knew my story and I knew hers. She was my secret keeper through my years as a First Lady as I was hers also.

And, as a bonus… she was Indiya's Godmother. Her smile was as wide as the ocean, and as bright as the sun. She blew me a kiss, lovingly.

"You may have your seats. It's an honor to be in the house this morning. I'm glad to see a familiar face in the house. And, Greater Faith wouldn't have it any other way than to ask if she would come and bless us with a solo. Lady Sheila, would you do us the honor of singing a little something for us this morning?" Brian invited.

"Sing Baby." My mother encouraged from beside me as I finally stood from my seat.

My *Stuart Weitzman* heels seemed to glide across the carpet as I made my way to the front of the church. Once upon a time, music was my first love. But, being soured into ministry made me shy away from it.

"Come on and help me bless the lord all over this place. Certainly, my heart is overwhelmed with nothing but genuine love for my Brother and Sister for the invitation this morning although the request to sing was left out. I count it an honor to stand before you." I joked.

The next words I bellowed were ones I had sung on many occasions. It was the song I would sing on sleepless nights, when I paced the floor all night long. It was even the song I sung during my seventy-two-hour hospital stay following my nervous breakdown three years ago. With my eyes tightly shut, recalling all that my Rock had brought me through; I sang these words.

"Where do I go when there's nobody else to turn to? Who do I talk to when nobody wants to listen? Who do I lean on when there's no foundation stable? I go to the Rock, I know he's able I go to the rock. I got to the rock for my salvation, I go to the stone that the builder's rejected. I run to the mountain and the mountain stands by me. When the earth all around me is sinking sand, On Christ the solid rock I stand. When I need shelter, when I need a friend I go to the rock."

CHAPTER EIGHTY-THREE

Love You Forever

"Your Goodness, Your Mercy and your kindness towards me.....Your love is so amazing it brings me to my knees...Oooooooo gonna love you forever."

Myka

Finally, we had arrived at my all-time favorite day of the week, Sunday.

Sunday's had long been reserved for me. It was the day that I pressed to the house of the Lord for the fuel I needed to make it through a long week. I put the finishing touches on my outfit and took one last look in the mirror. I was looking a lot different physically, these days. Everything was bigger, but I counted that as a blessing because I was carrying brand new life and that was a blessing.

The doorbell startled me a little as I reached the last step. I peeked through the curtain to see Sean on the other side. We had been communicating a lot more in the past few weeks. I was working to show him that I was more into him, just as he had shown me. I opened the door with a smile as he stepped in. He was dressed in a three-piece suit, impressing even me.

"Hi, baby. Don't you look handsome," I complimented.

"I just wanted to look good on your arm at church, today." He explained.

I was shocked. I usually had to pull teeth to get him to attend church with me.

"You're going to church with me?" I asked as I reached for my handbag and coat.

"Correction, we are going to church as a family." Sean rubbed my growing belly.

I felt flutters in my belly. I took it as a sign that our baby agreed.

"You just made my day, you know that." I cooed as Sean helped me into my coat.

"And, you make my life complete," I turned around to see Sean down on one knee.

My heart was about to leap outside of me.

"Myka, will you marry me?' he proposed.

"Absolutely." Was the only word I could speak through my tears.

CHAPTER EIGHTY-FOUR

That's The Way Love Goes

"Like a moth to a flame, burned by the fire...My love is blind can't you see my desire...That's the way love goes."

Sheila Denise

Thunderous applause sounded as I walked casually into Kelis's office. The funny thing is, she was the only one clapping and cheering. By the sound of things, you would have sworn it was no less than a football stadium full of eager sports enthusiast. But, no… It was simply my loud mouth, happy-go-lucky, can't keep a good woman down, girlfriend.

"And, there we have it ladies and gentlemen… She ain't come to play, Sheila Denise always comes to slay. My God, Reds… Do you always have to do me like that when you come here?" Kelis hugged me quickly before stepping back and placing her hands on her hips.

"And, just what have I done First Lady?" I asked, amused at Kelis's antics already.

"Honey, besides doing your good, good churchy singing this morning. You have officially put every natural born woman in the congregation to shame from the moment you walked through the door, serving a big ole' cup of flyness. Come in here and have a seat." Kelis offered, finally moving away from the door.

"My humblest apologies to you and the old hags of this here congregation. But, I Sheila Denise only know how to come through one-way Sis, and that's slaying," I winked as I took a seat beside her on the plush tufted sofa.

I smoothed my hands over the butter soft ivory leather dress I wore, taking a slight glance in the mirror at the Fox fur stole that sat perfectly on my shoulder beneath the weight of my *Chanel* Brooch.

"Alright, enough with the politics. What do I owe the pleasure my darling? I haven't seen you in a month of Sunday's Sheil." Kelis said, with her hand atop of mine.

"Girl, did you not just hear the song I sang? I said, whipping my head in her direction.

"Chile, you needed to go to the rock of your salvation I heard. However, what navigation program lead your ass to this here church is the question. Not that I'm not glad to see you," Kelis rolled her eyes hard in my direction.

"Where the spirit of the Lord is, there is liberty right? I mean damn… Did you not get your breakthrough this morning? Besides Mom told me Brian asked about me and invited me to Family and Friends day," I revealed eyeing her.

"Sheila, I have broken down, broke out and been flat out broken but breakthrough is a stretch. It's hard to be led into his presence by a no-good trifling dog." Kelis spat venomously.

"You meant that thing, huh?" I said trying to hold myself back from laughing.

Kelis and Brian warred more than the Bloods and the Crips. I swear, that Ike and Tina scene in *What's love got to do with it* was a scene straight out of their lives. There was one exception though, Kelis was Ike. She would be all over Brian with just the mere thought that he was doing something low down. You couldn't convince her that every sister in the church with a set of eyes didn't want her damn man.

"Chile, his ass ain't low. I bet you them fly shoes on your feet that he is skinning and grinning in some heifer face as we speak. *humph*.... I love him though." Kelis spoke so hard that time, she had to laugh at her own self.

"I don't know what kind of Black Magic Brian got that makes you as crazy as you are, but I will tell you this much... I pray a nigga never cross my kitty serving it. You are certified loco, baby." I laughed in unison with Kelis.

"Men will make you this way Sheil. You know how it is?" Kelis said, as more of a rhetorical question since she began speaking before I could even agree with what she said.

"Sheila, you were married to one of the most influential pastor's in the city for thirty long years. And, if there is one thing you learned in that marriage I'm sure it was this... Women are drawn to a man with a collar like a bee is to honey. And two, no matter how much love you shower on some of these men; your love will just never be enough for a man that's greedy. I have come to accept that Brian is greedy, but please don't think that my acceptance means I don't try my best to restrict his diet every chance I get." Kelis finished.

"Gregory and I, have been seeing each other." I admitted, shocking Kelis.

"I'd love to say it was accidental. But, after the first time… The love making became intentional. My greatest intent was to show him that I'm all the woman he ever needed. And, for this next statement Kelis you may call me a fool but I believe he finally gets it. That no matter how many skirts you get under and how many notches on the bed post you gain, ten whores don't equal one good woman."

"Damn it, Reds. You never cease to amaze me. That was deep, but allow me to be shallow for just a minute. Is it good to you?" Kelis asked with a sly grin plastered on her face.

"A-MA-ZINGGGG!" I emphasized every syllable.

"They say all good things come full circle, right? Who would have thought Gregory would ever cheat on the same woman that he was creeping with? It seems like yesterday, we were staking out old girl's house and doing drive-by's during his business trips." Kelis said taking my mind back to a place I tried not to remember often.

"That's the way love goes, I guess. At some point, every decent man has to come into the reality that the good woman he did wrong; was the right one all along." I shrugged.

"When I grow up… I just want to be half the woman you are, Sheila. If Brian had taken me through a third of the things Gregory took you through, I may have never left the mental hospital, like you did." Kelis admitted.

I felt a twinge of pain shoot through my body that I couldn't explain. I had never spoken to anyone about the breakdown that I had behind those walls. But, what I retained in my heart about that time in my life was this; If it had not been for my breakdown, I may have never experienced a breakthrough.

Sheila Denise

Padded walls and medicated residents, along with the paper slippers and white assigned scrub uniforms worn by every resident; were more depressing then the actual reason I was here.

Today, was my final day in this place. Not just in a physical sense, but emotionally and mentally as well. I had never been to prison in the natural, but I sure as hell knew what prison felt like mentally.

"Sheila McClure." The health care worker spoke softly, as she poked her head into the small room I had occupied for the last week.

I stood from the edge of the bed that I had stripped of its linen, in anticipation of making my final exit from this place.

"Time to go." She smiled as she placed her hand on my back, helping to guide me towards the door.

"Sign these for me." She handed over a clipboard with the keys to my release safely nestled under the clip.

I took a breath before inking my signature by every X.

"Promise me that you're going to take care of yourself" she said as I returned the clipboard to her hands.

"I absolutely will." I said with a reassuring hug.

Seconds later, she opened the door and my face was kissed by the brightly shining sun. Awaiting me was Kelis, who sat in her Lexus ES 300, with a bright smile adorning her face. I tugged the door handle slightly and the door opened, allowing me to slip inside.

"I wanted to wait for you outside the car but baby... I was sweating like a whore in church, standing out there." Kelis said, as she reached over and hugged me.

"Thanks for coming to pick me up." I said humbly.

Thinking on the fact that I had no idea who else to call.

"You owe me nothing, baby. All I want you to do in this moment, is to blow a kiss to this place and promise me that you will never return here again unless it's to minister to the souls and minds that are behind those walls." Kelis said with her hand atop of mine.

I looked to the right and did exactly as she asked, me blowing a kiss not only to the physical building that stood erect beside me, but to every haunting painful memory I laid to rest behind those walls. Kelis pulled off slowly as I snapped my neck into a forward position.

she asked, " Where to Sheil?"

"Are you in a rush, Kel?" I asked as we approached a red light.

"Not, at all. My day belongs to you, friend." She returned.

"Pull over and let me take the wheel." I instructed politely.

Kelis didn't question me. Instead, she pulled over and surrendered the wheel to me, and climbed into the passenger seat. I had a mission to complete in my head and I needed my friend beside me, not in the way.

My first stop of the day would soon be Exceeding Faith Ministries. I wasn't going to pray or shoot it up like Columbine, I was simply going to pack what was mine. There was now a new reigning Queen, who would soon take over the office that belonged to me. And, I was going strip it bare. There wasn't a cold chance in hell that I was going to allow Sis to build off my legacy.

Kelis was staring at me like a nut when I pulled up at Lowe's to buy industrial garbage bags and duct tape.

"Don't worry Sis, we won't be hiding no bodies today.' I winked as I fished through my bag for my credit card.

"I ain't gon lie bitch, you had me nervous. I was filming a First 48 episode in my damn head." Kelis laughed.

"No need. This bitch will bury herself, sooner or later." I assured her as I wrapped up my I purchase.

"What about him, Sheil? Do you forgive him and just let him live happily ever after, after all you've given to him?" Kelis questioned.

"No dog can serve two masters, Kel. So, yes, I forgive him for leaving. But, he's a smart dog. Sooner or later, he will understand that it takes more to keep a man than a cute shape and a wet mouth." I finished as we reached our first destination of the day.

CHAPTER EIGHTY-FIVE

How Did You Get Here

"How did you get here, nobody's supposed to be here……I tried that love thing for the last time."

Nadira

2004…

"How the hell did you get here Nadira?' I questioned myself.

I stood at the alter with the phoniest smile I could muster, plastered across my face. Church members began marching through the sanctuary to greet the new members class of which I happened to be a part of. The smell of peppermint and White Diamonds perfume swarmed me as the parade of handshakes and hugs began.

"I'm so proud of you." Myka my best friend, whispered into my ear before hugging me tightly.

I could choke her ass. After all, she was the reason for my black ass being here.

"Thanks," I said offering her a little stank eye.

If not for Myka's constant nagging to find a decent church home, I would have never visited Exceeding Faith Ministries; one year ago. It took some courting and a whole lot of convincing for me to take the leap and become a member. All I faintly remember, is my feet moving faster than my mind as I made my way to the alter just eight weeks ago. I was at the lowest point in my life, still struggling to accept the death of Darren aka Coke my boyfriend, best friend and protector of the past seven years who was killed in front of me a year prior.

I hadn't been able to shake the gruesome scene since it happened. My only saving grace had been throwing myself into work and coming here. I had yet to discern whether it was the preaching that came forth on a weekly basis or the fact that I liked looking at the Bishop; that made me just a little too excited to join. Don't get me wrong, I'm not a heathen. I just wasn't raised in church. I was forced to go whenever I stayed at either Myka's or Isha's houses as teenagers, because Holy Rollers raised both of them.

"Congratulations and welcome to the family, Gorgeous!" First Lady Sheila Fortune greeted as she stepped in front of me.

She was always dressed to kill, at least as far as churchwomen were concerned. She was a pretty lady with deep dimples and beautiful hair that touched the middle of her back. Today, it was pressed straight with a long part down the middle, instead of pinned up under a sparkly hat for a change. She was dressed in a Coral dress that had flowing sleeves, that hit her just past the knee and complimented the Swarovski Crystal embellished peep toe shoes she wore so well. Her neck and wrist were draped in eye catching Traci Lynn pieces.

She was well put together, for a woman who typically looked like something smelled bad or she was sucking lemons. I couldn't quite clock what was up with her but in due time I'm sure it would register. I hugged her back gently and she made her way to the next person in line.

"Well, Sister Nadira. You are officially a new member of Exceeding Faith Ministries. "Bishop Fortune said as he approached me.

"That I am." I responded with a smile.

I couldn't quite explain what it was about this man that was so intriguing and sexy to me."

"Following the benediction, I'd like to speak to with you in my office; if you have time," he said as he slowly let go of my hand.

I nodded my head in agreement as he made his way to the gentleman standing beside me. The line had finally come to an end and all the new members were escorted back to their seats.

"Welcome!" Isha said extending her hand to me.

Nadira

That flashback in my mind, took me back to a simpler time.

I sat, occupying the same seat that Sheila had once upon a time. Today, I felt very much like I had in those days when the whole church was walking around; whispering and gossiping about me. Calling me a whore and every type of nasty hoe you could think of. I couldn't focus on the sermon if I'd tried... There were too many internal conflicts raging on the inside of me.

My husband stood, preaching his entire face off under the unction of the Holy Ghost and I was squirming in my damn chair praying that no one noticed. In the pit of my stomach, I felt my breakfast churning as he made the alter call. I stood to my feet, keeping my eyes on the *Christian Louboutin's* I wore on my feet. I was having the time of my life, lifting my head and looking out at the congregation. I felt like all eyes were on me. I wondered if they thought he made that alter call for me.

I pushed back my own thoughts and smiled happily as the alter call ended and the newly converted took their seats. Service was slowly creeping to an end as most of the members were digging in their handbags and pulling out their wallets; a sign that it was offering time.

Gregory walked over and grabbed my hand, leading me to his office. The two of us were followed by his armor bearer, which was protocol to say the least.

"You alright from here, Bishop?" he asked Gregory as he unlocked the door to his office.

"Yes, we are fine." Gregory answered coolly.

I took a seat on the couch while Gregory removed his robe and hung it on the hook behind the door. He loosened before taking his seat.

"You look like you got a lot on your mind, Smooth." Gregory commented looking over at me.

Tears were forming in my eyes. I knew this moment would come but I still wasn't prepared for it.

I took a breath while smoothing my hands over my pantsuit. Before I could find the words to say, a soft knock at the door stole both of our attention away. An usher walked in, handing a manila envelope to Gregory before backing out the door to leave. Gregory regained his seat while opening the envelope. His eyes grew wide as he fixed his attention back on me.

"You've got to be kidding me!" He screeched.

I swore you could see smoke rings coming from his ears as I rose to see what had angered him. Before him, were pictures of Keon and I, taken just a few days ago when he asked me to meet him. Though these weren't pictures of us in compromising positions, I knew he would see them as more signs of infidelity.

"Before you speak, let me explain." I began to plead.

"What could you possibly say to me?" Gregory voice boomed as his anger seethed.

"I slept with him, Gregory. Yes, I did. I allowed my own lust to get the best of me. While we were apart, I found comfort in him on the nights I couldn't sleep. Was I wrong? Yes, absolutely." I answered rhetorically.

"These pictures, Gregory… Are from a few days ago when Keon called crying and begging for me to meet him. And, because I needed answers; I went to meet him. Nothing happened, other than him explaining to me that he wasn't the one who did this to me. Gees, please understand that I would hurt myself before I hurt you, again. I didn't mean to bring this kind of pain to our family. Please forgive me." I begged.

Tears and snot ran together, down my face.

"Smooth, have your attorney contact me." He said with little fight in voice.

I watched his back as he walked out of the doors of his office. I knew I had wounded him deeply. I picked up a bottle of water from his desk and chugged it back, praying that the clear content was something much stronger. Reluctantly, after my swallow I looked back at the bottle… It was just water and would do nothing to mask the situation I had only further created. I sat on the couch with my head buried in my hands, crying helplessly. I was hoping that my tears were interpreted as the words I couldn't say, to the only one that could help me.

Indiya

"Grace, mercy and peace the love of God be with thy people. Keep us all living free from sin, hence forth now and forever more. And, the people of God say. Amen." Like clockwork and in unison, the church sang out Amen.

Church was officially dismissed, I watched as my father was escorted down from the pulpit

I had a pocketbook full of candy that I needed to deliver. And, we all know church folks like candy… But, I discovered something in my new occupation. There are quite a few brothers in the church, that like hard candy. I found my customer standing off to the side, looking hella country. I shook my head while walking in his direction.

He smiled, exposing his gold tooth as I got closer.

"*Cam better not have set my ass up.*" I thought as I reached him.

I leaned in for a church hug and dropped the merchandise in his oversized pockets, quickly.

"Sister Indiya, how you are doing?" He asked pleasantly, looking over his tinted frames.

He quickly passed off a brown envelope, that I tucked into the small bible that safely tucked under my arm.

"Tel Cameron, Uncle B and Aunt Shirley we send our love." He said as an older woman approached the two of us.

"We will be in touch this week to set up that visit for you." He touched my shoulder and moved towards the door, with the woman in tow.

"Chile, this some foolishness. I'm sure I'm tap dancing at hell's front door." I thought as the room began to clear even more.

I took a walk around the sanctuary, and started mingling with old church members that I hadn't seen in a while as I waited for my dad to finish his meeting. Cam warned me this week when I went to see him that I needed to appear friendly and inconspicuous, if I wanted to make it in this business. That was only after he told me hell no twenty times.

I'd batted my lashes and licked my lips enough to get him to change his mind and hook me up with his connect by the end of the visit. This game was more complicated than I originally thought, but I was willing to give it a shot until I got my coins up.

CHAPTER EIGHTY-SIX

Tears Of A Clown

"Now if I appear to be carefree it's only to camouflage my sadness.... And honey to shield my pride I try to cover this hurt with a show of gladness, But don't let my show convince you that I've been happy since you."

Gregory

When a man inflicts pain on the woman he loves, he reasons with himself that she will soon get over it and forgive him even. But, when a woman inflicts pain on a man; he sees no sign of forgiveness or relief in sight.

The more that was revealed to me, the more I felt like a fool. The congregation was already talking.

"*How embarrassing.* T*he one I traded my all in for, turned out to be the one who'd betrayed me."*

"Aye, Daddy-o." Indiya said, walking up behind me as I sat in the empty sanctuary.

"Hi Princess." I greeted her as she came and took a seat beside me.

I was so caught up in my head that I forgot she attended service this morning.

"So, are you and Jesus having an after party?" Indiya asked, with her eyebrows raised and a chuckle.

"Yeah. I needed to holler at the big guy alone." I said, trying to force a smile.

"Oh sorry, Dad. Do you need a minute?" Indiya asked, a little more seriously.

"Nope, I'm through for now." I answered as I put arm around her.

"How about dinner, then?" She suggested.

"Sounds like a winner to me." I stood up and Indiya stood beside me.

"Dad, I know that you're the Bishop and all… But just in case no one has reminded you lately, in all things God has a plan. It's just up to us to be quiet enough to hear it. And, be obedient enough to follow through with it." Indiya advised as we reached my car.

"Spoken like a very wise woman, I know." I smiled hard after hearing Indiya speak.

She reminded me of her mother at her age, wise beyond her years.

"Now, where to for dinner kid?"

"Toss me those keys, I think I know a place you'll love." Indiya said as she walked around to the driver's side of the car.

I wasn't exactly a fan of her driving but I did as she asked and helped her inside the car.

CHAPTER EIGHTY-SEVEN

Cry

"I deserve to get my point across, Before all we had was lost……Now we are both hurt by the one we love….I know it's wrong but I want to see you cry, Cry, cry, cry……You gone cry, you gone pay me in tears…..You gon cry, you owe me for all these years."

Sheila Denise

I was listening attentively as Vic poured out his last spill. But, we inched closer and closer to the front door. I was praying that he would say his last words on the other side of it. I had a wonderful time in church this morning, I felt like I had released this pile of bricks and here was this selfish ass man; piling them back on me.

I guess guilt was his method of the day because he was laying the shit on super thick.

"Sheila, this is a once in a lifetime opportunity. How many times have you said you wanted to travel the world and just live carefree?" He asked as I swung open the front door.

My hand now rested safely on my hip and my head was cocked slightly to the side.

“I absolutely want to travel the world and live carefree, that isn't the matter at hand, Victor. Doing it in your time, is.” I finished as Gregory’s Maybach came pulling in through the gates of my home.

My heart sank to my toes, still I showed no signs of panic though I knew this could be sticky.

“Well, I’ll be going. Just remember… Time isn't forever, Sheila.” Vic said dropping his head slightly and giving me some relief.

“No, but London is. Have a good trip, Victor.” I called out as he reached his car.

He didn't bother to acknowledge the other car now in my driveway. Instead, he backed up and drove around them as if they weren't there at all. Seconds later, Indiya and Gregory strolled up the path to my home; together talking and laughing. She had always been a daddy's girl.

“Afternoon, you two.” I greeted pleasantly.

Indiya hugged and kissed me on the check, and Gregory did the same. I looked up in his eyes and instantly knew something was bothering him.

“How was church?” I asked, as the three of us walked toward the kitchen.

“You know... They were shouting, they were hollering, new members were joining…” Indiya said before she was interrupted by her dad.

“And, Indiya was sleeping.” Gregory finished her sentence.

I couldn't help but laugh, not much had changed in twenty years. Indiya never could make it past the choir singing. Today, I was just proud she dragged herself out of bed and made it to church.

"I went to church today as well." I said shocking the both of them. "No wonder it's particularly warm for November," Indiya added sarcastically.

I eyed her long and hard before laughing, along with her and Gregory.

"Now, now… I had to go in my own time." I defended.

"You're missed at EFM, Reds." Gregory revealed.

"Well, there is a new First Lady on the roster." I answered softly.

"Not for long." Gregory sighed.

Shocked, I dropped the glass that I held in my hand.

Indiya stood beside her dad fighting back tears.

"I'm sorry, Gregory." I said sympathetically, as I began to clean up the wine I had spilled on the counter.

"I'm going to let you two, talk." Indiya excused herself from the room.

I was at a loss for words. Gregory sat at the island, saying nothing at all. His head rested in his hands, momentarily.

"You want to talk about it?" I asked as I finished my task of cleaning up the mess I made.

"I think it's time that I give Nadira her freedom. It hurts like hell, Reds to have the woman I loved; make a fool out of me." He spoke slowly.

"Well, damn... If this doesn't sound familiar." I shook my head, realizing I had spoken my thoughts out loud.

It was too late to take them back and if I were brutally honest, it was the damn truth. I really wanted to turn to Gregory and remind him that Karma don't miss. Her shot may be delayed but her sting will never be denied. What I did feel bad for, was the family. Divorce isn't ever pretty. Especially, not for the children involved.

"I guess I deserve it huh, Reds?" He asked finally lifting his head.

"Would you be terribly offended if I said yes?" I asked with squinted eyes as I studied him.

Gregory nodded his head no, but I knew he would change his mind in a second after I spoke my mind.

"When you met Sis, you couldn't see past the thrill. You were a fool for the old cliché, thinking the grass was greener on the other side of town. And, yes.... I do hope you now realize that what you were running to was simply turf. And, in a moment's notice; it's superficial surface could be snatched up from beneath you. Leaving you, with nothing but possessions. Once upon a time, just three short years ago I sat where you're sitting... Trying to figure out how the hell it was I could go on and figure out this thing called life without the partner I thought would be beside me for the long haul. But, you know what baby? I bossed up." I took a pause.

"I dusted myself off and got back to living. And, in due time you will too. But right now, Gregory... I hope you cry. I hope you cry real tears and feel some of the same pain that I felt. And, finally... I hope you cry so hard that you think long and hard. So, the next time

God sends a good woman into your life; you treat her properly and handle her with care. Doing any and everything to keep her." I finished before wiping my hands on the dish towel in front of me and exiting the room.

Today, was the first time I ever spoke my truth to Gregory.

Usually, I coveted and acted as if I was never wounded by him.

The words of Queen rang loudly in my ear, "We overcome by word of our testimony."

I knew his pain all too well. I couldn't really tell you if I was thankful to Karma or ready to wipe away his tears and dust him off my damn self.

CHAPTER EIGHTY-EIGHT

Bad and Boujee

"We came from nothing to something nigga (hey), I don't trust nobody, grip the trigger....Call up the gang.....They come and get you....Cry me a River, Give you a tissue."

Nadira

Dressed in *Joe Fresh* jeans and a destroyed free People sweatshirt, I hopped out of my car and trekked up a grassy hill. On the top of the hill, was Isha's final resting place. I hadn't made any effort to visit her here in the last few months, partially because I was caught up doing my own thing. Today, I needed to talk to her. She was my one friend that knew how to play devil's advocate well.

"I feel like you just rolled over in your damn grave just now, seeing me here." I joked aloud.

"It's been a long few months, and I miss you. Life isn't really the same without you. I don't have anybody to check me when I'm wrong like you did." I admitted painfully.

I sat down in the grass, my back beside Isha's grave marker. Tears were overwhelming me, as I cried out.

"Ain't no use in crying man, you can't kill her twice." June chuckled as he made his way up the hill.

This guy was the last person I needed to see, today. I struggled to pull myself together. He laid flowers down on Isha's grave and took a seat beside me.

"You don't really feel like I killed her, do you?" I asked June through my tears.

"Nah, I just think you're selfish as hell… That's all." June retorted.

"Always have been. Whatever Nadira wants, she gets no matter what or who it cost."

"What do you mean by that?" I frowned.

"Just what I said. You want what you want, no matter what the cost. Coke paid with his life trying to make you happy." June informed me.

"That's not true," I argued.

"Man, that big head of yours can't see past nothing but your own needs. You just had to go to A.C. and to please you, Coke rode right through the enemy's territory." June reflected.

C H A P T E R E I G H T Y - N I N E

03' Bonnie and Clyde

"But Girlfriend work with the kid, I keep you working at Hermes' Birkin Bag, Manolo Blahnik, timbs, aviator lens, 600 drop, Mercedes Benz, The only time you wear Burberry to swim……And I don't have to worry, only worry is him…. And I do anything necessary for her, so don't let the necessary occur."

May 2002

"It's Freeway in the place with Be Sig and I got what it takes to rock the Mic right yeah, Still watch what you say out your mouth. Cause 50 shots still will turn the club out, ho!!! It's Mack Daddy young scrappy, No he ain't the OG gangsta. Yes, I is! Come on don't test the kid." Smoke rings and the sound of ROC Nation filled the car.

My fingers were safely intertwined with Coke's, our palms were flesh to flesh. Today, was one of the happiest days of my life. I proudly walked across the stage and received my four-year degree, in just three short years with a 3.97 GPA against every odd. Product of foster, dope dealing boyfriend who was ten years my senior. And, best of all; I did it without getting pregnant or going to jail for killing all the ghetto hoes who constantly brought Coke's acts of infidelity to my attention.

"I feel my best when you're smiling." Coke tucked his index finger into my deep dimple, causing me to smile even harder.

"You give me a reason to smile." I gushed.

I grabbed his hand into my a small hand and held it against my lips. Today, was not only graduation day but it was the day that I would give myself away to Coke. Coke made me save myself not by choice. Hell, if it was up to me; he would've gotten this kitty a long time ago. But, whenever I pushed the issue of sex he would remind me, good dick is a distraction and you don't need no distraction while you are working on our degree.

"You love me baby?" Coke drifted from lane to lane, while eyeballing his rear and side view mirrors; never letting my hand free from his grasp.

"Do you doubt it?" I licked my lips slowly, looking him in the eye.

"Nah. But, sometimes a man likes to hear it." Coke countered.

"Tell Daddy how much you love me." His hand moved into my lap and rested on my left thigh.

"I love you to infinity baby." My reassurance brought a rare smile to his face.

Coke was serious guy who rarely showed any emotion, that would make him seem weak.

"And, how long are you going to love me baby?" His hand massaged my thigh, sending my body into a whole other feeling of orbit.

My nipples grew hardened and I could feel my panties becoming wet.

"Forever and a day baby. Forever and a day." I said as I sat up on my knees.

I pressed my lips against the side of his neck. My kiss didn't stop there, seductively I kissed the side of his face until our lips met. I knew I was obstructing his view but I wanted him. And, I wasn't sure if I could wait another twenty miles to reach Atlantic City.

"Slow down, girl. You're gone get this dick." Coke joked, pinching my nipples as I sat upright in my seat again.

I watched as he grabbed his blunt from the ashtray. As if on instinct, I grabbed the BIC lighter and met the end of his blunt with it. He took a pull, blowing smoke rings in my direction. Coke was at his coolest when he was blowing trees. It was his only vice. He didn't drink or engage in any other drug.

"You beautiful, you know that?" His question was a rhetorical one as he started speaking just as I opened my mouth to answer him. "As a man, I've done somethings that I shouldn't have. Broke your heart a time or two since you been down with me. But, I prepared you well for this world. Don't always allow yourself to be led by your heart, you have a head for a reason make sure you use it. Listening to your heart will kill you. Have you ending up in the arms of a pussy nigga while you got Prince Charming waiting on the other side of the door.

"The only prince I want is you." My eyes welled with tears at the thought of being with another man.

It was no lie, I had been on dates with others out of curiosity but I loved Coke; he owned my heart.

"If the day should ever come and I'm no longer here to hold your heart, just remember the words I'm telling you." I nodded my head to let him know I understood.

"When we pass the toll booth, I want you to do me a favor. Climb into the backseat behind me and get low. You got your gun on you?" He asked, his hand intertwining with mine as he lifted it to his lips and kissed the back of it.

He took a long pull of the blunt that dangled from his lips. I reached in between my legs into my Louis Vuitton Speedy bag and pulled out my .45 as I saw the lights of the toll booth approaching. Every nerve in my body was on edge.

"Give me a kiss baby." Coke handed the toll booth attendant four dollars and drove through the raised arm barrier. On my knees in the passenger seat I kissed him in the mouth, in a way I had probably never kissed him before.

"What's going on baby?" I questioned from the floor behind Coke.

My hands were shaking like a leaf. The answer to my question came in a barrage of bullets crashing through the windows of the car. What felt like an eternity, in the middle of a war stopped as Coke hit the exit ahead of him. Shaken, I climbed from behind the seat and into the front seat only to be met with the horror that he had been hit multiple times. Still, a smile adorned his face.

With a slight shrug, he placed his hand over mine and said... "It's appointed unto a man but once to die, but after death there is judgement." Our car came to a complete stop while I rummaged through my purse for my cell phone.

"Come here." He tugged on my jacket, urging me to sit in his lap. With tears rolling down my face, I moved into his lap my hand covered the wound to his shoulder as he stroked the side of my face.

"Tell me how long you're going to love me, baby?" Coke coughed.

"Forever and a day, baby. Forever and day." I pressed my lips to his face as tears continued to stream.

"Even death won't take away the love I have for you. And, the coward that pulled the trigger still will never have you. I got you in life and in death, forever and a day baby." Coke said as he closed his eyes.

His head rested against the head rest. With my head pressed to his chest, I listened as he took his last breath. My body shuddered and tears fell violently.

"Forever and a day, baby. Forever and a day." I repeated over and over until I heard sirens in the distance.

Nadira

I snapped back from the painful recollection, feeling even more hurt than I did when I came here. It's funny, when you hear someone on the outside give their opinion on the person they think you are. I wanted to deny the truth but I couldn't I recalled all the days I asked Coke to got to A.C. and he would constantly say no to me. The one-time he said yes, was his last day with me.

"You can't be selfish always. You're going wake up in a world, alone." June admonished me as he lit his weed.

"And, money ain't everything. Sometimes, the more money only leads us to more greed. That's why I don't even chase the money no more. What prospers a man to gain the whole world and lose his soul or die empty." June said quoting the scripture his own way.

"It's something's money can't replace, baby girl. Hold on to those things." June finished as he passed his blunt off to me.

I took a couple tokes before returning it to him. He had given me a rude awakening and who would have thought my dose of reality would come from the person I viewed as an enemy.

CHAPTER NINETY

B&%$# Better Have My Money

"B%$#@ better have my money, Y'all should know me well enough.....B#@$% better have my money....Please don't call me on my bluff, Pay me what you owe me....Ballin Bigger than Lebron.....B%$#@ give me your money.....Who y'all think y'all frontin' on? Like Brrrap, Brrrap, Brrrap.......Don't act like you forgot, I call all the shots......Like Blah....Braap, Braap....Pay me what you owe, don't act like you forgot."

Sheila

Light taps on the other side of the door, startled me just a tad. I'd wanted to sneak out of the house today without rendering any explanations. The handle on the doorknob jiggled a little and in walked Gregory, carrying a full set of luggage under his eyes. He'd been tossing and turning nightly since Sunday.

"Good Morning." I said as he stepped over to the toilet.

"Morning, Reds." He uttered his voice full of discontentment.

I wouldn't dare ask him how he was doing today, because I already knew the answer to that.

“What do you have planned for the day?” I asked instead.

Gregory moved beside me to wash his hands before answering me.

“I need to check on my baby girl.” He answered sincerely.

I nodded my head before excusing myself from the bathroom. I had somethings to tend to myself. I walked straight into my walk-in closet and began to dress for the day. A sheer *Balenciaga* Bodysuit, black leather pants and calfskin *Versace* boots were on in minutes. I grabbed my Rolex from the jewelry tray along with a simple pair of diamond earrings before walking back into my bedroom. I heard the water running in the bathroom and decided to make my exit before Gregory finished his morning ritual.

“Your father is upstairs in the shower, I’ll be out for the better part of the day.” I said as my feet touched the landing.

“Good Morning, to you too, Mother.” Indiya said with her face frowned at my abruptness.

“I'm sorry. Good Morning, Sweetheart. Have a good day,” I said before opening the front door.

“Well, go on and get to the money Big Sheil,” Indiya chuckled as she closed the door behind me.

However, she had no idea how true her last statement really rang for me; I was about to get to the money indeed.

Nadira

I made my return to the office today, dressed a lot more modest than usual. My talk with June did something to me. No one had ever called me on my shit that way except, Isha. Hell, I almost felt like he had embodied her when he came and sat beside me at her grave site. After that conversation, I turned the microscope on; examining every part of me. I couldn't hurt another person I loved, at least not deliberately.

"Mrs. Fortune, you have a visitor." Janelle chimed over the intercom

"Janelle, can you pick up line one please?" I asked, pulling the telephone receiver to my ear.

Before I had the chance to say a word, the doors of my office were flying open. There stood Sheila looking like quite fly, although I'd never admit it to her. Her style of dress had improved drastically over the last few years. She was no longer the homely looking, church lady she used to be.

"I see you lack all kinds of respect for protocol, huh?" I asked as she took a seat in front of my desk.

"The quote is, "well behaved women rarely make history." She shrugged, crossing her leg over the other.

"How can I help you today, Sheila?" I asked humbly.

"I know that you're busy around here, so just thought I'd drop bye and remind you that you have something for me." She smiled.

"I do?" I raised my eyebrows in confusion.

"Yes, ma'am. I know it may have slipped your mind seeing as though you've been busy with all your extra-curricular activities." Sheila jabbed.

"I will have your check for you this week. I apologize for the delay," I said trying my best to sound humble.

"Well, not so fast pumpkin. Due to the unforeseen wait, I think it's only fair that you and I renegotiate the terms of our agreement; don't you agree?" Sheila asked, with a smirk lining her face.

"That depends on what it is you'd like to renegotiate," My answer came swiftly, still I knew she was about to give me hell.

"I want the severance money plus a silent seat at the table," Sheila projected as if she were asking for something small.

"So, you want your cake and the opportunity to eat it too?"

I'm sure my face gave way to the *what the fuck?* That was floating in my mind.

"Ain't that what you're supposed to do?" Sheila winked.

I was growing increasingly tired off her shenanigans by the moment. I bit down on my lip while staring back at her. I was still at a loss for words.

"You looked overwhelmed sugar, so I'll leave you to mull things over." Sheila said tapping my desk before standing to her feet, as Myka appeared in the doorway.

"She's all yours, Doll. You two enjoy the rest of your day." Sheila waved as she sashayed toward the nearest exit.

"Boss Lady, Boss Lady. Good to see you back." Myka projected as she waddled her way over to hug me.

"Good to be back." I forced a smile as I watched Myka struggle a little to take a seat.

"What brings you by, Sis?" I asked, rather annoyed with unexpected company.

"Just came you to check you out is all. Oh, and to show you this new ring." Myka flashed her ring finger in front of me.

"Congratulations." I screamed.

I was taken aback, so caught up in my own world that I had no idea Sean and Myka had mended things.

"Thank You." Myka said bashfully.

"Let's pray the second time is a charm." She gushed.

"For you, it most certainly will be." I assured.

"Why are you so down, Dee?" Myka connected with my tone almost instantly.

"So many things. Losing the baby is emotionally draining, daily. And, now the thought of losing Gregory is consuming me."

"Have you two spoken?" Myka inquired solemnly.

"His last words to me outside of the conversation we had about Heaven, were have your lawyer contact me." I confided.

"Let's just pray. Maybe he'll come around in time. He may just need time to forgive. I remember my grandmother use to always say' *When a man cheats they expect to be forgiven instantly. But when a woman cheats the relationship is broken irreversibly.*' We are going to believe that Gregory is so much bigger than that cliché'. He loves you, Nadira." Myka whispered reassuringly.

"But is love enough?" I rationalized.

"What do you mean?" Myka studied me.

"I mean, Myka. I love Gregory, God knows I do. But, then there are days where I want to be free. I feel like when our worlds collided, he was looking for some relief and I became the escape that he needed. And, as for me I made him my project without assessing all his needs. We work well together in two places, the boardroom and the bedroom. But is that enough for a perfect matrimony?" I reasoned.

"Sheesh." Myka sighed.

"Sis, I don't have the answer to that. Only your heart knows and whatever the answer is, holds the key to the freedom your heart needs. Now, come on and take me to lunch and feed your new Godson." Myka smiled.

"Really? You want me to be his Godmother?" I replied.

"Did you think I would have it any other way? You're a great mother and friend Dira. Don't let your "right now" overshadow everything that you've worked your whole life to be." Myka reached in and hug me as tears fell from my eyes.

Although, I wasn't up for visitors today… God knew that this was one visitor I needed to see.

"He said me haffi.... Work, work ,work, work,...He see me do mi dirt, dirt, dirt, dirt.....And so mi put in work, work, work, work, work, work."

Indiya

For the first time in months, I drove to my old apartment on campus.

Khadijah and I hadn't spoken outside off a quick Hello' when we passed one another in the hallways. However, in my visit with Cam yesterday he told me to smarten up and find a partner that I could trust. There was no friend in the world I could trust more than Dij. Dij may not have always agreed with my choices but the one thing she and I could agree on was money. She was much more connected than I, when it came to the streets and that was just the connect I needed.

I braced myself as I rang the bell outside the apartment.

"*Let this bitch be in a good mood."* I sighed.

A few seconds later, I heard laughter and footsteps from behind the door as it crept open. A chick with long Brazilian weave tossed her hair over her shoulder as she stepped out the door; leaving Khadijah and I standing face to face. She wore no expression for a second while studying my face and then a smile emerged as she reached out and hugged me.

"Get your ugly ass in here." She giggled, pulling me inside.

"I knew your dyke ass missed me." I joked as I stepped inside.

The apartment was clean and neat, not much had changed since I'd been gone. I flopped down on the couch while Khadijah sat on the other end rolling a blunt.

"So, is that your new habit PK?" I teased as she licked the blunt closed and prepared to spark it up.

"Yup, just like pushing Booger Sugar is yours." She remarked casually.

I slapped my hand over my mouth in disbelief.

"*How did she know that?*" I wondered to myself.

I guess the streets really be talking.

"Don't be so naïve, church girl. You know people talk, especially when it comes to the good shit. But real shit… What brings you to see me today, Sis?" Khadijah took a hit off the blunt and passed it my way.

I refused.

“Aye man, this shit here is your true best friend. Take one hit, and I guarantee it will change your life.” Dij said, putting the blunt in my hand.

I took a pull and choked instantly.

“Take another pull, and hold it this time.” Dij encouraged.

I did as she said, taking a pull and holding it for a second before I released it into the air. There was a feeling of euphoria that fell over me. All the thoughts swimming in my head, became clearer by the second.

“I need your help.” I admitted finally.

“I got some work, but I'm not trying to be a worker. I'm too much of a lady for that hand to hand action. I just want to be a boss and get in where I fit in.” I said, passing the blunt back to her.

“I got you.” Dij said grabbing a bag of kettle chips from the table.

“So that's it?” I asked shocked it didn't take much to convince her.

“Yea, that's it besides us speaking of my compensation.” The smile on her face made me want to hit her over the head with the pillow on my lap.

I knew she was about to spit something crazy off her lips so I sat back and waited.

“What do you want for your services yo?” I said finally breaking the silence.

“Eh, a couple dollars… you to ride my face maybe? It all kind of depends on what you're willing to give up.” Dij smirked at me.

“See, this is why I stopped dealing with you in the first place; you freak. Don't you think that’s kind of incestuous anyway?” I rolled my eyes in Dij’s direction.

“We are God sisters, for God’s sake.”

“I'm playing.... Loosen up, Shawty. Besides, I know how you get down. You might want your lil boyfriend to join us and I’m selfish.” Dij sang out.

I couldn't help but to laugh. She was as silly as she ever been. It felt good to bond with her over something again.

CHAPTER NINETY-ONE

No Pain, No Gain

"But love is a flower that needs the sun and the rain……A little bit of pleasure's worth a whole lot of pain…..If you learn the secret how to forgive….A longer and a better life you'll live."

Sheila Denise

My palms were sweating and my heart was beating a bit faster than normal as I sat in the waiting area. I skimmed over the pages of a magazine, trying to pass time as I waited. Nothing seemed to calm my nerves. You would have thought I was going into the confessional, instead of into the office to see my shrink. Maybe, my nerves were in overdrive because I really did have some confessing to do.

"Hi, Gorgeous. You can come on back.' Anita jestered cheerfully.

"We weren't scheduled for this week, does that mean you're about to tell me something good?" She questioned with a smile.

"I do have something to tell you, but how good you see it all depends on your view of things." I retorted.

"Fire away, whenever you're ready."

"I'm no longer seeing Quentin, he's engaged. Vic gave me a ring that I returned. He also invited me to London but I haven't yet accepted the invitation because Gregory and I have kind of rekindled our flame." I divulged quickly.

Anita's eyes were bugged out and her handed rested on her chest as if she was trying to catch her breath.

"Whew. You couldn't have prepared me for all of that if you gave me three warnings." Anita laughed.

"Lady, you have been very busy. But, I'll tell you one thing you look happy.

"That assessment would be right." I agreed.

"Well, what else is there to talk about?" Anita cackled.

"His wife." I countered.

The room grew still for a second, making me realize it was all good until it was all bad. The tables were turned and regardless of how bad the terms Gregory and Nadira were on… She was still his wife, just like I had been once upon a time.

2003

"How can you do this Sheila?" Sha asked, her face twisted with disappointment as she stood on the other side of the counter in the kitchen.

"Do what?" My confusion showed on my face as I bent down to place a tray of biscuits in the oven.

"Cater to a man that you know is no good. I mean he didn't even come home last night and here you are cooking dinner for his trifling ass." Sha spat venomously.

"He's still my husband, Sha." I reasoned calmly.

I knew she wouldn't understand if I explained to her anything otherwise. I did my best to keep it moving through the house, in effort to complete my wifely duties and possibly thwart this conversation with Sha. The fact that she was hot on my trail as I reached the laundry room was a strong indication that she was not letting up this time.

"I mean Sheila, don't you feel like a fool in this house? Day and night, caring for a man that doesn't give a dam about you?"

"Nope. not at all. It makes me a good ass woman to a selfish ass man. All I Sheila Denise know is, never ever will Gregory David Fortune say that the sole reason for his actions are because mine." My words ended as I slammed shut the top of the washing machine.

"Is that what you tell yourself when you wash that nigga drawers as he lays up with the next bitch?"

"Humph, not at all. You what I do remind myself of though, Sha'? A very brief lesson I was taught by someone dear to me. I

could throw hot grits on that nigga when he comes in the door, or put all his stuff outside, maybe even put him on the blast for all the world to see. But, none of those things will bring me the same resolve as this one right here. The only true way to kill the enemy is with love, there is no better way to teach the enemy a lesson than to show him that despite the low-down things you have done to me, I still choose to fulfill my duties and obligations to you righteously." I shrugged off.

"Ha. Girl, please! And, who taught you that shit?" Sha laughed hysterically.

"Kat did." I answered sweetly.

"Chile please, Kat was a hoe. What the hell does she know."

CHAPTER NINETY-TWO

Since I Lost My Baby

"The sun is shining there's plenty of life……A new day is dawning sunny and bright…..But after I've been crying all night the sun is cold….. and the new day seems old…..Since I lost my baby."

Gregory

"Sheila, what did you come here for?" I asked, becoming more agitated by her presence each second.

"Why don't you let me make you feel good again," Sheila said, and walked over to me.

She dropped to her knees and ducked into the space between my desk and lap. I couldn't believe what I was seeing. She tugged on my belt and I pushed her hand away. I could smell cognac on her breath. It was clear that she had been hitting the bottle.

"Come on, Gregory. Don't you miss me?"

"Hell no, I don't miss you. Get up and get yourself together. Have some decency, Sheila. Please,"

"So, just like that you're going to just throw us away, Gregory?" Sheila asked, struggling to maintain her bearings.

"All I want from you is a divorce. Long gone are the days of you and me. I've moved on and so should you."

"What about, Indiya? She needs you."

"And, she has me." I stood up.

"I will never stop being a father to her. And, it's imperative that my children know one another. She's welcome into our home anytime and she is aware of that."

"What do you mean, your children, Gregory?" Sheila asked, obviously stuck on what I said.

"Nadira, is pregnant. And, as soon as you sign the papers; I plan to make her my wife."

"So that's it, huh? You got your little whore pregnant and you're just going to pretend I never existed?"

"No, not at all. But, first things first. Don't you ever address her as anything outside of Nadira again. And, secondly, if you're looking for a scapegoat that led to the demise of this marriage, take a long hard look in the mirror."

"You know what Gregory, you are completely right." Sheila reached into her bag and pulled out a Manila envelope and slammed it on the desk.

"You got just what you wanted and I hope you're happy. But remember, I made you into the man that you are today, and without me you wouldn't be half the man you are.

I stepped closer to Sheila, as I wanted to look her square in the eye when I said, "You are right. A lot of the things that got me to where I am today, you made it happen. I was broken, unhappy, and on the verge of losing our home and this church, all because of the place you brought me to, both mentally and emotionally. But, I guess you've forgotten about that?" I continued.

"Allowing Nadira in my life, was one of the greatest things I could have ever done. I truly did not know what real love was until I met an extraordinary woman when I was dead broke with nothing to offer.

"She helped me to build an empire and accumulate wealth, the same wealth that you've been living off by the way. She spoke into existence, the King in me. Unlike you, who foolishly plucked down what took us years to build before. So yes, if you want to take credit for something then with all due respect there goes your claim to fame. Now, if you'll excuse me... I must go," I picked up the Manila envelope and my briefcase from the desk.

Sheila was dumbfounded, and could barely move. I stepped around her and made my way out of the door and down the hall. I felt every emotion known to man. I checked my messages when I reached my Benz. Nadira had left a voicemail sounding upset. I sent her a text, letting her know I'd be home soon.

The memory I just recalled was like a shot of vodka to my system. It was bitter and intoxicating. It reminded me of the words Indiya spoke to me a few days ago in the car on the way to Sheila's house. She placed her hand on my shoulder and said, "*Dad you never trade your rider for a slider.*" I had all the proof otherwise yet I still didn't see Nadira as anything but right.

Just days ago, I had packed my bags and left for the second time this year. Except, this time was voluntary. Nadira and I had become like strangers in the night, in our own home. She did her best to show me that she had walked away from the affair she was having. But, there was something to me that just didn't feel right. It could've been that she told me, she didn't believe all the things the media was saying about her little lover were right. Even at the cost of our son, she still saw some light in this guy.

And, then there was my relationship with Reds that was tighter than ever. She was my peace and my place of refuge on a lot of nights. But, I felt a little conviction in my heart knowing I was now doing the same thing my wife had done just a few months earlier. I made up in my mind that I wouldn't hurt Reds ever again in life. She deserved nothing but the best, because that's what she was to me. My thoughts halted as Nadira's car pulled up beside me. She and I didn't communicate much but Heaven was at the center of our bond. I brushed off all I was feeling and put on a smile as I got out the car to greet her and my little piece of sunshine.

CHAPTER NINETY-THREE

Fake Love

"Somethin ain't right when we talking, Something ain't right when we talking....Look like you hiding your problems.....Really you was never solid....No you can't son me, you won't get to run me....Just when S@#$ is out of reach I reach back like one three......Like, One, Three, yeah."

Keon

I took a long pull of the blunt in my hand, hoping that the clouds of smoke would take away the pain I was feeling in my heart. Still, the pain was worse than being stabbed through the heart with an ice pick. I lost the one woman I had been waiting to meet my whole life. The kind of woman I could build a life and a family with, over a woman I should've let go of a long time ago. Dani couldn't compare to Nadira if she tried. She was evil, mean, jealous and a cold-hearted guttersnipe.

I waited until I was lifted to the highest abyss before making my exit from my vehicle to building in front of me. I braced myself, because I knew I was about to be met with a conversation orchestrated by the deception who wanted to ruin my life. I used my left hand to cover the peephole and my right hand to knock at the door. Heavy locks on the other side began turning right after I knocked.

“Take your hand off the peephole dummy, I saw you pull up.” Danielle said cracking the gum in her mouth.

“What's good?” I said opening my arms to her.

“Your lil girlfriend must've put the trash out, today or your ass finally came to your senses since that court date coming up.” She remarked as she sashayed back into the kitchen.

I took in her body even with ball shorts and a t-shirt on, she couldn't hide her shape. Her assets weren't as pronounced as Nadira’s but they were talking loud. I walked up behind her and moved her hair to the side so I could kiss the back of her neck. She resisted my touch, instantly pushing me away. She pulled me back to her by the elastic knot in the waist band of my ball shorts.

As much as I hated this chick right now, my dick didn’t get the memo. I threw my hands up in surrender as she dropped to her knees, tugging my shorts to my ankles with her. She wet her lips with her tongue before forming an “O” with her lips and guiding my stick inside her mouth.

“Chew it, baby.” I encouraged through a hiss, as my hand rested on top of her head while she swallowed me hole.

“You like that daddy?” Dani moaned, deep throating me like a pro.

"Hell yea." My stomach was contracting and my legs felt weak just before a jolt of pain shot through my body.

Dani skinned the head of my piece with her teeth, causing me to jump back in horror.

"Yooo!" I screamed.

"Play with my heart again, and I'll Lorena Bobbitt your ass." She spat as she stood up from her knees and wiped her mouth with the back of her hands before disappearing out of my view. Leaving me checking my member for permanent damage.

"Now, let's get down to business." She said throwing some paperwork on the table.

I needed a plan B. Messing around with this chick was going to land me twenty-five to life.

CHAPTER NINETY-FOUR

"I remember when loving you wasn't easy, It wasn't easy, baby...But I stuck on in there with you and we made it... Sugar we made it, Through it all... Now let's keep it up Cause I ain't had enough."

Gregory

"*Shoot your shot.*"

In the confines of my office, I rubber my hand over my head trying to muster up the confidence to do something I felt like I hadn't done in a million years… Ask someone on a date. Not just anyone, but my ex-wife. I had been quiet since the incident the other morning with Nadira, while Sheila was there through it all. I felt a bit of corny romance spring up inside of me as I grabbed the keys to my car and walked out the door hurriedly.

I was sure I was smiling like a man who had just hit the lottery when I hit the parking lot in pursuit of my vehicle. I remembered when Sheila and I were in high school and I would call her on the phone at night and play music through the phone.

Music was always one of our connections. I scrolled through my phone for the perfect song. My smile got even bigger when I finally found it. "*We Go a Long Way Back"* by Bloodstone was the one for sure.

"Hello." She answered, her voice smooth as honey.

She was met by the voice of the lead singer as he sang;

"*I know you remember when trying to love me wasn't easy, it wasn't easy baby. But you stuck on in there with me, and you see, huh, we made it. Just me and you we love each other so. Girl we can't let each other go, no girl.*"

My heart was smiling as I heard her giggle lightly on the other end.

"*Shoot your shot man.*" The voice in my head repeated.

I switched the call from the Bluetooth to the handset, and pressed it against my ear while simultaneously lowering the volume on the music.

"Reds?" I finally spoke up.

"Yes." She sounded like the teenage girl I met in high school, again.

"I was wondering if you would go on a date with me, tonight?" I paused clutching my chest and bracing for the rejection I'd hyped myself up to believe was coming.

"Absolutely." She spoke. Her words were like medicine to my aching heart.

In effort, not to drag on the conversation, I answered…

"I'll pick you up at eight." Before hanging up the phone.

My day had been made. I put the car in gear and reversed out the parking lot with a little piece of my confidence back in place.

CHAPTER NINETY-FIVE

Oh Me, Oh My

"We'll blow a genie from a cigarette, And then we'll take a magic carpet ride…….Yes we will… And we'll tell our smokey friend, Hey don't you forget…..Because you've got to keep us side by side…. Oh Me, Oh my I'm a fool for ya baby……..Oh me, Oh my….Oh you You know that I am crazy, crazy baby."

Sheila

"What time does that cloud you're floating on, land child?" Kat remarked as she poured a cup of tea for she and I.

"What ya talking about' Old' Lady?" I replied, hoping she didn't mind the fact that I was playing slow.

I knew it was the truth, I had been floating on cloud nine since Gregory called me this afternoon. It was strange, he had been taking up residence on my sofa and/or in the guest room. Sometimes, even right beside me. Still, there was no pressure for him to make a move. I missed his company so I welcomed him, even when my conscience disagreed.

“Baby girl, I’m old not slow. Some man done stole your heart or reclaimed it. Which one is it?” She said with a little bit of a side eye.

I sipped my tea with the craziest smirk on my face at the latter part of her sentence. But, I already knew Kat was far from slow and wasn't nothing dumb about her either.

“Why can't I just be happy? It's a brand-new day, and I'm alive and well?” My finger whirled around a loose curl and my eyes were dead locked on the coffee mug in front of me.

“Ha. Girl how long did it take you to practice that lie in your head?” Kat shook her head. She was just too damn sharp witted for me.

“*Damn did she ever miss anything?*” I wondered to myself.

“And, for your information… No, I do not miss a doggone thing.” She answered, scaring the day lights out of me.

“Sheila Denise, I know you like you know yourself. So, cut to the chase and stop all this pussyfooting around, who is he?” She questioned bluntly.

I looked to the right of me to avoid her gaze while deciding if I was going to start lying to my mother like a teenage girl at the age forty-nine.”

“I’m over here, Toots.” She whistled cutely, causing me to turn back to her immediately.

“Gregory and his wife are separated right now, Mom. And, he's been staying at the house.” My admission sounded terrible outside my head.

“Is that so?” Kat never lifted her head from her mug.

I knew she was about to hit my heart with something deep.

"All I'm going to say Sheila Denise, is they're still married. Don't go doing nothing to someone else's vows that you wouldn't want done to yours and before you say anything; I don't care who he is. Because, the one thing that time should've proven to you about that man there and God know I love me some Slick… But, you never can be too sure what you're going to get when it comes to him."

"Mom, I'm not asking the man to marry me. Nor am I sexing him nightly. I'm just being a shoulder, that's all." I quickly dismissed.

"Girl, you must think I suffer from Dementia. I ain't forgot a thing. And, I sure ain't forget the face of a woman that is in love with a man. And, sure as the sky is blue… You love still love that nigga." Kat head and shoulders shook in unison as she held her belly while laughing heartily.

"If I turned off all the lights in this room, your face alone would illuminate it. He got you glowing, don't try and fool me. You done let him give you the magic stick." Kat continued laughing.

Momentarily, I felt like fool seeing my Mom laugh so hard. I felt like internally she was saying, "*Abra Cadabra... he gave you the tool now you're back to being his fool.*"

"Lighten Up, Reds. I'll say this one last thing and then I'll let this go because I don't want to spend time dwelling here. Sometimes, in life the assignment of our past is to distract us presently; so, it kills our progress towards the future. In the words of the young folk today, stay woke." She concluded.

CHAPTER NINETY-SIX

I Pray We All Be Ready

"I pray we'll all be ready, I pray we'll all be ready……I pray we'll all be ready for his return, I pray that we get our business straight so we can all meet at the gate.... I pray we'll be ready for his return....Man and his wife in their bed, One of them by the spirit lead.... The rapture came and took one above....The other one rose on the next day and found their loved one ruptured away....Oh what away to lose the one you love.... I pray we'll all be ready."

Myka

Wednesday night women's ministry meeting was on fire. The spirit was moving mightily through the speaker. I watched in awe as the women who pressed their way here tonight, shouldering burdens turned their all over to God. Beside me, Nadira held my hand tightly. To my surprise, it didn't take much convincing to bring her out tonight. Nadira, wasn't really one for church services on a weeknight, heck she barely liked church on Sunday morning. But, one thing I know for sure; people pressed their way when they need something from God.

Tonight, she wasn't the Bishop's wife or her usual fly girl self. Tonight, she was naked of all the makeup and camouflage, just straight up Nadira before God. As The alter call came, my heart leaped from within as I slowly watched Nadira move from her spot. She made her way to the alter with both hands raised and a face covered in tears. There were whispers in the room but the only voice that mattered was God's.

I kindly checked the chicks beside me who were inquiring whether that was Bishop Fortune's wife.

"Hey, Hey! You'd have less time talk if you started praying." I admonished while being met by their rolled eyes.

I wasn't affected in the least, I kept right on praying and joined Nadira at the alter as she pressed her way into the presence of God.

CHAPTER NINETY-SEVEN

Angel

"If I could I'd give you the world.....Wrap it all around you, Won't be satisfied with just a piece of your heart......My angel, Oh, angel.....You're my angel.....Dreams are dreams, some dreams come true.... I found a real dream baby when I found you, You're so strong tender too....You're my angel."

Gregory

There was something serene every time I pulled into this driveway; it was a place full of peace.

I reached into my pocket and pulled out my cell phone which had been buzzing and vibrating like crazy for the last thirty-five minutes. Displayed on the front was a text from my soon to be ex-wife, that read: *Call me please.*

"Is Heaven, alright?" I replied.

Moments later, a text came through that read... *Yes, she's fine.* That was all I needed to know, to go on about my evening in peace.

I stepped out of the car and grabbed the fresh lilies I had picked up from the back, along with a gift bag from *Hermes*'. If my relationship with Nadira had taught me nothing else, it taught me women like to know they're on your mind. And, nothing says I thought of you like an expensive handbag.

I turned the knob and walked inside the house. The sounds of Anita Baker filled the air, complimenting the scent of *Tom Ford Café' Rose* candles that burned in the room. I walked up the marble stairs two at a time, in a hurry to see Sheila's face. The bedroom door was slightly ajar as Sheila's voice escaped the room.

"*Love the way we touch, I love the way it feels. Every time you're near me my poor heart just won't keep still... No doubt about that this love I feel is real, ask me to go with you, you know I will.*"

I stood in awe for a moment, listening to her voice. It had been years, since I heard Sheila sing. The hairs on the back of my neck were standing at full attention much like my manhood. I swear everything about her was overwhelmingly sexy in that moment. She swayed from side to side, applying lipstick and singing every word as if she wrote them herself.

I stepped further into the room and wrapped my arm around her waist while pressing my lips onto the back of her neck. She turned her head to the side slowly, as a sexy smirk made the corner of her mouth curl.

"Good Evening, Mr. Fortune." She said, as our embrace released.

"These are for you, Beautiful." I lifted my arms to hand her both the bag and the flowers.

Her smirk became a full smile, as she pressed her nose to the bouquet of lilies.

"Thank You." She said bashfully.

She took a seat on the end of the bed and pulled the box from the bag.

CHAPTER NINETY-EIGHT

When I Met You

"When I met you, I never knew bout all the things you'd see me through... When I met you, I never knew bout all the things that we would do... Then I met you, When I met you... I met me too."

Sheila Denise

Dinner was nothing short of amazing, Simplistic, to say the least. Dinner, wine and a man I loved for the better part of my life. I borrowed a minute of time and snuck away upstairs the moment we got in. As I entered my bedroom, I took a minute to admire the beautiful gifts Gregory had given me earlier. However, I was nothing like his current misses. I didn't need material things, hell these past three years should have shown him that I could finance myself. I sat my packages to the side and went into a drawer, I long overlooked. Tonight, had to be special.

I decided to put on for old time sake. The last time I dressed up for Gregory, he fell asleep on me. But, tonight would be nothing boring. I gathered *La Pearl* everything before making my way to the bathroom. When all was aligned and lifted perfectly, I returned to my bedroom to find Gregory sitting on the bed; his head buried in his cell phone and his glasses sitting on the tip of his nose.

I grinned just a bit knowing he hadn't even noticed me in the doorway. I dropped the black silk robe I wore to the floor, and walked over to Gregory, taking up the space in between his legs. His eyes were leveled with my snatched waist which was covered in only the black sheer material of the *La Pearl* bodysuit I wore.

"Wow." Gregory mouthed as he looked up at me.

In that same instant, I confiscated his phone and carried it over to the dresser; on the other side of the room.

"You didn't have to go through all that trouble for me," he smirked.

"It was the least I could do to get your attention." I teased.

Gregory's lips pressed against the delicate lave that laid flatly against my stomach. My hands ran along the side of his face, as my lips had their own encounter with the top of his head. In the next moment, I inhaled his scent and exhaled everything that fought to keep me from enjoying it. My hands moved slowly from his face down his neck and rested at his shoulders. I tried ever so gently to lie him down flatly against the bed, but Gregory had other plans as he lifted me off my feet instead. He kissed me on the neck before lying me down on the bed. I reclined back with ease.

I watched with hungry eyes as he unbuttoned his shirt. He leaned in between my legs, kissing me on my nose first before whispering to me.

"I want to make love to every part of you." He said.

With the flick of my pointer finger, I urged him to come closer to me. He smirked a little before his body towered over me. He kissed my forehead and then my eyelids and lastly my lips.

"You've been running the show, a lot lately. Tonight, you submit to me." I couldn't fight him if I tried.

I Sheila Denise was now putty in the hands of the only man besides God that I would humbly submit to, while I watched him mold me.

Within minutes our bodies were so intertwined you couldn't tell where I began and where he ended. The passion between us was raw and intoxicating. I was entranced by the smell of *Creed* cologne, and the taste of big red gum in which he chewed. I watched him kiss a trail down my center as he made his way to my middle.

There was a puddle of wetness in between my legs so deep, his expert tongue couldn't help but to swim in it. My squeals only encouraged him, as he explored me the more. I laid beneath him, an open portal awaiting his arrival; that we may both ascend to abyss. Gregory slipped into my wetness and was greeted quickly by a hug from my slippery tight walls. The moan that escaped from his lips, let me know that he too was putty in my hands.

With his hands safely nestled around my waist and my legs wrapped around his waist, he kissed my neck before whispering.

"I haven't felt this happy and safe in a long time." He began stroking me into oblivion.

His next question was one I didn't know I was even ready for until the answer rolled off my tongue. He pressed his lips to my ear and whispered while gripping my waist tightly.

"When is the last time you felt loved like this, Reds?"

A tear rolled down my face, staining my cheek as I released the orgasm that had been building in the pit of my stomach and whispered with a trembling voice of truth. "When I met you."

CHAPTER ONE HUNDRED

Do You Know

"Do you know where you're going to? Do you like the things that life is showing you……Where are you going to? Do you know?"

Nadira Sy'Mone

Today, was a momentous one.

The red *Versace* suit I was wearing was symbolic of many things. The first was BOLD Brand Inc. The second was the blood covering I was under and the experience I had with the Holy Spirit last night. In my thirty- three years of life, I had felt many feelings but none that could compare to the feeling I felt last night. From my back, all the burdens I carried into the service were lifted away. The weight was lifted off me and my sins had been washed away. Today, was indeed a new day.

With my new found confidence in God, I stepped closer to the NYSE podium; prepared to push the button that signaled the opening bell to ring. Today, BOLD Brand would officially become a publicly traded company. A life-time achievement to some… To think, this was a company that started as a mere thought so that I could escape the woes of regular ministry; some thirteen years ago. To date, I'd made quite a name for myself as one of the youngest CEO'S to run a multi-billion-dollar company. I was breaking records in *Fortune 500*, *Forbes* and now on Wall Street. But, I'd gladly surrender it all to have my family happily back together.

As the members of the Board of directors gathered around me, I looked in both directions; hoping to see Gregory who was noticeably absent this morning. I was certain he had gotten my text regarding today. We had even spoke when he came to pick up the baby.

"*Where could he be*?" I wondered, as I straightened my suit jacket and returned smiles to all of those around that were smiling and nodding at me.

I looked down at my watch, seeing I had a little over thirty minutes before the opening bell would ring. I excused myself to call Gregory. As I stepped around the many people gathered, my heart felt some relief as I spotted him walking towards me. He offered a smile and a light hug before joining me in front of everybody. The countdown began before the opening bell ring.

C H A P T E R   O N E   H U N D R E D - O N E

Going In Circles

"I'm an ever rolling wheel... Without a destination real... And I'm an ever spinning top... Whirling around 'till I drop."

Gregory

My drive to New York was a whirlwind.

As I walked in to the New York Stock Exchange, I realized in my heart; it was the last place on earth I wanted to be. Fifty-one years on this earth had finally shown me that all the money in the world couldn't buy me peace. Seeing, Smooth this morning reminded me that I was once again the man I said I would never allow myself to be. Smooth shined in red, she was the boss I had always known her to be; standing poised as she prepared for the opening bell to ring. The more I stared at my wife, the more I searched for the answer as to whether the woman I surrendered my old life for was the woman for me.

Was I guilty of falling head over heels with temporal things? Lusting after the one, who too lusted after me. In the past thirteen years, I learned a lot of lessons. Some good, some bad and even some ugly truths about the man in the mirror. But, all in all... These years made for a better me. I stood in awe of those who had gathered to celebrate this occasion, with a twinge of sadness that the two people who stared out on this journey with BOLD Brand weren't present to see it birth out a brand new horizon. Bernie, who was now resting in eternal sleep and Sheila... Who declined the invitation for fear of the situation being peculiar between She, Nadira and myself.

My thoughts were brought to the present as a boisterous countdown began all around me. With a gracious smile, Smooth placed her hand on top of mine. At the sound of the number one, we pressed the button and for the first time BOLD Brand stock was being bought, traded and sold publicly. With open arms, Smooth hugged me tightly. I gave her a peck on the lips to satisfy the camera's recording the interactions of she and I for T.V. Internally, war was waging for me. I no longer craved a facade. I just wanted to be the man that God called me to be. I spent far too long leading people with who they believed me to be.

"Mr. Fortune, Mr. Fortune. What does this mean for BOLD Brand?" A reporter held her mic to my mouth.

"A brand new day." I answered smoothly.

"Bishop Fortune, What is the recipe for maintaining a happy marriage, ministry, business and family?"

"God first. He's the head of all things." I responded as I strategically pulled Nadira in front of me.

I'd had enough of the spot life for the day. And, center stage in the corporate world; was the place my wife lived and breathed.

CHAPTER ONE HUNDRED-TWO

You're A Big Girl Now

"You can love, girl, if you must......You can kiss, girl, if you must.....What you'll see day by day.... All the realnessin your way."

Sheila Denise

I listened to *KYW News* in the car, with the most bittersweet feeling in the pit of my stomach.

I received an invitation from Nadira to attend the launch of the IPO today but declined. I listened to much of the opening ceremony on the radio. This morning, I needed to be in the presence of someone familiar. The sprawling green lands and the massive solid gold gates of the estate before me, quadrupled in sized in comparison to my home. As a child, my sister Sha and I often told our friends we lived in a castle during the summer and this was no means a far cry from one.

I pulled up to a second set of gates and was pleasantly greeted by an armed security guard wearing an all-black uniform. He offered me a wink before hitting a button, inside the small booth he occupied. And, like magic I was offered access to the grounds. I marveled as I rode through the gates. Not one hedge out of place as I reached the center court. I smiled widely. Looking at the fountain that overflowed with fresh water, cascading over giant mermaid statues in the center.

I killed the ignition and opened the car door. I began to saunter up the marble stairs, outside. I took a breath, while standing in front of the oversized oak French doors that stood before me . I ran my hand along the Lion's head door knock before I actually used it to knock on the door. Nothing but fond childhood memories began to swarm me. The door opened slowly, and the greatest man I have ever known stood before me.

"Ciao, Papa''" I greeted. He smiled a smile that could light up a room as he hugged me tightly.

"Mio Caro" meaning my darling, he spoke in his heavy Italian accent.

His hands touched the sides of my face warmly just as he kissed my forehead.

'My… look at how beautiful you are, Reds." He complimented, taking a step back to look at me.

"Thank You, Daddy. You don't look half bad yourself old man." I smiled.

"Mighty were the winds that blew my favorite girl my way, today. I have missed you so much, Princess." My father chuckled.

"I've missed you too, Papa'" I agreed.

"Not too much… You haven't come by to see me in ages, Sheila Denise." My father reprimanded.

I took in his words as I walked further into the house behind him. There was one thing about the castle that I hated and that was the evil stepmother that lived here or used to at least. She'd passed away, just shy of a year ago.

"I apologize, Papa'. Sometimes, life gets away from us. I promise I will make more time for you" I acknowledged.

"That's all I ask, Princess." My father said as he led me down a long hallway lined with childhood pictures of me and Sha'

"It smells amazing in here, Papa'. What is your chef preparing?" I asked, savoring the smell in the air.

"No. No, chef today. That's good ole home cooking you smell in the air.' My father revealed.

My eyebrows raised at his last comment. I didn't have a moment to inquire who was cooking for him since he began to lead me in the direction of the kitchen.

"Katherine Denise, we have a visitor." My dad said, stopping just shy of the doorway of the chef's kitchen so I could enter. My confusion only grew, seeing my mother standing there preparing a meal on the stove.

"Sheila Denise, what a surprise. I hope you're staying for lunch," She winked.

"Hey, Ma. I wasn't expecting to see you here." I revealed, as I hugged her.

"Well, the day brings surprises of its own. Take your father in the den and talk until I'm done with lunch." she shooed.

For now, these two were off the hook since I needed my father's advice more than anything.

"Come on, Papa'. I need to pick your brain a bit." I lead my father down the hall to one of sitting rooms and cozied up in a chair next to him.

I felt like a teenage girl coming to my father for advice. Truth be told, my father didn't have the best track record when it came to women, but when it came to his daughters; he gave sound advice.

"What's on your brain, baby girl?" My father rubbed my hand.

"Men, Daddy….Men." I sighed.

"Oh, I see."

"Gregory and I, have been kind of seeing each other again. He's going through some woes in his marriage and well… We kind of found our way back to one another." I explained.

"*Hmmm..* soul mates usually do." My father added.

"Soul Mates? Daddy, do you think Gregory is my soul mate?" I questioned.

"Indeed, I do. Sheila Denise, soul mates have a way of finding their way back to each other regardless of what separated them." My father advised.

"I want the best for you. You're my favorite little girl in the world, so I'm going to reveal something to you. You my dear are poetry. And, Gregory can't read. But, something in my heart tells me that he's learning." My dad concluded, as my mother appeared in the doorway.

"Lunch is ready." She sang.

I suddenly wasn't hungry after all… My dad's words left me with a lot to chew on.

CHAPTER ONE HUNDRED-THREE

Set Me Free

"There's a special place in hell for you.... You gon pay for what you did to me..... Ima tell you cause the truth will set me free, ohh."

Myka

A Few Weeks Later…

"God dammit, man!" I screamed aloud, hitting my open hands on the steering wheel.

An onlooker would have thought I was raving mad. Instead, it was simply the effect Mary J. Blige had on a woman. Her music was the kind of music you could feel in your soul. If you had a man problem, she had a song for it. I had arrived at the thirty- nine week mark effortlessly. This pregnancy had little difficulty and truly proved God's healing virtue to me. My swollen feet hit the pavement as I prepared to walk into my meeting. A meeting, that would either set me free or send me straight into labor.

I fed the parking meter before waddling my way down the street, it was no easy task lugging around a massive stomach full of baby. A few short steps away was *Starbucks,* but in the mind of a pregnant woman; I had been walking for an eternity. I walked into the coffee house, not overly enthused about the options they had to offer me as I perused the menu.

"*A nice juicy steak and potatoes.*" Sounded a lot better to me, I thought before the cashier offered to wait on me.

A muffin and a latte would suffice for now. I placed my order and moved to the end of the line apprehensively. I practiced a few breathing techniques to calm my anxiety. The words to Mary J's Set me free still played in my head. My nerves subsided as her voice crooned, "*Oooh Ooh... I'ma be alright, I'ma be alright.*"

"Myka," The Barista called out, cheerfully as soon as my order was ready.

I politely thanked her for my ordered and turned to find a seat. As I spun on my heels, I was met by the face of the person I had come here to meet today. My words got lost as we got in closer proximity. He looked nothing like the skeletal sickly figure I thought I was coming here to see.

"Wow! You look beautiful. And, congratulations are in order I see." He said hugging me gently.

I fought with nausea as I hugged him in return before taking a seat. I took him in once again. He looked like the guy I had married. Clean shaven, suave, and well-dressed with snazzy shoes on his feet.

"Thanks Trent. You look very well." I complimented, sweetly.

It was no lie, he looked better than I had ever seen. This might sound strange, but prison had obviously been good to Trent from the looks of things.

'It's so good to see you. It looks like life has been treating you well and you have been keeping busy." He said nodding his head at my belly.

"God has been very good to me." I shared.

"Myka, I don't want to take up too much of your time today. I know that the last place on earth you want to be is somewhere, drinking a latte with me. I didn't even think that you would show up today, to be honest with you and the fact that you did really means the world to me. I needed to see you today, for my sanity. You were so good to me. I can never take back what I've done to you, and a million I'm sorry's wouldn't kill the pain of the hurt I brought to you through my own greed. I didn't mean to ruin you, Myka. I swear I didn't." Trent confessed before pausing.

"It's funny you said that you needed to see me, because I needed to see you as well, Trent. You know a few seconds ago, you said you ruined me but the truth is you didn't ruin me. You did however, capture and imprison me. I left my freedom in your hands and allowed you to control me, even from prison you had a hold on me mentally. The bondage I was in almost made me miss out on so many things. I almost lost out on the greatest thing that ever happened to me because I couldn't get free from you. So, when you called me the other day… I knew I had to answer and it's not for you. This one is for me. See, when they opened those prison gates; it allowed a part of me to go free too.

"Do you forgive me, Myka?" Trent asked, near tears.

I paused to gather my words. That was a loaded question. How could I forgive the man who tried to kill me with his scandalous deeds?

"The important thing is that you forgive you. As for me, as much as I want to hate you; the God in me won't allow me to. The answer to your question is yes, I forgive you. I used to want you dead for what you did to me but as God began to change my heart, my prayer changed too. I want you to live. I want you to live to see the damage living a secret life can do. I want you to live every day with the choices that you've made. And, most importantly… I want you to live long enough so that you help some of these younger brothers in the closet to not be like you." I concluded taking a deep breath.

My last sentence came with a surge of pain that engulfed my lower extremities.

"Are you okay?" Trent asked, after he noticed me wincing in pain.

"Yes, I'm good. It's time I get going." I stood to my feet, met by a gush of wet liquid that poured down my legs.

"*Well, ain't that nothing.*" I thought as I reached for my phone to call Sean.

I guess God works in mysterious ways. I got set free and sent right into labor. Maybe God didn't want this baby to be born while I was still in my mental captivity.

C H A P T E R O N E H U N D R E D - F O U R

Lick

"Bank Tellers asking for info.....Cause now my deposits on Kimbo."

Indiya

The sound of my heart beat was so loud, I could barely hear the announcement being made over the loud speaker as I walked through a busy New York Penn Station. I followed the directions to a tee. Still, I was nervous. My stomach was doing back flips as I made my way to the baggage check. I handed over my claim and three minutes later, the baggage agent came wheeling my bag through small door.

My mission didn't end there. I began wheeling the bag down a long hallway. My stomach was really doing a number on me as I ducked into a women's restroom in the corner of the station. I hurried to do my business and skate; I had one last stop to make. I was heading up the escalators that lead to the entrance of Madison Square Garden when I heard radios, dogs panting, and heavy footsteps behind me.

I was tackled to the ground, losing a shoe in the process as one officer held me down and the other unzip my bag; allowing the dog to begin searching. It seemed like hours as I lay there on the ground, hands cuffed behind me. I looked up to see the officers, who all wore puzzled looks on their faces.

"Ma'am, we are really sorry. There was a report of drugs being transported in a bag that is identical to yours. We take every precaution to ensure our passengers safety." The chief explained as he opened the cuffs I was wearing.

The other officer zipped my bag and pulled out a business card to give to me. I regained my composure as they shook their heads in confusion but there was no one more confused than me.

I walked out of the doors that led to busy Thirty-Fourth Street with a look of sheer panic engulfing me. A whistle from across the street diverted my attention as I looked up and saw Dij. I crossed the street hurriedly. When I approached her a little closer, I saw that she was standing with the same bag as me.

"What's better than one bag, you ask? Two. Those cops were hot on me. I had to throw them off." She explained.

I wanted to kill her for having me tackled to the ground. But in reality, this girl just saved the day for her and me. I looked up to the sky and vowed to God that this would be the last drop I ever made. I was about to flip every dime of the money I'd made in the last few weeks.

CHAPTER ONE HUNDRED-FIVE

If I Were A Bell

"If I were a bell, baby, I would ring....Tell the whole world that you are my everything.....If I were a bell baby you would know....That you are my only lover and it's wonderful."

Sheila Denise

"Reds, you are simply beautiful. Will you save your old man a dance?" My father asked as he entered the bridal suite.

The butterflies in my stomach were having a field days as they fluttered away.

"Sure thing, Papa'." I answered sweetly as Sha adjusted my veil.

"Hi Papa'. I'm going to leave you two alone for a second." Sha kissed my father's cheek before walking out of the suite, closing the door behind her.

"You remember I always told you that I was going to dance at your wedding even if I were in a wheelchair." My father recalled.

"I remember." I agreed, smiling at him.

"Well, God gave me the opportunity to walk you down the aisle today on two good legs and give you away once more because this time will be the last time you'll ever have to marry. I am most happy for you. You make a gorgeous bride and you are already everything a wife needs to be. That man is a lucky one to have you." Papa' finished.

"Thank you, Daddy." I brushed away tears, from fear of ruining my makeup as Indiya walked into the suite dressed in a sapphire blue gown.

Today, both she and my father would give me away though untraditional.

"Don't you look darling?" I gushed, admiring Indiya.

"Thank You, Mom. You look pretty too. I wanted to tell you, I'm honored to walk you down the aisle today into the arms of the man that deserves and cherishes you." Indiya revealed before kissing me on the cheek.

I dried my fresh tears as the music began to play in the sanctuary. The doors of the sanctuary opened as the voice of the soloist rushed out sing my favorite song. The altar was full with people who were my trusted confidants, sister, friends and my one and only true love. I couldn't stop the tears from falling as I prepared to say I do.

When we reached the front of the alter, Indiya took her place beside me as the Bishop asked, "Who gives this woman to this man?"

"We do." My father and Indiya said in unison.

"Gregory, you have some vows that you would like to read?" The Bishop acknowledged

Gregory grabbed hold of my hands tightly, looking me in the eye he began to speak.

"Reds, I searched high and low for the perfect woman. During my search, I uncovered many things. Heartache, pain, disappointments, counterfeits, lessons, blessings, growth, change, and ultimately myself. It wasn't until, God helped me to find myself that he allowed me to come back and rediscover you. I have never made a better discovery in my life. Daily I thank God, but today I want to say thank you." Tears escaped my eyes and rolled down my face.

"Sheila Denise, your vows to Gregory." The Bishop said, opening the floor for me to speak.

"I have loved you forever and now today my life is now comp" A high pitch beep sounded beside my bed, awaking me from my sleep. My eyes fluttered open as I fought to hold fast to my dream.

"Damn it." My heart was suddenly broken.

Sometimes our dreams appear better than our waking life. Maybe I should go back to sleep.

"*Get up, Sheila.*" I told myself as I pushed myself out of the bed. I felt like I was being held captive by the soft Duvet and sheets. I didn't want it to let me be free, but what I did know is great things were awaiting me.

First up on my agenda, a BOLD Brand meeting and then some errands. I slipped into the shower , praying it would invigorate me. My other prayer was that things wouldn't be awkward and/or tense during this meeting. Slick and I, still communicated daily though we'd been spending far less time together because he'd gotten himself a condo in the city and that was alright with me. In the back of my mind, I was fighting thoughts that things were on the mend between he and Nadira.

BOLD Brand was thriving on the market, which made a fool out of me not believing. But, I wasn't mad in the least. I still owned my shares and a seat at the table, now a firm believer. I dressed quickly. *Donna Karan* business suit and *Prada* shoes were on the wardrobe menu for me.

C H A P T E R O N E H U N D R E D - S I X

Blessed

"I'm so blessed, yes yes yes yes………My son was born healthy and beautiful, yeah yes."

Myka

"One more big push, Myka. He's almost here." The doctor said, from behind his mask.

After twenty-six hours of labor, I was most fatigued and drained. I took a breath before pushing one final time with all my might. The next sound was like music to my ears. Happy tears ran a river down my face as I heard my son cry for the first time. Nadira stood to my right and Sean on my left, equally as emotional. The baby had finally made his grand entrance into the world.

"Here he is, Mommy. A healthy boy, eight pounds and eight ounces." The nurse said, as she laid my son in my arms.

I was too overwhelmed with gratitude for words as I felt his tiny heartbeat. Looking into his eyes, was a brand new world for me to get lost in.

"Nadira, will you name him?" I asked innocently.

Sean and I decided after Nadira's incident, we would give her the honor of naming him. He was her godson, which made him our baby.

"Are you sure, Myka?" Nadira asked, with her finger resting in the baby's hand.

"Absolutely." I looked to Sean, who was also shaking his head yes.

"Messiah Chase." She said quickly and confidently.

I didn't have to question her choice, it just felt right instantly. I handed the baby back to the nurse so they could do handle all the necessary medical stuff.

"Thank you so much for being here with me." I said, as Dira leaned over and kissed my cheek.

I knew she had other things to get to today.

"Thanks for having me. I'll be here with plenty of gifts, a little later to spoil our baby." She said as she grabbed her handbag to leave.

"We did it." I sighed with relief.

"You did it!" Sean said, kissing me.

I guess all things really do come full circle. After my diagnosis three years ago, who would have ever thought so many beautiful things could happen for me. I surely never did but I'm ever so grateful that God doesn't see things the same way as me.

CHAPTER ONE HUNDRED-SEVEN

Prove It

"Prove that it won't bother me..... To become your used to be....Prove that I can just ignore all the love we shared before."

Nadira

I sat in the parking lot of EFM, swimming in tears.

I was crying myself a river and from the looks of things, it was endless. The birth of Myka's brand new baby, brought remembrance to the hole inside of me. The void of my son, who was cruelly ripped away from me. To make matters worse, his father and I were now estranged. Gregory made sure I that I knew what I had done, hurt him in a way that left us broken irreversibly. Still, I did everything that I could to restore Gregory's faith in me these last few weeks but he was treating me as if I had some incurable disease like leprosy.

We were back to sharing the duties of parenting. We no longer even did business together, he left most of the dealings of BOLD Brand solely to me. I gathered myself, dabbing my face with my MAC powder; hoping it would refresh me. I noticed my eyes were a bit puffy and red from crying as I added Visine. I was finally ready to get out the car as I gathered all of my belongings from the seat; careful not to leave behind anything.

As I walked into the boardroom, I was greeted by only Gregory; who was seated in his chair. He watched as I approached, never even smiling at me.

"Good Morning." I said as I walked over to him hesitantly.

"Good Morning." To my surprise he stood to greet me, hugging me loosely.

"How are you?" I asked as I took a seat beside him.

"I'm good, Smooth. How are you?" He asked staring over at me.

"I'm okay." I lied.

Inside, I felt like I was crumbling.

"You must've slept well. I stopped by the house this morning, before dropping Heaven off at Pre-K." He said sarcastically.

"Myka was in labor, Gregory. I spent all day and night at the hospital, you don't have to be condescending." I retorted.

"Hey, whatever floats your boat baby. You no longer have to answer to me." Gregory pushed a Manila envelope in my direction, tapping his fingers on top of it.

I pulled out the contents of the envelope while holding my breath. My heart sank to my shoes as I read the words across the top, **Separation Decree.** The tears in my eyes that threatened to fall, were held up by BOLD Brands Board entering the room one by one.

"So, this is what you want to do?" I leaned in and asked Gregory before standing.

Gregory rose to his feet with me. We found our way to a corner in the room to have our conversation a bit more privately.

"Nadira, I'm only following your lead." Gregory backed away a little from me.

I walked up on him again. He wasn't about to get away that easy.

"So, are you saying that you don't love me?" I asked near tears.

"I will always love you, Smooth. But, my love obviously wasn't enough so I'm setting you free." He kissed me on the forehead and hugged me tightly.

Sheila

"*Well, I'll be damned.*" I swore inwardly.

If this wasn't a church, I wouldn't have held those words captive inside of me. I felt like I interrupted the moment, as Gregory and Nadira released their embrace and turned to their seats. I took my seat without greeting anyone. A fire had ignited inside of me and any little brush the wrong way would only further ignite that flame.

"Good Morning, everyone." Nadira greeted, as she rose to stand behind the podium.

I didn't even look up to see Gregory's face once he took his seat. But, by the hole that was being burned into the side of my head; I knew he was looking at me.

"I'm going to get right down to business, today. BOLD Brand is killing the market. We are thriving as expected. Our stocks have soared in comparison with others, over the last few weeks. I have created the blue print and now I believe it is time for someone new to lead. Bishop Fortune will continue to occupy the role of CEO, while I step down as acting COO." Her announcement caused a lull across the room. *Nadira created BOLD brand who better to lead it.*

"The Office of COO from this point forward, will be filled by our silent chair. Who better to lead then someone knowledgeable who has been a part of this company since the very beginning? I will occupy a seat on the board and will continue to advise at the discretion of Bishop Fortune. Nothing stays the same forever right? Now, I will be stepping into a bigger role with my firm and believe that I have brought this brand to the height and level that God has called me to. And, I proudly relinquish my role as acting COO as of today." Nadira took a minute to sign some paperwork before taking her seat.

"*What the hell just happened? Did she really just relinquish her seat to me? Who the hell told her to do that? Gregory?*" A boat load of questions befell me as, Ronald Mayer BOLD Brand's secretary stood to his feet.

Everyone in the room wore a look on their face like me. I guess they were all wheeling and dealing in their head who the hell the silent chair could be?

"Do we have any further questions?" Ronald said opening up the floor.

The room was silent.

"If there are no further questions, we can stand to be dismissed." Ronald gave the benediction as everyone still shocked by today's events, prepared to leave.

I lingered for a minute wanting to speak, but Gregory and Nadira were caught up in their own communication. They moved away from the table to the same corner they had been occupying when I walked in.

I grabbed my YSL bag from the table and disappeared out the door and to my car within the blink of an eye. As hard as it was to admit, it was painful watching them communicate today. I guess this answered my questions as to where he'd been.

Gregory

God really had a way of lining up the chips to fall in place. Never in a million years, did I think Smooth would relinquish her chair just before signing the separation decree. When she gave her chair to Reds I was blown away. I stood face to face with Smooth once again, as she handed the paperwork over to me.

"As you asked previously, I'll have my attorney contact you." She seethed before turning her back to me.

The tension in the room was thick and only increasing. I scanned the boardroom for Reds amongst the BOLD Brand members who stood around lingering. When I didn't see her, I bolted out the room as fast as my feet would carry me.

My sprint led me to the parking lot, where I found her getting inside of her Maserati.

"Reds!" I called out, with my hands in the air.

She drove fast toward me. She rolled down her window just enough to talk to me.

"Where are you going so fast?" I asked, looking at her face that was hidden behind big shades.

"London." She answered driving off faster than the speed limit allowed.

"*What was in London? She never even gave me the opportunity to tell her that I filed for separation.*" Defeated, I walked to my car.

Today, had become even more bittersweet. I watched as Smooth exited the building, never even making any eye contact with me. We were on the road that she chose, back to living apart and co-parenting.

CHAPTER ONE HUNDRED-EIGHT

Put You Up On Game

"Lemme put you up on game every man is different but the game won't change….Lemme put you up on game, so you won't make the same mistakes I made."

Indiya

A knock at my bedroom door caused the trance I was in to be broken. I was plotting and planning like a mad woman. I had made plenty of money in the last few weeks but my last run was really my last run, it was time to put this money to good use. I dropped all the money on my desk into the drawer, while calling out to my mom to come in.

"You're up early." She smiled, as she entered fully dressed for the day.

"I didn't want to miss saying goodbye. I'm going to support, Nadira today in court as well." I confessed.

"Good girl. I'm sure she could use you by her side." My mom kissed me on the forehead and pulled me over to the ottoman in front of my bed to have a seat beside her.

"Indiya, there are days when I look at you and I still see that ten year old girl I had to fight to keep out of my bed. When I woke up this morning and started preparing for my journey, the only thing in my heart that made me feel apprehension was the thought of leaving you behind. And, then I looked over at the nightstand and saw your picture and realized you are no longer ten years old. You have had twenty years of my unconditional love, care and guidance. And, you will continue to have that until the day I close my eyes. However, my dear. Today is the day, mommy will test you on all the things that you've learned to make sure that you know how to apply it." She paused to take a breath.

"I will never be too far away to guide, protect and/or lead you. I promise. Show me what an amazing child I've raised." My mom said as we both began to cry.

"Mommy, I love you and I promise that I'm going to make you so proud." I laid my head on her chest.

"I know you are. Mommy has to be going now. Everything you need is here for you and I am only a phone call away." She said, as she rose to her feet.

We shared a long hug and my mom planted one last kiss on my forehead before we walked out the room and down the stairs where her luggage was.

"Oh and Indiya… The very next time you bring drugs and/or dirty money to my house it will be you who closes their eyes. Got me?" She winked as we both grabbed her Louis Vuitton luggage and began to pull it outside.

"*I swore my mom was a spy when I was a child and she just proved my theory correct with that last comment.*" I thought as her driver began loading her luggage into the trunk.

As the car pulled out from the driveway, I reached into my pocket; pulling out my phone that had begun vibrating.

"Good Morning, Dad." I spoke cheerfully.

"Aren't you happy this morning? Good Morning, baby girl." He returned.

"Not too happy… My mommy is leaving me." I pouted.

"She's leaving?" He asked, surprised.

"Yes, she's leaving for London today." I divulged, wondering why she hadn't told him.

"When is she returning, do you know?" he asked me.

"No dad, I don't. She just left for the airport. Don't tell me, you miss her already." I teased

"Indiya, what airline is she traveling? "My dad asked in a hurry.

"Jet suite, I think." I said trying to recall the information my Mom had given me.

I was met by silence on the other end. I removed the phone from my ear only to realize that my Dad had hung up on me. I shook my head laughing.

"Dang and I thought young love was crazy!"

Nadira

"All Rise. The honorable judge Salvatore Peruto, Senior will be presiding over this case." The bailiff began to speak as the judge emerged from the chambers.

My stomach was in knots. I had been practicing all types of breathing techniques to get me through this. My lawyers advised if it became too much, I'd be excused from the preceding.

"Your honor, we are here today to try the case of the State and Fortune VS. Keon Walsh." The state's attorney informed the judge as he put on his readers and began to look the rough the dockets.

After the day I had yesterday, I felt all alone even though my mother, Indiya, my partners, Janelle, Emilio and even June were by my side. Keon sat at the table beside his lawyer dressed in a three-piece suit. He appeared nervous as his attorney whispered something in his ear. Dani had the nerve to show up to court today, doing her best to appear like a model girlfriend while gritting at me from across the room.

I stared back with pure hatred in my eyes, I wouldn't dare drop my gaze and let this bitch out stare me.

"*Nope... not this time.*" I said in my head.

"Aye Dira. Just know that if this pussy get off, the whole hood got him, both of them." June whispered in my ear from behind me, after noticing that Dani had been staring at us the whole time.

I patted June's hand as he sat back in his seat chewing on a toothpick. Who would have ever thought he would show up in my time of need? His loyalty to Coke, made him and I put all the bad blood behind us.

I stared down at my shoes as the State's attorney began to recall an account of the day I was poisoned, which also signified the day my son died. I was trembling as he read through the papers in his hands. My heart was beating out of control. I just kept thinking how could someone who claimed to love me, be so damn cruel. The State was charging Keon with a murder charge for the death of my son, still nothing would suffice.

My head began spinning as the defense began with their opening statements. My eyes welled with tears as Keon took the stand and made eye contact with me. I couldn't sit through this even if I put in ear plugs. It was just too painful for me. I gave my mother the signal we'd discussed, and in seconds we were excusing ourselves down the row to leave.

CHAPTER ONE HUNDRED-NINE

Take It All

"Didn't I give it all? Tried my best……Gave you everything I had everything and no less….Didn't I do it right? Did I let you down?Maybe you got to use to having me 'round…..Still how can you walk away from all my tears….It's gonna be an empty road without me here."

Sheila Denise

Why was I torturing myself? I'd asked the driver to play Adele. The moment her voice began to croon through the speaker, I felt my heart and soul open up. My heart was gushing with blood while my soul released an ocean of tears. I pulled my black *Chloe* shades from my handbag beside me as I rolled up the partition. I needed to be one with my emotions.

"But Go on and take it, take it all with you…..Don't look back at this crumbling fool. Just take it all with my love." Adele's words were everything I wanted to say.

But, really who was taking it all from who? I felt like in this game we were playing, when it came to matters of the heart; we were all loosing.

My iPhone began to vibrate beside me as I looked up to see signs welcoming me to Philadelphia International Airport. The caller ID display read *Slick.* I kicked myself a little as I hit the answer button. I'd long missed the flight that Vic booked for me by two weeks, so today I wouldn't be flying international commercial but by way of private jet.

"Hello." I said, after a bit of a delay.

"Hey Reds, what time is your flight today?" He asked immediately.

"In just a few, Gregory. I really need to go." I said anxiously, too afraid of becoming emotional and overwhelmed.

"Reds, do me one favor? Just wait for me at the tarmac." Gregory said before I hung up the phone and dropped it in my bag.

I tried to wipe away the tears before my driver opened the door but it was too late, I couldn't hold them back. I was silent yet an emotional wreck. With my glasses covering my eyes, I grabbed my *Celine's* bag and prepared to kiss the city goodbye. I tipped the driver as he unloaded my belongings from the SUV. The captain stood in the doorway of the jet welcoming me. I took one last look behind me, throwing a kiss in the wind; hoping it would land on the face of all I was leaving behind.

CHAPTER ONE HUNDRED-TEN

A Song For You

"You taught me precious secrets of a true love, you wanted nothing...You came out in front and I was hiding...Now I'm so much better, And if my words don't come together...Listen to the melody...Cause my love is in there hiding."

Gregory

I was driving like a madman, dashing in and out of lanes. I was Bo guarding every opportunity to cut in front of cars that were lagging, while praying that God held back the state trooper who would write a huge ticket if he caught me flying by him. My mind was in a frenzy as I did what I hadn't done a long time ago... For once, I was placing my pride aside. My heart knew where it belonged, and finally I knew too. A true soul mate was hard to find and I was determined not to let Reds go this time.

KYW was airing the news, distracting me slightly as I listened to the details of Nadira's trial today. Although, I felt some responsibility to be beside her; things were complicated enough. I sent my love and prayers, knowing that she had the support of many behind her. Then, I hit the off switch on the radio. I needed to take the remainder of this ride in silence.

Sheila was so closed off to me over the last twenty-four hours, it hurt. I had no idea what could be in London, or even an estimated day of return. If it weren't for Indiya, I'd have no idea of her flight itinerary either. What I did know was, I wasn't letting that plane leave without telling her that she is the only woman I have ever really needed and that I could no longer live without her.

I arrived at the private gate, it was the private tarmac reserved for Jet-Suite flights. I honked my horn to the guard, awaiting the gates to be opened for me. He waved his hands signaling, no, to me. Confused, I got out of my car and hurried to the gate to find out what the holdup could be.

"I'm sorry, the pilot is preparing for departure. Cars aren't allowed behind the gate at this time." He informed.

My heart was in a panic, but defeat wouldn't be allowed. I grabbed the roses from the passenger seat, and ran through the smaller gate; leaving my car behind. My Italian made dress shoes beat the ground as I ran toward the jet, whose engine began to roar. The flaggers were staring at me as I ran wildly towards them.

"Hold the plane! Hold the plane!" I called aloud.

My voice was no match for the engine that was sounding loudly. I watched as the plane began to move forward on its wheels, making its way to the runway. Chasing behind it was a lost cause. Still, something on the inside of me wouldn't allow me to slow down.

The Jet stalled for a second mid runway giving me a second to catch up, I begin running with everything within. I walked away from the love of my life once, this time I would chase her across the land and the sea to make things right. I understood God's law now. I needed to love that woman with all of me and everything else would fall in line.

Like someone had punched me in the gut, I bent over with a roar as I watched the nose of the jet soar towards the sky. I threw the roses to the ground, crushed by the agony of defeat. Tears began to escape my eyes. I now knew what it felt like to be left behind by the person you were meant to be with your whole life.

CHAPTER ONE HUNDRED-ELEVEN

One and Only

"I dare you to let me be, your, your one and only…….I promise I'm worthy……..To hold in your arms……… So, come on give me a chance to prove I am the one who can walk that mile until the end starts."

Sheila Denise

I tuned into the news as I waited for my flight to leave the ground. I watched attentively as the newscaster explained a continuation had been declared in the Fortune Trial. I turned my iPhone on airplane mode. I slid back the Venetian from the window just as the pilot began to pull forward on the ground.

Anxiety rushed over me as I saw Slick running toward me. I wanted to scream out like they do in the movies.

"*Stop the plane!*" But, the words were stuck like glue inside of me.

I felt a panic attack building inside of me as the engine revved up more, the wheels went up and the jet took off from the ground. Tears the size of gumdrops fell, still I could make no sound.

"*I made the right decision.*" I tried to convince myself.

I'd been right in Gregory's face for thirty- three years, and the moment I leave the country… He decides to chase me down. Was this fate of true soul mates or just irony?

"Mrs. Fortune, are you okay?" The stewardess asked, as she stood beside me with a drink on her tray.

Tears were seeping from behind the oversized frames I wore on my face as she sat the drink on the tray table in front of me. We were now soaring high above the clouds, while my thoughts were far away.

"Yes, I'm fine." I managed to say.

"But, please do me one favor?" I asked removing my glasses from my face.

"Anything?" she welcomed enthusiastically.

"Call me, Mrs. McClure." I said with confidence.

"I apologize. I thought you were the Bishop's wife?" She said shamefully.

"Darling, I am the Bishop's wife no more." Speaking those words was like swallowing a ton of bricks.

I have long been all in when it came to Slick. But, his interactions with her yesterday told me there was something that I had missed. A reconciliation maybe, or were my eyes playing tricks on me. There was a piece of me that kept nagging and pulling, telling me that everything wasn't always what it seemed. Still, I wasn't sure.

I, Sheila Denise had long been the ball in Slick's ping pong game. A game that went heavy over the last thirteen years. It was time that I gave my all to someone who was willing to give their all to me. I couldn't belong to someone who wanted me to settle for just a piece. Revelation is one hell of a truth serum. I wouldn't and couldn't settle for anything less than being a man's one and only.

CHAPTER ONE HUNDRED-TWELVE

He Won't Go

"Wake me up, Wake me up when all is done……I won't rise until this battle's won…….My dignity's become undone……But I won't go…..I can't do it on my own……If this ain't love, then what is this…….I'm willing to take the risk."

Nadira

"We are live here at Justice Juanita Kidd Stout Center For Criminal Justice in Philadelphia. Where preceding in the highly publicized case of former Pro Star Wide-Receiver, Keon Walsh has been accused of attempted murder and involuntary manslaughter of an unborn child in the Poisoning case of Newly Appointed President of Shipman and Thales, and wife of renowned Bishop Gregory Fortune, Nadira Fortune. Late this afternoon after returning from lunch, the defense submitted both video and audio evidence attained by the private detective; acquitting Mr. Walsh of all charges.

Ironically, in a strange turn of events… Mrs. Fortune will get justice. As Mr. Walsh's former girlfriend, Danielle Sutton, was just escorted out of the building in handcuffs and led into the van behind me. Mrs. Sutton has now been charged with attempted murder, involuntary manslaughter, extortion, blackmail and a host of other crimes. Ms. Sutton is set to stand trial in the near future. This case is one that I am sure we will continue to follow as the plot thickens.

Mr. Walsh, today is a free man. As for Mrs. Fortune, she has requested privacy as she still deals with the loss of her son, and the new developments of this case. I am Casey Oldham. Reporting Live.

Some tastes are too bittersweet to be savored. I sat in front of the television watching the news still reeling from the information my attorney delivered to me just an hour ago. Though insane to most, the events of today were everything my heart already knew. Dani was a human being unworthy of a social security number, just downright malicious and evil. I guess that's the place love could drive you to. I prayed to God above that I never experienced love like that because only he knows the level of suffering I'm going through.

I had the world to some… A new appointment as acting president of my firm, an amazing home, a beautiful daughter, good friends, a reasonable portion of my health and strength, unmeasurable wealth, and a mastermind that knew how to make a dollar from a vision alone. But, today I felt alone. Like I had it all, and nothing at all. I risked it all for the love I thought I wanted, the love I'd became addicted to… A love that turned out to be attached to a psycho. My husband gave up the fight for our marriage and I couldn't blame him.

Gregory, did yesterday what I didn't have the strength in my body to do and that was let go. I could have never set him free on my own. An eighteen year age difference, was all good in the beginning. Except, while caught up in the rapture of love; I forgot that he too would get older. Things changed… Our conversations grew boring, our love making grew shorter and my interest in him became miniscule. Yet, there was some beauty. A child, that was the best part of both him and I. A multi-billion dollar company, and we both found ourselves even. Even, if it lead to the end of the road.

A ringing doorbell pushed my thoughts to the back of my mind. I wondered if it were the movers here to pick up the rest of Gregory's things as I hurried to answer. I bypassed a mirror and doubled back to take a look. Somewhat rare, but I was sporting the natural look. Hair in a bun and not one stroke of makeup.

I opened the door, and my hands started to shake as butterflies in my stomach began to flutter. As he reached down and hugged me, I could feel electricity as our lips met. After all that has happened, there was still something special about his energy.

"I can't fix the past, baby. But, I'm here right now… Asking you to give the future a chance with me?" Keon swept me off my feet, kissing me repeatedly.

I pushed the door close with my hand as he carried me inside. This wasn't a perfect ending to a love story, but at least it was happy.

CHAPTER ONE HUNDRED-THIRTEEN

I Gotta Get Her Back

"I should've kissed you longer, I should've held you stronger……..And I'll wait for forever for you to love me again."

Gregory

I've never been the man to take defeat lying down. I watched the woman I wanted so bad, fly right out of my world and into the clouds. Everything was unfolding and taking on a new meaning. I guess Smooth got her happily ever after, knowing lover boy wasn't guilty. I wasn't mad anymore, she freed me to love completely. And, that's just what I was preparing to do.

"Good Afternoon, Mr. Fortune. Are you checking in today?"

'Yes, I am." As much as I traveled, I was known at the airport by name.

"Where are you headed to today?" The agent asked from behind the counter as I handed her my passport.

"London." I answered with confidence.

"Awesome! Going for business or leisure?" She pried.

All I wanted, was for her to hand over my boarding pass. Instead, she was grinning from ear to ear while talking to me.

"A little bit of both, business and leisure. I'm going to get what's mine. My lady." I smiled, finally letting up.

Those words were medicine for me. They jumpstarted my heart as I went running towards the gate. With just ten minutes to spare, I made it. I had no luggage, just me. And, a mind to bring back the woman that God kept for me. My countenance was light as I reclined back in my seat. There was a countdown until take off, going on inside of me. The sooner we got in the air, the sooner I'd see my baby.

The pilot came in over the loudspeaker and welcomed the passengers on board as we prepared to leave. In just seven hours, we'd be arriving in London, United Kingdom. For the first time ever, I was chasing a forever thing. I'd had enough of what temporal satisfaction could bring… Scandal, heartache, and loss had all had their way with me. The aftermath was a lesson to me, to build my hope on things eternal. The return would be a lot longer lasting.

CHAPTER ONE HUNDRED-FOURTEEN

If Only You Know

"I must have rehearsed my lines, a thousand times……Until I had them memorized…..But when I get up the nerve to tell you the words……Just never seem to come out right."

Sheila Denise

There goes that walk again; so smooth yet alluring.

Landing in London, had done something incredible to me. After checking into my hotel, I showered and changed. There was no time for rest as I had a surprise visit to make. I'm certain Vic wasn't expecting me, especially after the way we left things off. As I walked through the hotel lobby, I double checked the itinerary; remembering the exact hotel Vic had told me weeks ago he would be staying.

My *Creed* perfume was almost intoxicating as I pressed the elevator button, inhaling my own scent. I had to do some heavy buttering up to get the front desk attendant to divulge Vic's suite number to me. I told her I was his wife, here to surprise him for our anniversary. When that didn't work, I slipped the bitch a fifty.

As the elevator doors opened, I stared at myself in the mirror. I was near tears as I stared at a brand new me. My hair was long again, hanging past my shoulder blades in an edgy cut with a part down the middle with Ombre' hues.

I exhaled all my fears as I walked off the elevator. Suite 1437 brought a smile to my face. This was something different for me. I rang the bell with my nerves, all over the place. Still, I stood firm. I'd come too far to feel jittery. The door began to open slowly.

"Hi, can I help you?" A Caucasian woman with brown hair greeted me.

"I'm sorry. I must have the wrong suite. I was looking for a friend." I said, batting my eyelashes in confusion.

"Oh, what's their name?" She asked, extra friendly like.

"Uh, Victor." I replied, still confused.

"Oh, are you his business partner? I'm Megan, his fiancé. What's your name." She said, as she extended her hand to me.

You could have knocked me over with a feather in that second. *Did she just say Fiancé?*

"Sheila, and no not a business partner just a friend. Please tell him that I stopped by." I said, backing up onto the elevator.

Damn, I guess when he said time wasn't forever; he meant that he put an expiration date on him and I. I reached the lobby, retrieving my phone from my purse. I hadn't looked at it since I arrived. I was certain there was a slew of text and calls from those who were concerned if I arrived safely.

Still in shock, I took a seat in the lobby to wait for my car service that would be arriving shortly. The first text I opened caused me to almost need a defibrillator right there in the lobby. I looked down at a picture and a text Gregory had sent me. The text read, *I'll cross the ocean, land and sea to be where you are.* My eyes were glued to the document he sent me a picture of, it read at the top: Separation Decree.

EPILOUGE

For You I Will

"I will cross the ocean for you, I will go and bring you the moon……I will be your hero, your strength anything you need."

Sheila Denise

Still adjusting to the time zone difference, I stepped out onto the balcony wearing my white silk robe. It was just past eleven p.m. in London, while still early evening in the US. I had been avoiding my phone since earlier today, afraid of any more surprises befalling me. I looked down at my phone and decided to call Sha. My twin sister had been phoning me since I arrived. She was worried about me. I was her other half undoubtedly.

"Oh… Finally your service is working again, I see." Sha started in the moment her mouth hit the receiver.

"I needed a moment to settle in." I lied.

"Is London all that you thought it would be?" Sha gushed.

"It's beautiful. The hotel is amazing. I can't wait to explore and go shopping." I retorted excitedly.

"But enough about me, what are you up to lady?"

"Just watching the news. You know daddy is the presiding judge in Gregory's wife's case." She shared.

"No, I didn't know that." I rolled my eyes at the phone as if she could see me.

"Yep, just saw him on the news a few minutes ago. This is all such a tragedy. I can't imagine what she's going through." Sha said sympathetically.

"Sha, that girl was cheating with that man." I cut in.

"Sheila, she lost her child. You could be a bit more sympathetic." Sha announced, scolding me a bit.

"Hmm." I sighed.

"Why you so damn attached to this case anyway. Things like this happen every day." I was a bit annoyed that Sha was taking this case to heart.

Sha took a big breath and sighed. I could tell she was stalling.

"I just feel bad, she could use a bit more compassion and grace."

"Aright, Mother Theresa. Bestow some grace." I joked.

"Seriously, Sheila. At least show some empathy." Sha was really getting on my damn nerves already.

"My... You are quite the humanitarian today." I retorted sarcastically.

"Sheila, remember that day when you asked me if there was anything that I regret." Sha asked, her voice now lacking confidence.

"Yes." I replied, wondering where she was going with this.

"The more I watch this case unfold, the more that regret grows." Sha admitted.

"Oh?" I said, becoming confused a bit.

"She's my daughter, Sheila." She confessed.

The phone went dead.

Stay Tuned For

The Pastor's Wives Chronicles

Million Dollar Baby

Up Next

Made in the USA
Middletown, DE
22 September 2017